THE RUINS

A NOVEL

STEVE WICK

PEGASUS CRIME
NEW YORK LONDON

ALSO BY STEVE WICK

The Long Night: William L. Shirer and The Rise and Fall of the Third Reich

Heaven and Earth: The Last Farmers of the North Fork

All That Remains: A History of a Long Island Farm Labor Camp

Bad Company: Drugs, Hollywood and The Cotton Club Murder

THE RUINS

Pegasus Crime is an imprint of
Pegasus Books, Ltd.
148 West 37th Street, 13th Floor
New York, NY 10018

Copyright © 2025 by Steve Wick

First Pegasus Books cloth edition February 2025

Interior design by Maria Fernandez

ISBN: 978-1-63936-815-0

10 9 8 7 6 5 4 3 2 1

Printed in the United States of America
Distributed by Simon & Schuster
www.pegasusbooks.com

For Lena, Alice, and James

"When you have eliminated the impossible, whatever remains, however improbable, must be the truth."

—Sir Arthur Conan Doyle

41 08'29" N/72 08'46" W

ONE

Lindenhurst, Long Island—September 30, 1954

Morning arrived too early for a man who had too much to drink the night before. He'd had too much beer, sitting on the couch, feeling sorry for himself. It was often that way, since he'd come home from the war, gotten married, had their son, separated, and began his work as the police chief of the village in which he grew up. He could hear his ex-wife saying, "Lay off the beer, Paul. Get a hold of yourself." At this stage in his life, which he regarded as mostly a dismal failure, he was a man awash in his past, unable to pull free. The past was his prison. Any form of self-reflection was to be avoided at all costs.

The agony of night brought with it the intense claustrophobia of being trapped in a small space on the sea floor. Smothering blackness. Men shouting out prayers, begging. And every so often—he could not predict when it would reveal itself—a particular nightmare returned. His Irish mother and his German father shouting at each other about a man's execution. Their son, their only child, just a boy, huddled in fear in the dark of his bedroom. The walls of the house vibrating with the electric violence of his father's voice. His mother's agony. Her voice: an unlocked bedroom window, a ladder leaning against the side of a house, a stolen child.

❖

He only fell into bed when he was certain he would fall asleep quickly. Most nights were the same. Sit on the couch, drink to numbness, stumble to bed, wait for the horror to return. Count the hours until sunrise.

Sitting up on the edge of the bed, he surveyed the empty beer bottles scattered on the floor, the dirty clothes heaped in a corner by his dresser, the overall mess around him that reflected his inability to focus on even the smallest routines that might improve his outlook.

He had removed the mirror that was on the wall over the dresser because waking up, standing up from the bed, he loathed seeing his reflection. He no longer knew himself. The gaunt face, the sunken eyes, his was the image of a man on the wrong road, wherever it was leading. The mirror was now banished to the back of his closet.

In recent months he had avoided going to the barber in the village because of the big mirror on the wall in front of the chair. He loathed what he saw. His was the image of a man giving up, of a man who couldn't outrun his past. To maintain some control over his appearance, he cut his own hair, which most times looked rather pathetic to someone who knew him when he was growing up in the village. That handsome, dark-haired man was gone.

Beyond the lack of personal hygiene, he could not remember the last time he took the bedsheets to the laundromat in the village. Last month, probably. Nor could he remember the last time he woke up, made the bed, cleaned up the breakfast dishes, and happily went off to work. It was no wonder his wife ordered him out of the house. A man who doesn't look after his own well-being is incapable of being wanted by someone else.

The bungalow on the salt creek he'd moved into after the separation was dark, except for the light he always kept on above the stove. The glow was a beacon, a lighthouse on a dark sea, and it gave Paul Beirne hope that what he missed the most would one day come back into his life.

He went to the bathroom, pissed, and splashed hot water on his face. Seeing himself in the mirror brought him no comfort, the ugliness in his life staring back at him. Removing this mirror would have been an additional act of self-deception, so it remained on the wall.

He was relieved not to hear the rain pattering on the roof. He'd gotten to bed after midnight, having spent hours at the railroad crossing in the village. A drunk had fallen on the tracks after stumbling out of the Alcove Bar and Grill on West Hoffmann Avenue into a heavy rain. The eastbound train cut him in half at the waist. The upper half landed ten feet from the lower half, the gutter flooded with blood and crushed organs like the washout from a slaughterhouse. No identification on the body, and no one in the bar claimed to know who he was.

That did not surprise Paul, as the Alcove was a hangout for Krauts getting liquored up on a Saturday night. Most spoke no English or claimed they didn't if anyone asked them for a particular piece of information.

The village was a place of secrets, of a hidden-away past few people talked about. Paul had lived here his whole life and he understood early on how closemouthed the longtime residents were. There were pockets of Germans, pockets of Irish, pockets of others, but there was no mixing, no sharing of stories, nor a common story. Paul regarded the village as a ghost story.

The only possible clue to the dead man's identity was the item Doc Liebmann had found in the man's pocket. It was an odd looking German medal with the date 9 November 1923 on it. Doc called it a "Blood Order" medal and seemed repulsed to hold it in his hand when he showed it to Paul. As for the dead man, Paul figured he was one of the workers at the defense factory in nearby Farmingdale, but that was just a late-night guess. He didn't see any mystery in the death.

While waiting on Doc's review of the scene, and wanting to get out of the rain, Paul had gone into the Alcove to listen to game one of the World Series at the Polo Grounds between the Giants and Cleveland Indians, playing on the big radio on the back of the bar. The radio sat between rows of cheap liquor and next to the poster for Rheingold Beer featuring Ed Sullivan proclaiming, "My beer is the dry beer!"

Paul had been in the bar a hundred times on business, as well as a customer looking to numb himself with whisky and a night of not sitting alone in the creek house. He walked in when the game was in the eighth inning, a 2–2 score. Don Liddle on the mound. A monster hit sent the ball four hundred feet into center field, where Willie Mays turned and ran it down, catching it on the warning track. The bar erupted in shouts.

Outside the bar, he pulled a cap out of his coat pocket and draped it over his wet head. He stared at the sheets of rain-soaked plastic draped over the two halves of the body and the lumpy blood flushing into the gutter. Shaking his head, he suppressed the image that flashed in front of him of a headless American sailor lying in the dirt alongside a sandy road near the prisoner of war camp, the torso and legs shaking in spasms. If he lived to be one hundred, he doubted he'd ever lose that image. It pulled him out of bed, his face wet with sweat.

He forced himself back to the present. Standing over the top half of the body, his feet spread wide to avoid stepping in its fluids, he stared at the face of a middle-aged man, gray hair above the ears, mouth open, eyes half shut the way they always were with a corpse. Brown eyes.

Who are you?

❖

In the kitchen, as he got the coffee going, Paul went over the details from the night before. The lack of clarity at what he was dealing with, confusion over what steps to take to find his way to any answers, rattled his well-being. He knew he'd made a mistake leaving the scene and coming home and drinking until early the following morning. But doing anything to correct the mistake was something else entirely. He was glad Doc had gotten to the scene; he was always relieved to see him, since he had so little confidence in his own abilities to examine the dead and come to any firm conclusions. But it at least seemed cut-and-dried: a drunk stumbles out of a bar and gets run over by the late-night train from Manhattan. Accidents do happen.

While coffee percolated, he fried his last two eggs. To toast two slices of Wonder Bread, he placed them over the gas burner. After he piled the dishes and frying pan in the sink—he told himself he would clean up later—he filled the thermos and wrapped two peanut butter and jelly sandwiches in aluminum foil. That was all he would need, as he planned to be back at the marina by noon.

Everything went into the canvas bag he used to store shotgun shells during duck hunting season, along with an unopened pack of Camels and his Zippo lighter. He'd bought the lighter at the commissary at the base in Pearl Harbor, the day he set out aboard the USS *Grenadier*. Etched on the lighter's side was the ship's launching date, November 29, 1940, from the Boston Naval Shipyard, and his name, PAUL BEIRNE. The *U* in Paul and the *R* in Beirne had faded.

The Japanese had somehow overlooked the lighter when they stripped him of his clothes and any personal belongings before the long march to the camp. That he still had it with him gave it a special quality, like a religious relic. He took the pack of Camels nearly everywhere he went but had not peeled open the top to pull out a cigarette in months. It was more of a prop, a leftover habit, and a reminder of life on the submarine, where everyone smoked. That was, at least, one thing he had gained control over. His mission was to bring discipline into his life, even if he had so far failed miserably as it related to his drinking and cleaning up after himself.

His .38-caliber service revolver sat on the kitchen table. It shouldn't have been there. Its presence brought him confusion. His practice was to put it high up in one of the kitchen cabinets. Why would he have taken it down? Next to it was an empty White Horse bottle, a monument of sorts to a life without the necessary guardrails to live it smartly.

He picked up the gun and placed it behind a cereal box on the top shelf of the cabinet. His ex-wife had insisted the gun be hidden from their son, and he had followed her instructions to the letter. In the year he had been living alone, he continued many habits forged when they all lived together, as he often found himself speaking to her and Pauli even though they weren't in the room. The light left on above the stove every night was for his son. He reached up and flicked it off.

With everything in the back of his four-year-old Ford truck, he drove south through the village and parked near his boat slip at the marina. He made sure he had plenty of gas for the boat. He turned when one of the marina workers shouted, "Hey, Chief—did you hear the Giants game last night?"

"Part of it," Paul shouted back.

"That boy made an amazing catch!" the worker said. "I hear you found a body on the train tracks. Anyone I might know?"

"Nah," Paul said. "Another accident."

The goal this morning was to fish underneath the new trestle connecting the mainland to the barrier beach. There were stripers in the bay feeding in tight schools on tiny anchovies. He'd caught a thirty-pounder a week ago and screamed for joy so loud he was sure they heard him on the mainland. He brought his fly rod, a nine-foot bamboo beauty with an eight-weight line. The reel, which he considered a work of art, had been handmade in Maine. He loved the feel of it in his hands and the imperceptible weight of the rod.

The cloudless sky glowed a deep, rich blue. It was the kind of color, when sunlight bounces off salt water—his uncle out east called that "wet light"—that stilled the angriest mind and brought peace to a troubled man's life. He'd brought along a slicker but shed it as the air was warm for late in the month. Breathing deeply, the rich smell of salt water and tidal mud happily filled his lungs. That lovely smell. He could motor out of the marina seven days a week, and each time he would marvel at the saltwater world around him. Soon, as fall deepened, the salt grass would begin to fade from a rich green to a pale yellow.

A welcome calm settled over him. The bay, the saltwater world surrounding him, was where truth came back into his life. His truth, his past, the present that seemed so unpromising, a path forward, everything found a different place in his mind as he floated across the bay. The deep-seated belief that had held him in its grip for so long now, that he was a failure, receded as he took in the clear water under the boat, the sandy rim of the barrier beach to the south, the sky overhead.

Here, he was a man not frightened about the future or haunted by the past. His mistakes, freely admitted, retreated. The past was in its place. Memory's ball and chain receded. Not entirely, of course. That was not possible for Paul, and of course it was temporary. But as he motored out into open water, he knew he loved this place and the way late summer held jealously to its charms and pushed into the first weeks of fall. He could see for miles across the Great South Bay. Far to the east, a sailboat heeled into the morning breeze.

All summer when he fished on the bay, he saw ospreys circling over the water looking for a meal. He loved their presence, their focused purpose on the water below. They were gone now, headed south. Once or twice he had seen a bald eagle gliding above the clear water. A pair had nested atop a light pole at the marina.

His luck was pretty good when he fished around the concrete pilings of the trestle, so he steered the boat in that direction, revving the outboard to full speed because the bay was flat.

As had long been his practice, he fished with light tackle unless he was surf fishing on the barrier island and sleeping on the beach overnight. He did that often in the summer and fall, mostly for the joy it brought him to stand in the surf wearing heavy waders, to cast out beyond the breakers, the salt spray in his face. When midnight came, he set up a sleeping bag above the high tide line, built a driftwood fire, and was lulled into sleep by the sounds of the ocean splashing onto the beach, the Milky Way a shimmering mystery above him.

Those nights on the beach were the only time his mind was free of horror. Fishing began again at sunrise. Several times he had fished and slept on the beach with Pauli, but the few times the boy's mother had allowed it came with so many conditions that it had only made his attempts to establish a good relationship with the boy more difficult.

"You keep talking about police stuff as if he's an adult," she lectured him one morning as they stood in front of the house. "A boy needs to hear the details of someone who put a gun in his mouth? You really think that's an appropriate conversation? You don't understand, do you? He's a very curious boy. When I ask him what he wants to be when he grows up, you know what he says? A cop. Just like his father. Imagine that! And don't be drinking anymore in front of him. You understand, Paul? Get off the bottle. You keep doing that, we'll be back in court. You have too many demons following you around. You need help to get it straightened out instead of trying to drown the memories. Between the Japs and your old man and why your mother walked out on the both of you—you don't have a lot left in you anybody could possibly care about."

In spite of everything that had gone on, the pain of leaving the family home, he yearned for her company. Granted, it made no sense, but he could not tame it. That lecture was even more memorable because his ex-wife's new beau was standing on the front step of the house like the lord of the manor. He even had a beer in his hand. A self-anointed player in local politics, he was the editor of the local weekly, the Lindenhurst *Star*, whose editorial policy each week was to make nice with the powers that be and curry favor with the advertisers. Don't rock the boat. Don't stick your nose where you don't belong. He smirked at Paul and said, "Maybe if you put the bottle down, you'd start to think straight."

Maybe if I smashed your head in with it.

Ever since the separation, at least one weekend a month, he drove east to his uncle's potato farm on Oregon Road in Cutchogue, a hamlet on the North Fork, a nearly ninety-minute drive on country roads. He went there to calm the loneliness, to be with people he knew, to be away from his troubles. It was his retreat. The farmers around his uncle at the eastern end of the road were Irish and Polish. Most of the Poles didn't speak English, and the clannish Irish acted like they were still in Ireland. His uncle talked about the English as if they lived around the corner and were waiting to bang on his front door and demand rent payments. There, Paul could keep work away, sit with his aunt and uncle, and walk the farm road up through the woods that edged the bluffs overlooking Long Island Sound.

With his mother gone—she was Uncle Martin's sister—Paul was next in the family line to run the farm if something happened. For so long, going east was to get away; in recent months, all that had changed. Now, Paul felt that he had to go. Martin's health had been failing. There was an urgency in his aunt's letters about Martin's condition and ability to manage the farm. Her letters always ended the same way: *Please come out and see us, Paul. Martin needs you.*

Years had gone by without Martin mentioning his sister. Now, he brought it up all the time. It was obvious to Paul that Martin did not want to die without knowing what happened to her. Nearly every trip east, Martin asked, "Will I ever see her again? Where is she?"

Paul knew the maintenance on the farm was not up to his uncle's standards. Martin could no longer keep up with it. Besides the farm, Martin's eighty-foot dragger, the *Predator*, was moored at the commercial dock in Greenport, unused and rusting away. During slow times on the farm in years past when income was scarce, Martin put together a crew and they took the boat offshore for squid, which he sold on the dock to buyers who packed them in ice and trucked them to the Fulton Fish Market in the city.

Since his teen years, Paul had gone out with his uncle many times, and it was on those trips, when they passed the northeast side of Gardiners Island, that Martin would point out the piles of rocks and concrete on a small island the locals had nicknamed "The Ruins." A nineteenth-century fort had once stood there, Martin always said, reciting the history of the area he knew so well. All that was left was the rubble, reduced each year by the force of the sea.

Paul carefully draped the fly rod across the seats of his boat. He tied a bright streamer to the end of the leader that was meant to look like bunker. The bamboo rod was so delicate, he could break it with one hand. He loved the feel of pulling the rod tip high overhead, throwing the line forward, and mending the line with the tide to fool a bass into thinking the streamer was bait fish.

He could see the tide was nearly at flood stage. The water was clear. He looked down at the sand and pebbles and water-smooth rocks at the bottom. If he watched long enough, he was sure a bass would swim by, its nose facing the current. Standing in the boat, cradling the rod, he heard the chime of church bells pealing on the mainland, the music rolling over the bay like a call to prayer. After eleven o'clock, he steered back towards the marina and fished in coves on the north side of the barrier island.

By early afternoon, the boat was tied off to the dock near a freshwater hose and gas pump. He pulled up the Evinrude and flushed out the engine with clean water, removed the spark plug, and ran a wire brush over the contact point, then put a drop of oil on the threads and returned it to its rightful place. He finished cleaning up the boat and refilled the gas can. Climbing up to the dock, he hosed down his rod and reel with freshwater. He walked fifty yards to a shack where an old-timer sold clams out of a bucket.

"Good morning, Chief," the man said.

"Hello, Mr. Doyle," Paul said. "Got some fresh little necks?"

"Yes, I do, sir," he said. Uncle Martin spoke in the same melodious voice, rising and falling as if controlled by the moon and tides. "Not an hour out of the water. You had a death last night, I hear?"

"Yeah, outside that bar by the railroad tracks," Paul said.

"Any idea yet who it is?"

"He had no identification on him," Paul said.

"Could be someone took it, right?"

"Possible, but I doubt it," Paul said. He didn't want to think the death was anything more than the falling down actions of a drunk.

Doyle opened a dozen of the smallest little necks. He slid a paper plate of the clams and two slices of lemon over to Paul. He lifted a cold beer out of a bucket of ice water and popped open the top. Paul drained it. The clams went down smoothly, salty, the essence and beauty of the bay.

After one more beer—three would be pushing his luck—Paul drove along the bay to where his father lived. The old man's truck was parked by the house. His father was seated in a chair in the sun behind the house reading a newspaper. Paul knew him to read a German-language paper from New York City. Paul passed the Harding Avenue School his son attended, then turned around and went by the house where he had lived with his wife, something she had warned him repeatedly not to do. Phyliss's Pontiac Chieftain was there, as was the blue-and-white Oldsmobile 88 he'd seen on previous occasions.

The asshole must have moved in.

Feeling a wave of hurt, he turned around and drove to his house. He removed his gear and returned everything to the back of his garage.

As he walked to his back door, Roger Cantwell pulled into the driveway, honking the car horn and shouting, "Paul! Paul! We got us a big problem!"

A house fire? He was certain he had not heard any alarms sounding in the village when he was out on the bay. A fatal car wreck? Another person run over by the train?

"Oh, Jesus, Paul," his deputy said as he climbed out of the car. The look on Cantwell's face was that of an overwhelmed man. "You are not going to believe this."

"What's up?"

"Well, holy shit is all I can say. We got a serious problem."

"Okay, okay. I get that. What?"

"A father and his boy." He stopped to catch his breath.

Paul said, "Come on, calm down."

"Okay. Okay. So, they were driving up Wellwood. Going to early-morning Sunday Mass in Huntington. Lots of cars had gone up that road and seen nothing. But the boy sees something at the edge of the field on the east side. Just north of the entrance to the new Catholic cemetery. You know where I mean, Paul?"

A new cemetery owned by the Brooklyn diocese was being laid out on what had been until recently potato and cauliflower land. Paul used to hunt rabbits there when he was a kid.

"Calm down! Finish the story, Roger." His deputy could not tell a story in a straight line to save his life. "What did he see?"

"A white mound."

"A what?" He wasn't sure he'd heard him right.

"A big white mound of human flesh. Naked. Some clothes on the grass. The father stopped. Told the boy to stay in the car. He walked maybe fifty feet into the field, and he could see it was a woman's body.

A dead woman's body. Sort of twisted. A lake of blood on the ground between her legs. Legs pulled apart. I'm telling you. Holy shit. I mean, someone just ripped into her and . . . shit."

"Good God," Paul said. His own feeling of being overwhelmed began to keep pace with Cantwell.

He tried to remember the last murder in the village. Nothing since 1945, and nothing during the war years that he knew of, even though he'd been in the South Pacific and Asia. He knew of an unsolved murder from the late thirties. 1938. A young Jewish woman. A thin file on the death marked OPEN in faded black marker sat in a dusty cardboard box on top of the filing cabinet in Paul's office in the basement of Village Hall. It was there when he took the job. Its neglect and thinness suggested that no one before him had particularly cared about the death or put any effort into making an arrest. Cold cases in a village reluctant to deal with its past remained cold.

"Who's up there now?" he asked. He wasn't entirely sure what questions to ask.

Cantwell tried to control his breathing. It seemed to Paul he was in danger of hyperventilating and passing out. His deputy was a tall, gangly man, thoroughly uncoordinated, with long, wide feet that had a poor relationship with the ground. He was also the sort of man who, when faced with a puzzle of any kind, gave up without even trying. His method of dealing with problems was to turn his back on them and go on as if he had not been confronted with any.

"I couldn't reach you, Chief, so I called the state trooper barracks for backup. They got Schmidt up there, keeping people away until you get there. You know which one I mean? There are several Schmidts. This is the one who's lazy and dumb and speaks Kraut when he don't want people to understand him. A big fat guy."

"Go to the office and get the Speed Graphic," Paul said. "You know how to use it? You've done the training with the DA's office? You finished it, right?"

When Cantwell didn't answer, Paul felt certain the answer was no. "And call Doc Liebmann. Tell him to meet us up there. He was up late last night with me, but he should answer his phone."

"I've used that camera once," Cantwell said, his voice swallowed up in insecurity and worry. "Remember that car wreck down on Montauk Highway? That lady went right through the windshield and got run over by a bread truck. Never seen such a mess. Those pictures didn't turn out so good. I don't know if I can make sense of it, but I'll give it a try. Hell, Chief. You know I was driving a truck delivering mattresses to the summer houses before I became a cop."

Paul knew very little about Cantwell's experience during the war years. Cantwell never brought it up, and Paul never questioned him. Nor did Cantwell question Paul about his past. Some stories were better left alone. Paul guessed, from snippets of overheard conversations, that Cantwell was a gunner on a B-17 based out of England. But that was all he knew.

"We'll need a lot of photographs, so it's up to you to get it right," Paul said. His deputy was showing signs of panic, which in no small measure he was feeling himself. "I'll meet you up there. Understand?"

Paul passed through the village going north on Wellwood, over the railroad tracks, and past the cemeteries. From a hundred yards out he saw the trooper's car, the dome light bright yellow and spinning, parked on the grass twenty yards from the road. Paul climbed out of his truck. Behind him, Cantwell drove off the road towards the mound of flesh that at first glance gave Paul the impression of a huge rotting fish that had washed up on the beach.

To his disgust, Paul saw that the trooper had driven over tire tracks that ran from the road in a loopy half circle to a location next to the body, and then back to the street. He wondered how someone who called himself a member of law enforcement could be so stupid. Seeing Schmidt answered that question.

"Quite a mess here, Chief," the trooper said as Paul approached the body. "You certainly are going to have your hands full. Think you can handle it?"

"Did you notice the tire tracks in the dirt?" Paul asked, not looking at the man. "This is a crime scene. And you drove over the tire tracks?"

The trooper did not respond as Paul tapped his right index finger on the side of his head to reinforce the point. He had been around Schmidt enough times to have a negative view of the man. A fat man with a fat mouth who fancied himself a ladies' man, a big man in a tiny sandbox. He'd grown up in a house in the village where his parents spoke only German. Every time Paul ran into him, he felt repulsed.

The man was too stupid to get a private-sector job. Without patronage, without the public payroll, he'd be pumping out septic tanks. Paul always marveled at how Schmidt would wear shirts that were part of his trooper uniform that were two or three sizes too small, so buttons in the middle of his gut wouldn't close and the skin would stick out as if desperate for fresh air. His torso was perched atop stubby legs; his head was the size of a fall pumpkin left in the field because it was too big to pick up. And always the food stains on his uniform, even on the pants. He was one of those men who liked to drape a hand over his crotch as if concealing a secret weapon. Rumor in this insular, gossipy village was the man ran a blackmail ring and extorted people desperate for public jobs.

Schmidt's father had worked the meat counter at the *King Kullen* store on Wellwood. His friends called him *der Metzger*—the butcher—and thought of it as an inside joke. On May 1, 1945, he'd thrown a rope around his son's swing set in the backyard and hanged himself. On the kitchen counter, he left behind a copy of the German-language newspaper with the headline that Hitler had killed himself in his bunker.

Cantwell, breathing so heavily Paul could hear him from ten yards away, hoisted the Speed Graphic to his face.

"I can't promise anything, Chief," he wheezed.

"Just get it right," Paul said.

Standing at the woman's feet, he snapped pictures, the process slow and tedious before he could take the next one. As he pressed the shutter, the body and the soaked grass around it exploded in a white glow. Gingerly, watching every step, Paul moved closer to the body. Dark stains covered the grass between her legs. As his eyes settled on the body, his head rolled back in disbelief at what he was staring at.

Last night a man cut in half. Now this. Dear God.

"No, no, no," he said out loud. Along with panic, a hot liquid climbed up his throat. "What happened?"

"Ripped her pussy out, Chief," Schmidt said. "That's what he done. Ain't no blood left in that broad."

Paul's contempt for Schmidt was rising to new levels. "Roger, where is Doc?"

"Should be here any moment."

"Herr Liebmann?" Schmidt said, dissolving into a raucous laugh he made no effort to control. "That fuckin' Jew? You think he's got anything to do with the Liebmanns who run the Rheingold Brewery in Brooklyn? Is he one of them rich Jews?"

"I wouldn't know," Paul said.

"Maybe they're cousins or something," Schmidt said. "He must have all kinds of money, so what's he doing looking over dead people, anyway?"

Paul stared at Schmidt, hoping he'd get the message to keep his mouth shut. He stepped closer to the body. Blood stained the grass from the woman's groin to well below her feet, flooding either side of her knees. It must have represented every drop of blood she had in her body. He touched her right knee. Cold, damp. Not quite stiff yet. The ripped mass of skin ran from her groin to nearly the navel.

"You can leave now, Schlitz," Paul said. "We don't need you here."

"It's Schmidt, Chief. Not Schlitz. That's a beer made in Brooklyn." After a long silence, he said, "What were you doing this morning, Chief?"

"I don't work for you," Paul said.

"Me having to wait on you," he said.

"Doesn't sound like much of a hardship for a hard-working man like you," Paul said.

"Why you telling me to go?"

"Because we don't need you here anymore. Nor do I need your mouth. This isn't your crime scene. You understand that?"

"Hell, Chief, you sure don't know what you're doing. Being in over your head is a daily experience for you. You should be grateful I showed up this morning to cover for you."

The trooper raised his right hand, his middle finger extended straight up. "You know what I do, right, Chief? Besides work for the state police?"

"Are you threatening me?" Paul said.

"I've blackmailed people far less than you, Beirne," Schmidt said.

Cantwell said, "Shit, man. Come on. Forget this. Maybe show a little respect for what we got here."

After a minute of awkward silence, the trooper stepped towards his car. He muttered, *"Dein Tag wird kommen, Arschloch."*

Cantwell stood to the left of the body, jerking his feet up and down as if the ground were on fire.

"Arschloch? Is that what he said?"

"Sounded like it," Paul said.

"It means asshole," Cantwell said. "Even I know that."

"Roger," Paul said. "Watch where you step. Just focus on getting the pictures we need."

He looked east towards a stand of trees. For an instant he thought he saw the profile of a man. He was about to say something to Cantwell, but when he looked again, it was gone. Beyond the woods was a small neighborhood where Negroes were allowed to live. None were allowed in Lindenhurst Village. The demographic engineering managed by the real estate people and their similarly minded fellow travelers in village government was a marvel to behold. A high wall topped with barbed wire and guard towers would not have been more effective. A quarter mile to the north, the Long Island Rail Road tracks ran east and west. In the distance to the west, an eastbound locomotive sounded its horn as it approached a crossing.

"Also, walk in circles around the body, between the woods and the road, and look for anything on the ground. An item of clothing. Jewelry. Anything like that."

"You can see, Chief, her purse is under her right arm." Cantwell pointed to where he wanted Paul to look. "Doesn't look like a robbery or nothing like that. And her coat is laid out under her on the grass. Maybe she or the guy stretched it out like they were here for a specific purpose. Don't you think?"

When Paul did not respond, Cantwell said, "Only an animal could do something like this, Chief."

"Yeah, I can see that," he said. Paul didn't need an education on what human beings were capable of doing to other human beings.

"One of them from the city coming out to rape one of our women," Cantwell said. "Think he brought her here to screw and something went wrong?"

"I wouldn't know," Paul said. "Just shut up and take pictures, Roger."

The smell of vomit and half-digested alcohol from the woman's stomach slapped Paul in the face. It stuck like wallpaper to the insides of his nostrils. Shaking his head did nothing to relieve it. A few feet to the right of the woman's head: enough puke to fill a mop bucket.

A Plymouth turned off Wellwood and onto the grass. Paul held up his hand to tell the driver not to go any farther. Doc climbed out of the car. When he was sure Doc was looking at him, Paul pointed to the tire tracks in the dirt and grass extending from the road to the crime scene.

When he arrived at the body, a gasp escaped Doc's mouth. Shaking his head, he hesitated for a moment. He gasped again. A small, thin man with dark hair fringed around his skull in a narrow band, a carefully groomed pencil mustache under his nose, his customary bow tie neat under his chin, Doc spoke with a German accent, using the words and crisp tone of the well-educated man that he was. He carried himself differently because he was different. He always wore a suit, no matter the day, usually light in color, which seemed to run counter to the man's seriousness and the somber mood he carried with him like a heavy weight he could not cast off.

To Paul's eye, Doc lived inside a shadow, a dark space behind a curtain, impenetrable and unknowable. It followed him around. There was no sunlight for him to step into. His pronunciation revealed that English was not his first language, but in the time Paul had known him,

Doc had never retreated into the safety of his native German. It was as if Doc wanted to forget it, get past it, not have it harass him anymore.

Doc had been born in Vienna and arrived in New York City with his brother in 1946 after a year in a DP camp. Beyond that, the man's biography was a blank. Early in their acquaintance, Paul thought of Doc as an iceberg: you saw only a tiny part of him. Knowing so little about him did not detract from Paul's appreciation of him and need for his skills.

Doc was everything Paul wasn't. Sure of himself, curious, a problem solver. Doc talked about books he'd read the way men sitting on barstools in the pubs Paul frequented talked about alcohol and the women who'd let them down. Doc was well-educated, and also self-educated. He conducted himself the way a newcomer to a new land unsure of the ground beneath him would, always careful not to draw attention to himself or violate any long-standing customs. He owned the funeral home on Montauk Highway. He also served as the village's official coroner, and as backup for Babylon Village and Babylon Town, whenever a dead body turned up in their jurisdiction and their people could not get to it.

"Morning, Paul," Doc said.

"Thanks for coming," Paul said. "I don't know what we are looking at."

"A tortured, violent death. Someone somewhere is looking for her."

Doc held a leather bag in his left hand and a canvas tool kit of the kind a plumber might bring to the job in his right. He stood over the body, staring at it the way a professional looking for insight would, starting with her head and working his way down to her feet. His feet were spread wide on both sides of the body's hips. He removed a spackle blade from his bag. Carefully, he reached down and parted the torn skin of her vagina. Paul looked away.

"She was torn open all the way to the navel. That's astonishing."

"With what?" Paul asked.

"Not a knife or it would look much different, with cleaner lines. This is very ragged, a deep rip. Not a cut or a slice. I'd say a fist. A big man with a big fist, a hand the size of a dinner plate and the arm strength to rip open the abdomen. She was alive through the whole thing. She bled to death, probably after he left. That explains all the blood on the grass. Her heart was still pumping."

Doc pushed down on her left shoulder so that her torso moved to a flat position. To the right of her left shoulder, half concealed under the coat, lay panties crumpled into a pink knot.

"When do you think this happened?" Paul said.

Doc dipped the tip of a finger into the pool of blood between her knees. Cold. He put one hand on her right foot and moved it sideways several times. He looked at his watch.

"Two or three in the morning, perhaps."

He opened the tool kit, took out a thermometer, reached below the woman's groin and inserted it into her rectum. That was too much for Paul; he jerked his head away. Doc retrieved a Leica M3 and began taking pictures of the body, beginning below the feet where the bloodstains began and working up towards her head. Back at the other end of her body, he pulled out the thermometer and read it.

"Maybe midnight to two A.M.," he said.

Eight to ten hours ago, Paul thought. *Plenty of time for the killer to be far away. Someone must have heard her screams.*

Two vehicles appeared. One man got out of the first car and two out of the second, a black hearse. Doc stopped what he was doing and watched them for a moment. Cantwell combed the field, looking for anything that might have dropped. The men tried to pick up the corpse and put it on a stretcher but could not manage it. One of them gagged loudly. The other muttered what Paul knew to be the cadences of the Hail Mary. Her buttocks had been flattened against her spine from the weight of her body on the ground and were blue-black from the settled blood. The men lifted the body and pulled the stretcher towards the hearse as Doc and Paul looked over the woman's coat. Doc retrieved a bag out of his medical kit and, picking up a purse with two fingers of his right hand, dropped it into the bag.

"Do you want to open it now?" he asked.

"Let's do that back at your place."

Cantwell and Paul walked the grass in tight circles, working out from where the body had been until they reached the woods on one side and the road on the other. Dozens of cars had stopped along the road. People stood at the edge of the grass and gawked at the sight of the two cops examining the ground for any possible clues.

Someone shouted, "Who is it?"

"Roger, get over there and push these people back," Paul said.

He waved at the crowd to stay away, and walked towards his truck with Cantwell. When they got there, Cantwell opened his hand to show Paul a single earring, a silver hoop.

"I didn't look to see if she still had the other one," Cantwell said.

Paul put it in his pocket. They walked back to where Doc was taking pictures with the Leica. Cantwell and Paul kneeled on either side of the bloody grass and looked for anything that might be helpful. Paul saw it first: a row of false teeth from a lower denture under a layer of vomit that had been concealed by the coat.

"What do you make of that?" Paul asked.

Doc took a pen out of his pocket and pulled at the denture until it was closer to him. He picked it up with the pen, held it in front of his face, eyeing it closely to see if there was any blood or skin tissue on it. Then he dropped it into another bag.

"I can only think the killer pulled them out," Doc said.

TWO

Paul approached each day with uncertainty and dread. His daily life was a practice of dragging a heavy chain behind him; his past was a beast that feasted on doubt and insecurity. Anything that came at him out of nowhere, unforeseen, throttled his well-being. The unexpected was a curse.

He told himself he had multiple voices in his head—too many to count. He couldn't expect to even keep them straight. He was afraid of being overwhelmed, of not being in control of any outcome, and of being at someone's mercy. Yet he'd taken the job of police chief not long upon his return from the South Pacific after his father had suggested it to him. It was an odd choice for a man who had experienced what he had, and who in his first year back suffered panic attacks. He was told by the town fathers that the village was small, and nothing horrible ever happened beyond the normal tragedies. You'll be more of a caretaker than a law enforcement officer, they'd told him. They insisted on one firm rule: you work for us. Go along to get along. This isn't the sort of place where people ask questions. Keep to your business. With a new wife and child, he needed something more stable than the series of odd jobs he'd taken when he first came home from Asia.

Now he was standing over a dead woman who had been tortured and abandoned, allowed to bleed to death in agony and pain. His nights would now be filled with more horror. Headless American sailors. Smiling, sword-carrying Japanese soldiers. The inexplicable memory of his parents shouting about an executed man. A childhood fear of an unlocked bedroom window. Now a ripped-open woman in a field of blood.

A wave of indecision washed over him. He remembered the first death after he was sworn in—an old man dead in his bed in a nursing home—and how difficult he found it to look at the body before the funeral home took it away.

What do I do now?

When Doc had collected all that was available to be bagged and removed, Paul told Cantwell to stay for several more hours, at least until nightfall, to keep crowds from trampling the grass where the woman had been violated and murdered. The tire tracks also had to be preserved. That had been Doc's suggestion.

Finally, he choked out some words he hoped would make sense. "I don't want people walking on this ground," Paul said. "No flowers, no roadside memorials, nothing like that. Keep people away."

An hour later, Paul stopped by his house. He felt this was an odd thing to do at the start of a murder investigation, but he needed to collect himself. For sure he did not have the skills to find out who butchered the woman—the second violent death in his village in just two days. He wasn't even sure what his investigative steps should be. His "training" amounted to a one-page printout the village attorney handed him after the mayor swore him in. Standing at the sink, he picked up an empty glass and thought for a moment he would have a sip of whisky.

His hands shook. He put the glass down. A groan escaped his mouth.

Not now, not with all that has happened.

His side of the creek was a string of small, one-bedroom summer bungalows. In July and August, they were rented most weekends, except during the war years when no one came out to enjoy the beaches, which were closed except for civilian and Coast Guard patrols looking out for German submarines. When one was spotted just off the beach, word rippled through the village, house to house, like news of an impending invasion.

In his years growing up in the village, it had hardly changed. It had a small fishing fleet and a decent sized boat-building business that had doubled or tripled in size during the early war years. Otherwise, the village of 1940 was the same as the village of 1920, or even earlier. German immigrants had arrived after the turn of the century and that continued into the 1930s. The early fifties brought in a wave of blue-collar workers as subdivisions such as Levittown began to be built on former farmland.

But even with the gradual transformation of the landscape, from rural to eastward-crawling suburbs, the village remained the same close-mouthed place where people stayed in their groups. If pressed, Paul would say he never understood the place of his birth. He was the insider who lived like an outsider.

A half mile farther down the creek was the former fishing shack owned by Paul's father, Helmuth Baer. Baer purchased the shack in the spring of 1939, a month after his wife, Paul's mother, abandoned her family. Or went missing. Father and son could not agree on the correct terminology. Baer's word was *abandoned*. His bitterness was always present, always over the top, often in the form of a drunken rage. He lorded it over his son, who could never escape it. Paul felt his father was blaming him for his mother's absence.

Paul's word was *missing*. He was sixteen years old at the time, had no idea what had happened, except she was no longer there. If Paul brought her up, Baer shouted him down. Two years later, having turned eighteen, Paul enlisted in the Navy, out of a sense of duty after Pearl Harbor, but also to get away from his father and the memory of his missing mother.

A young man with a missing mother was someone with a wrecked present and no future that could be predictable and planned. Paul knew that the day he enlisted, and he thought about it every day in the prison camp. He was the son of a missing mother. She left him.

Over the years, Baer converted the shack into a year-round home that consisted of a small kitchen, with a table, a bed, and a tiny bathroom. He pulled down the inside walls and put in insulation. When the work was done, he moved in and this became his home. The house was partially built on cedar posts, and full-moon high tides and nor'easters washed sea water under the house. A corner fireplace made of fieldstone and a potbelly stove were the only sources of heat. Most winters the creek froze solid, the ice extending far out into the bay towards the barrier beach. It spoke volumes to Paul that his father had left the family home on the east side of the village off South Wellwood Avenue and moved into a house where there was no room for his son to stay, let alone live. Enlisting was an easy decision.

From the cabinet of his bungalow, Paul retrieved his revolver and shoulder holster. He infrequently wore it on the job, having never trained with it, aside from shooting beer cans and rats at the town dump. If it were up to him, he would never have taken it when he was sworn in. He'd only pulled it out once, on a Fourth of July weekend in 1949, when he broke up a fight at one of the packed beer gardens when a half dozen drunks had attacked a Negro man delivering ice.

A little before two P.M., he pulled into the parking lot behind Doc's funeral home. As he got out of the car, Billy Evans pulled in behind him.

"Chief, what do you want me to do?" Evans asked.

Well into his thirties and living with his widowed mother, Evans was rumored to have fathered a child with a fifteen-year-old girl from the village who lived with her grandfather. The baby had been turned over to the county and put up for adoption. Evans was one of those men who never matured past his late-teen years. He was a hanger-on because he had no skill sets he could possibly rely on. Heavyset, his hair cut into a military style as if to suggest something that wasn't true, he acted as though the world owed him something beyond his meager capabilities.

Evans's father had been killed in Germany in January 1945. His body was never recovered. Stories about what became of him as the US Army crossed into Germany abounded. One was that he was shot for deserting. The truth was elusive.

One of the conditions from the town fathers when Paul took the job was to bring Evans on as one of his two deputies, even though his prior work experience amounted to little more than lawn mowing jobs and house painting. He was said to be bad at it.

"Go up to the crime scene," Paul said. "Roger is up there keeping people away. While he's doing that, I'd like you to set up some traffic cones to slow down the cars. Ask anyone who might have seen the body this morning, or anyone who might have driven by last night and perhaps seen a car, or people standing around. Anything at all. I'm hoping someone saw something out of the usual. We need an identity of this woman. Did anyone report her missing?"

"Geez, really? Just stand around asking if anyone saw anything? What a waste of time. Got any better ideas? How long you want me up there?" Evans said.

"I'll let you know. And listen, Billy. There are tire tracks from Wellwood Avenue, onto the grass, and over to where the body was found. Don't let anything happen to them. I'll ask the district attorney's office to make a plaster cast of the imprints. Do you understand what I'm saying?"

Affecting the body language of a spoiled teenager, Evans nodded and got into his car. Paul had no confidence his directions would be followed. He entered the funeral home through the back door, under the awning that read LIEBMANN FUNERAL HOME. He took the stairs to the basement, where he found Doc standing over the body of the woman. The sight of something that had once been a human being, laid out on a steel table and gutted like a stockyard cow, knocked the wind out of him. His stomach seized up. His hands started to shake. He was looking at his own nightmare, on par with the one that had followed him around since childhood of being in his bed at night facing an unlocked window with a ladder leading up against the side of the house. He shook his head as if to clear it of demons.

The corpse's pale skin glowed under the hot, bright lights overhead. The table was tilted at one end so that liquids could drain down and through a hole into a bucket on the floor. The body looked like it had been attacked by a man-eater that feasted on human flesh. Her skin was white as snow, except for a blue-black cave between her legs and bruises on the inside of her thighs that looked like paint had been splashed on them. Her mouth and eyes were half open. Her lower gums were absent of teeth. Foul acid in Paul's stomach heaved into the back of his throat and threatened to overwhelm him. He equated the rising bile in his stomach, burning its way to his throat, as similar to the contents of an overused cat litter box. He covered his mouth and nose with a handkerchief, gagging loudly at the smell.

Doc ignored him, focused intently on his work.

Making everything far worse for Paul, the two halves of the train victim lay uncovered on a table pushed against the cinder block wall. The halves were lined up to make the corpse look whole, as if this were an exhibit in a freak show, along with a two-headed cow. Panic swelled in Paul's chest.

Doc's assistant, a baby-faced high school kid, stared at the woman's corpse with a strange look of fascination on his face.

"This boy should not be down here, Doc," Paul said.

Doc didn't hear him. Paul motioned for the kid to go upstairs.

"She has no blood left in her," Doc said.

At first, Paul wasn't sure what Doc had said, although Liebmann tamped down his accent and enunciated every word.

"You mean—what?"

"She would have been screaming the whole time. Someone must have heard this, Paul. She was alive through all of it. She died because of massive blood loss, after her assailant had left. Her heart was still beating when he turned his back on her and strolled away. She may have lived another twenty minutes. You understand the suffering involved here? The person who did this has very large hands."

"You can tell that?"

"Definitely."

He held up both of his hands, which were small and delicate, with the long fingers of a serious pianist, which he was. Even standing in a small basement room dominated by two ripped-apart corpses, Doc gave off an air of culture and education that Paul, who had been second to last in his Lindenhurst High School class, found impressive. His calmness, his ability to focus on the task before him without distraction, seemed unnatural.

"The killer's hand is larger than two of mine, Paul. I know this is a bit overwhelming, but you need to pay close attention to what I am saying."

How does a human being do something like this?

The temperature in the windowless room topped out. A Niagara of sweat poured down Paul's back. The cat litter box in his stomach kicked into high gear. He watched as Doc unclipped his silver cufflinks and rolled up the sleeves of his white shirt to reveal the inexplicable. Paul had seen this once or twice before. He knew what to expect. There was the capital A, followed by four numbers, tattooed on the forearm in bluish ink.

A1828.

Dear God, what is that?

Seeing it again jerked him up short: a man branded. He turned away. He did not want Doc to see him staring. He shook off the thought that in the six years he had worked with Doc, he had never asked him what it was, how it got there. Doc was as silent about his past as Paul was about his. The big difference between the two men was that Doc somehow managed his past, whereas Paul's past owned him. Doc's history showed on his face, in his eyes, his demeanor, and how he carried himself. Doc's past was there for Paul to try to discern. Still, somehow, Doc lived in the present, something Paul never learned.

With a scalpel in his right hand, Doc inserted it into the skin at the bottom of the woman's sternum. He leaned his shoulder into it and pushed hard downward, pulling the blade towards the lower abdomen in one long line, two inches deep, to below the navel. The sound was of thick rubber tearing, like cutting into a truck tire with a sharp knife.

Paul retreated towards the staircase, falling backward onto the bottom step, breathing in deeply through his nose. He watched as reddish, yellowish crud bubbled out of the woman's abdomen, spilled down the sloped table to the hole, and noisily dripped into the bucket. A pulsating nausea rippled through his body.

"Her stomach was filled with alcohol," Doc said. "She was very intoxicated."

Standing up, Paul moved around the back of the table, but kept his distance.

"There are signs of old bruising, on her arms, left shoulder, the upper part of her back. Not from someone hitting her; that would look different. They are no doubt from her falling down a lot."

Paul felt his attention turning away from what Doc was telling him.

"Are you following me, Paul?" Doc asked, his voice taking on a lecturing tone. "Don't look for logic. This is a puzzle piece. Horror doesn't have an explanation." He waved his hands about like a frustrated teacher. "Do you understand that? There isn't an answer to every question. Get used to that. Nothing here makes sense except pure human savagery. You see it once, let alone over several years, and you know that man is a beast capable of the worst possible cruelty. The man you are looking for . . ."

He paused, staring at the ceiling, then at the body spread out on the table. He lowered his voice. "Men who do things like this to women don't stop. He's done this before; he will do it again. If I were in your shoes, I'd look for a previous crime just like this one."

"What about the purse?" Paul said.

He pointed to the desk against the wall. The contents had been spread out and organized into small piles. Six nickels and dimes, a silver half-dollar with its image of Benjamin Franklin under the word Liberty, a five-dollar bill, a house key, a handkerchief, food coupons held together with a paper clip, and rosary beads.

There was no driver's license or anything with her name on it. The rosary beads made him think of the ones his mother had left behind at the Cutchogue farmhouse before she went missing. He could not fathom how she would not want them with her, as she kept them close wherever she went, and they were always on her bedside table. She had once told Paul they had been her mother's back in Ireland.

"That's it?" Paul asked.

"Look inside the purse," Doc said.

Opening it, Paul pulled out a locket attached to an ornate gold chain. Staring closely at it, he could see, under the glass in the front of the locket, a faded photograph about the size of a thumbnail.

"Don't try and pull it out," Doc said. "It's old and could fall apart."

"A small boy," Paul said. "Blond haired. Three or four years old? Did she have a child years ago? That's a very fancy locket and chain, Doc. It suggests something special, don't you think? Like maybe the boy died? I don't know."

He gently returned it and the other items to the purse.

"That's to be determined," Doc said. "A mother losing a child? I can see her doing that, Paul."

"Maybe whoever killed her went through it and took any form of identification."

"That's your job. But if she didn't drive, what identification would she have?"

Upstairs, he went into Doc's office and dialed the number of the police department. No one answered. Leaving the building, he walked across the parking lot and proceeded a block east on Montauk Highway to Village Hall. A white-haired man, so thin and gaunt he gave the appearance of an upright corpse, stood by the door to the police department smoking a cigarette, his hands shaking wildly.

As Paul got close, he could tell the man was either drunk or badly hungover. His hair was a nest of tangled webs stretched across the top of his bald dome and plastered to the mottled skin in an act of absurd vanity. His dark eyes had retreated deep into his skull, his cheeks depressions on either side of his narrow slit of a mouth. There were no lips to speak of.

Wheezing, the man exhaled stale cigarette smoke, and the harsh stench of half-digested alcohol. The cigarette dangled from his right hand, between the yellowish-brown tips of two fingers. His fingernails were long and dirty. He took a quick, hurried drag and dropped the smoking butt to the ground onto a pile of others, then in a rushed panic pulled out a pack of Chesterfields from his shirt pocket and lit another. The exchange, long practiced, took less than three seconds.

"I'm looking for the police chief," the man said. He made a loud gurgling sound and spit a gooey, gray-green blob onto the pavement.

"I'm Chief Beirne," Paul said.

"I'm Mr. McKay," he said. "I live on Liberty Avenue."

Paul thought it odd the man did not use his first name but identified himself as "Mr. McKay." It suggested he was once important and was still grasping the last vestiges of a former life that had long faded away to insignificance.

"The white house with gray shutters?" Paul said. As the chief of a small village police department, Paul knew every street and cul-de-sac.

"With a slumped-over garage on the right side of the house? What can I do for you?"

"My wife didn't come home last night," he said. "She . . . often leaves the house and walks into the village. She likes to sit in a bar and talk to people. Catch up on things. Very social, my wife. Yes, indeed. That isn't me. I stay at home. She likes the company, don't you know?"

The man's brogue had lost some of its thickness, but shards of it remained in the way the words exited his mouth in an undisciplined way. Paul retreated two big steps away from McKay to escape his breath and the smell that rose off his clothes like steam. This was the first time he'd heard of a woman drinking alone in a village bar.

"What is your wife's name, Mr. McKay?" he asked.

"Constance," he said. "Dooley is her maiden name."

He said her name in a flat voice, without any emotion. For a man whose wife hadn't come home, Paul thought that odd. He also wondered why McKay had bothered to tell him his wife's maiden name.

"She's done this before?"

"Oh, yes. That's Constance. A social butterfly, that one. She always comes home."

"You're okay with that?"

He hesitated. "Well. You know. We see things differently."

"Are you saying that your wife went out drinking at night by herself?"

He nodded.

"Against your wishes?"

"She did what she wanted to do," he said.

"Did you fight about it?"

The question was pro forma. McKay seemed incapable of doing anything more challenging than lighting a cigarette or refilling a whisky glass.

"I'm here to report that my wife did not come home last night, or this morning. But I'm sure she's fine."

Someone who doesn't come home isn't fine.

"Where were you last night?"

McKay's face tightened. "Why are you asking me that?"

"It's routine to ask questions, Mr. McKay. Your wife went to a bar to drink and socialize. What did you do last night?"

"I stayed home, if you must know. I like sitting in our living room, listening to Dr. Sixgun and the World Series on the radio."

"You didn't go looking for her?"

"Why would I do that? I don't understand why you're asking me this. She'd come home and I'd be glad to see her, and we'd go to bed. And that was that. She always made me a lovely breakfast in the morning. She knew I liked a whisky sour with my eggs and bacon."

The story seemed too pathetic to be concocted.

"You're retired?"

"For about fifteen years now."

Paul guessed the man was in his late seventies. "What did you do, sir?"

"During the war, I worked at a factory in Lower Manhattan that made airplane parts," he said. "Mr. Norden owned it. A particular invention of his was very top secret. Before that I worked in a eugenics lab in Cold Spring Harbor. Met some very interesting people there."

"Where were you living at the time?"

"We lived in the Hell's Kitchen area for many years. My parents went there when they came over from Ireland to get away from those English bastards. It's where I grew up, don't you see. When I retired, it seemed a good idea to come out east and start over. Away from"—with his right arm he pointed in a westerly direction—"the dark people. The

Jews. Dear God. If they police who lives out here, Long Island will be a lovely homeland for people like me."

"Did your wife work?" Paul asked.

"In the factory where I worked. She was the big boss's secretary. Mr. Norden. His private secretary is what they called it. All hush-hush, don't you know?" He paused for a moment, as if waiting for this to sink in. "She kept a lot from me, I found out later."

"What do you mean?" Paul asked.

"What don't you get? I am telling you all I know."

"Yes, I appreciate that. But are you saying she had secrets on the job that she didn't tell you about?"

"It was that kind of place. They were doing things only a few people were allowed to know. Mr. Norden was a very important man in government circles."

"And Constance was one of them?"

"Her boss trusted her. That's why she was his private secretary. He was probably screwing her at one point. I confronted Constance about that several times, but she never admitted it."

"Is that where you met?"

He nodded. "I was a widower. My first wife was crushed by a trolley car in Brooklyn. All she was doing was walking across the street."

And now this, Paul thought. A second wife who was no doubt stretched out on a slab in Doc's basement, her fluids dripping into a bucket.

"My neighbor tells me there was some excitement up Wellwood Avenue this morning," McKay said. "What was that?"

Paul knew that he should get McKay to walk back with him to the funeral home to identify the remains, but that felt too soon. Besides, the body needed to be prettied up before Doc would allow anyone down there.

"A woman's body was found. Murdered. She had been with someone. We don't know anything yet."

McKay's mouth fell open, a gaping, smoke-black furnace lined with discolored teeth tilting this way and that like aging gravestones. A birdlike screech managed to escape his throat before it was extinguished.

"That don't make no sense to me," he said after a moment. "That can't be my wife. No, sir. She drank like a fish, I grant you that. But are you saying she met some man, and they went off together and he killed her? No. I don't buy that. She is a sweet woman. Problems, sure. Who don't have problems? But such a good wife. Every Sunday she'd be up and walking to Mass holding them beads of hers. That's the kind of woman she was. Father what's-his-name at Our Lady of Whatever, he adored her. I have no use for the priests. The Irish ones are the worst. They can all rot in hell far as I care."

"I'm not saying I know who it is. I don't have an identification for the dead woman yet."

"I'm not interested in looking at any body, if that's what you have in mind." He stepped away from Paul.

"Does your wife drive? Did she carry identification?"

"No, she never learned. Where we live, she can walk to the King Kullen and into the village, all the places she likes." He covered his face with both hands. "I come here looking for help, and you tell me a woman is dead in a field."

I never said she was dead in a field.

"Do you remember what time you went to bed last night?"

"I don't know."

"She wasn't home yet?"

"No. Not unusual though. I knew she'd be home soon."

"How about if we go over to your house? I'd like to look around. Did you drive here?"

"No, I walked. I don't drive, either. Never had a reason to."

He turned and Paul followed him. They crossed South Wellwood and reached the house. McKay went through four cigarettes, leaving a line of spent butts behind him like a trail of toxic breadcrumbs. He wheezed so badly he had to pause every few steps to find his breath. A crumbling brick walkway extended from the sidewalk to the front door. On either side of the walk was a patch of weedy lawn. Long-ignored shrubs covered the area in front of the porch.

Coming through the front door, they entered a foyer, a living room to the left, a dining room to the right, every square inch of which was stacked with papers, boxes, and mountains of debris. The living room could have passed for an unlicensed landfill. Every place anyone could sit was stacked with overflowing boxes, old newspapers, and trash. The mantel above the fireplace held framed, formal photographs of a young man. In one of them, he wore an Army uniform. A second photograph showed an older man. A Virgin Mary statue stood at the end of the mantel. Paul thought of the rosary beads in the dead woman's purse.

McKay erupted into a fit of coughing. It took nearly a minute to get it under control.

"My wife has her problems, as I said. But she would not leave her home. No, no, no. She would not do that. Besides, unlike a lot of people, she could handle her liquor. Half the time you couldn't even tell she'd been drinking."

Paul stepped into the living room.

"The photographs on the mantel," he said. "Who are they?"

"The boy in uniform is our son," McKay said. His voice began to crack, and he fell silent for a moment. When he composed himself, he said, "The older man is Thomas Clarke, a relative on the Dooley side. He had a farm on Long Island at one time, before he went back to Ireland to fight the English. They executed him in a firing squad."

Ah, here we go. The bottomless Irish grievance.

The stench of alcohol and cigarette smoke hung in the air as if painted to the walls with a brush. As Paul walked towards the fireplace, navigating his way around the trash, he smelled urine and spilled alcohol. Nausea returned with a vengeance. The couple had stubbed out their cigarette butts on the arms of chairs or under their feet on what remained of a rug. Dirty dinner plates littered with spent cigarettes sat on the floor. Four or five empty bottles of Old Fitzgerald adorned what had once been a coffee table.

"Do you have a photograph of your wife?" Paul asked.

Reluctantly, he wheezed and groaned up the stairs to the second floor. Five or six minutes passed before he returned. He handed Paul a framed picture of a large, round-faced woman with an impenetrable helmet of hair atop her head.

The dead woman.

He stared at the picture to make sure he was right. Blondish hair etched with white strands and sprayed with some sort of adhesive gave it the appearance of boardwalk cotton candy. Pale, bloodless skin. Dark circles under the eyes. A large round face.

How could she have gone off with a stranger?

Perhaps they weren't strangers, after all. He could only speculate.

McKay's hand shook as he struggled to light the cigarette hanging off his lower lip. He kept missing the tip of it with his match. He stared at Paul with droopy, bloodshot eyes as if waiting for a declaration that the dead woman was not his wife.

When nothing came, he said, "What am I supposed to do?"

"Stay home," Paul said. "I'll come back for you later this afternoon. Okay?"

He stared at McKay. He took the match out of McKay's shaking fingers and helped him light the cigarette.

"What about a family member? Can someone come to help you?" Paul asked.

"The boy died in Sicily. Or we think he died."

Paul waited for an explanation.

"His body was never found. He's technically missing in action, but we were told dozens of bodies were so badly mauled they couldn't be identified. We think he and some other soldiers burned up in a fire. We just don't know. You can imagine how that made us feel. My wife took it very hard. Until recently, she thought he'd walk through the front door one day."

Dead first spouse, murdered second spouse, a missing soldier son. Paul thought of the tiny photograph in the locket in the purse. He knew if he asked about it, McKay would know the dead woman was his wife.

"You had just one son?" Paul asked. He could see in the man's eyes and sagging face that McKay was giving up, sinking deeper into his own hole.

"Yes," McKay said slowly. "For a while we wanted to adopt another child. We hoped it would happen. It was my wife who wanted it to happen. I wasn't so crazy about the idea. But it all fell apart. We was lied to."

Paul touched the man's arm. "I'll come back for you, Mr. McKay. This afternoon."

THREE

Black sedans sat on the grass alongside Wellwood Avenue, the road closed in both directions, north and south. A van from the district attorney's office was parked close to where Constance's body was found. Two men in overalls were mixing plaster in buckets to make casts of the tire tracks. Lindsay Henry stood giving directions to a man taking notes on a clipboard. He turned when he saw Paul.

"Hello, Paul," he said.

Paul had known Henry for several years and viewed him as a trusted advisor, even though he was a political figure. Henry was one of those laugh-out-loud types with whom Paul felt comfortable. He didn't carry himself with any air about him or act entitled or part of a separate or ruling class. Their interactions had been few—the village police chief and the county's top law enforcement officer—but from the beginning Paul was fond of the man. He also regarded him as a bit of an Irish stereotype.

The district attorney had the physical appearance—big round head, florid skin on both sides of the nose—of central casting's idea of a New York City cop walking a beat. He drank too much but by all appearances could hold his liquor, even when consumed in abundance. He wore cheap department store suits he never bothered to get tailored and shoes that were perpetually beat-up and should have been donated to the Salvation Army. He looked like someone who had difficulty looking after himself. Paul also knew the upside with Henry was his contempt for the politicians of both parties. Paul remembered with a near-smile Henry once telling him the chairmen of the parties were nothing but piano players in a whore house, that local politics was about getting even and having your hand on the spigot so you can control the flow.

"You have photographs?" Henry asked.

"Yes, sir, we took them this morning. I'm sure Roger is working on them now."

"A stranger? Someone she knew?"

"I've been thinking the former, but now I'm not so sure. There was an intimacy to the crime scene. A familiarness. As though they came here for a purpose. Maybe even been here before. She was drunk. Spread her coat on the grass. That was what we found."

"Was there sperm on her body?"

"I didn't ask Doc that specifically."

Paul heard loud voices and turned to see the village mayor, Olly Madden, climbing out of his Buick Skylark, his driver rushing around to pull open the door for him. Paul avoided him as much as possible, even though the mayor had appointed him and could fire him at will. Madden's driver and attendants followed him around like obedient pilot fish. The mayor, a stubby, ill-fitting little man, small in every category, waddled over to where Henry and Paul stood, his eyes on the ground, paying close attention to the tire tracks and the plaster casts being made. His sycophants trudged three steps behind him.

"Excuse me, everyone," one of the attendants called out, as if announcing the next speaker in a crowded convention hall. "His honor the mayor is here."

The mayor had the face of a down-in-the-gutter boozer you could spot a mile away, the red lines that crisscrossed his face a road map to the nearest barstool. His boulder-sized stomach was closer to the ground than to his chin, making it a challenge to keep his pants pulled up. Paul had never seen the man when his eyes weren't bloodshot. Oftentimes he walked around with his pants' zipper down because he couldn't see if it was up or down. Standing five feet away, Madden stared at Henry, who did not turn around and acknowledge his presence.

Waiting impatiently, Madden finally said, "Mr. District Attorney. Nice to see you this morning."

Henry turned and said, "You know, Mayor, this is a crime scene."

"Yes, sir, I've heard that. This kind of thing doesn't happen in our village. I am sure you understand our concern. What sort of outsider, and I think you know what I mean by 'outsider,' came into Lindenhurst to commit such an act?"

"What is the reason for your visit?" Henry asked.

"As I was saying, Mr. Henry, a woman's murder never happens in our village," he said. "I thought it important that I be here." He turned to Paul. "Chief, what's going on? I need some answers."

Henry glared at Madden. "As I said, this is a crime scene."

"Yes, Mr. District Attorney. You don't have to repeat yourself. I am not stupid. But you are on my turf."

"Your—what?"

How did he know to come here? Paul thought.

Stupid question: Billy Evans was the mayor's nephew. More likely Trooper Schmidt had filled him in. Besides, it was all over the village that a woman's body had been found. There were no secrets in this place, particularly among the ruling class. Gossip, backstabbing, even blackmail over sexual matters if it helped another member of the class, were commonplace. Bad things that happened to some people were seen as good things by others who could take advantage of it.

When Henry failed to show him any deference, Madden moved directly in front of Paul. "I'd like an update before the end of the day," he said.

"I am a little too busy for that," Paul said.

The aide scoffed. "You will show the mayor some respect, Chief Beirne."

Pointing to the aide, Henry said, "I imagine he wipes your ass when you're done taking a shit?"

Turning to walk back to his car, Madden said, loudly, "Paul, I will be in my office until six. After that, I will be at my usual table at Baloney John's. Feel free to stop by. A reminder: you report to me, not that Irish clown who somehow got elected district attorney."

Late in the afternoon, Paul joined Evans and Cantwell in the make-shift dark room that Cantwell had built in a utility closet in the basement of Town Hall. Liquid-filled trays covered a table, filling the room with the smell of chemicals and dampness. Enlarged crime scene prints, still wet, were pinned to a clothesline strung between nails driven into the studs.

Paul started at one end of the line, staring closely at each detail in the photographs. Three were of Constance's body lying on its side, the knees together. The fourth and fifth were looking straight down at her face. The remaining ones were taken from her feet looking towards her head.

"I've got another dozen to develop, mostly of the ground around the body where the purse was, the blood on the grass," Cantwell said. "You see something you want blown up a bit, let me know, Chief. I've figured out how to use the enlarger. I'm kinda proud of myself."

"Who in God's name wanted to get in her pants?" Evans said.

Waving both arms, Paul gestured Evans out of the darkroom.

❖

When Paul pulled up in front of McKay's house, the old man was sitting in a chair on the front porch, rocking back and forth in such a way that suggested madness had overtaken him. Several neighborhood residents were with him. When they saw Paul, they rushed down the stairs and up the sidewalk. McKay's hands were shaking uncontrollably. Cigarette butts and empty glasses littered the porch in front of the chair. A moan escaped his throat as Paul approached.

"I'd like you to come with me," Paul said.

"No, no, no."

"You have to come," Paul said.

McKay pushed on both arms of the chair in a feeble attempt to stand up. He fell back into the chair. He tried again, and this time got nearly out of the chair when Paul reached out and grabbed his right arm to hold him upright. As he did, Paul saw the wet circle on the front of McKay's pants. Paul moved to his side and, holding his arm, led him down the steps to the car. The old man wheezed so heavily, Paul thought he would collapse. He opened the car door. As he did, McKay's forehead came to rest on the roof of the car.

"My God! My God!" he cried.

A few minutes later they pulled up behind the funeral parlor. Paul helped McKay extricate himself from the car. The man stared down at the ground as if he had no idea where his feet were as he tried to light another cigarette. Paul navigated him through the back door and, one awkward step at a time, down the stairs into the basement. With all the overhead lights on, the room had the appearance of the Polo Grounds on game night. A sheet covered the body up to her chin. The train victim, covered with a blanket, lay on a table pushed into the corner. A right foot stuck out from under the blanket.

McKay took a dozen steps, looked up, and stopped. His mouth fell wide open, his chin collapsed, his cigarette landed on the floor. Gasps flew out of his mouth. His wife's hair had been washed and combed. Metal staples held the eyes shut. McKay's knees buckled. Doc took his right side and, with Paul on the left, led him closer to the body, his feet dragging along the floor. Paul's thought was the man was within minutes of dropping dead.

"Oh, please no . . ." he cried. "Oh, no, no, no . . ."

McKay suddenly jerked away, reached out and pulled back the sheet before Paul could stop him, revealing the naked and torn body, the gash from her navel to her groin stitched together with black thread as thick as wire.

He shrieked, "What did he do to her? What did this animal do to my Constance?"

As Doc re-covered the corpse, McKay collapsed onto the concrete floor. Paul covered his mouth with his hand as the smell overtook him.

❖

Paul met with Cantwell and Evans at the police station and told them the plan: visit every dive bar in the village, ask about a woman drinking alone, and whether anyone saw her leave with a man.

"The logic is, it would be walking distance from the McKay home," Paul said.

"Are you making that up?" Evans said. "You have no experience with this sort of thing. This is your first murder, for God's sake. You're just winging it. You should let the state police take this over. They will figure it out. You certainly can't."

Paul knew better than to respond to anything Evans said. The man was offensive without even opening his mouth, and when he did, Paul knew from experience the best policy was to ignore him. He knew he reported everything that happened back to his uncle. Evans was a spy in plain sight who made no attempt to conceal his role.

Paul knew of three bars within a ten-minute walk of the McKay home: the Dead Mallard, the Hungry Cod, and the Alcove Bar and Grill, which was tight to the railroad tracks on West Hoffman Avenue. His bet was on the Alcove, as it was a low-end joint selling cheap booze and fifty-cent glasses of beer, although it was a German gathering place, which might have kept the Irish woman from socializing there if she could not strike up conversations. The thought made Paul think once again that she must have gone there for a purpose, perhaps for a pre-arranged meeting, as it seemed an illogical place for her to drink alone with a crowd she could not speak with. Still, he thought that was likely where she'd spent her last evening alive.

"You'll have to stay up late," Paul told them. "We need to find people who were there after eleven P.M., probably guys getting off the eleven o'clock shift at the Republic plant. Someone saw her, some bartender served her. We need to find them."

"The DA got plaster casts of the tire tracks?" Evans asked.

Assuming the mayor must have told him, Paul said, "Yes, those are done."

❖

Past midnight, Paul drove through the dark village, up and down streets where the bars were open, where the working class sat on stools and liquored up. There was little money in Lindenhurst, no wealth to speak of, albeit plenty of social hierarchies that played off against each other. Perhaps it was leftover from the war years, when the village was home to a sizeable German population, but Paul thought there remained tight little circles of people who lived off the lies of the past. Secrets were kept. Enemies were not forgotten. Questions were not welcomed. There were too many unsettled grievances. As police chief, Paul was in the awkward position of having to ask questions some people didn't want answered. Even though he was born and raised in the village, he was someone not to be trusted.

Economically, everyone in the village was pretty much in the same boat, except for a certain segment of the good-old-boy political class. A new Caddy driving down Wellwood Avenue drew a lot of eyes. It was a village where everyone was pretty much the same, except some had English as their first language and others had something else, going back to when the village was named Breslau. People lived within their tribes.

People worked where they found work, and on most evenings, found a stool to sit on. With the World Series going on, the bars that had radios were packed. Paul checked in at several and lingered for a while at Baloney John's talking to the bartender. Madden's entourage was seated in the back, the room separated from the front of the bar by sliding panels and a cloud of cigar smoke. Laughter and loud voices drifted over the panels.

By two in the morning, Paul was asleep on his couch. On the table in front of him lay a stack of dog-eared *Field & Stream* magazines. No empty beer bottles littered the table; instead there was a plate that held a few pieces of the striper he'd fried for his dinner.

The first thing that stirred him was the alarm at the village firehouse going off, followed by loud banging on his front door.

"Paul! Paul!"

He jerked awake. Reaching the door, he saw Cantwell at the step, Evans behind him.

"You have to come," Cantwell said.

He grabbed a coat and followed them out the door. They were halfway to the street when Paul looked down and saw he wasn't wearing shoes. He ran back into the house. When they arrived on Liberty Avenue, four fire engines were in front of McKay's house. Hoses snaked across the street. Thick smoke poured out the second-floor windows. Paul got out of the car in the middle of the street and ran to the house.

The front door had been pulled down. He yelled at a fireman to give him his turnout coat and helmet. He peered inside. The staircase had collapsed. He took another two steps and, looking up to where the stairs had been, saw McKay's body hanging from a long rope tied to the upstairs banister. McKay's hands were tied behind his back.

Cantwell stepped onto the porch, then pulled up short. Evans came up behind Cantwell and let out a loud whistle that to Paul was thoroughly out of place. At that moment, sparks flew in all directions as the banister gave out. The body crashed into a heap of charred and smoldering wood that had been the stairs.

FOUR

The sky in the east peeked yellows and blues. Fire trucks from two neighboring departments had packed up and left the scene. Neighbors who had stood in horror as the blaze destroyed the house were back in their homes. Paul watched as firemen poked at the coals with their long hooks. Smoke rose as hot spots popped and flared. His nose and eyes burned; the back of his mouth was basted with smoke. He was grateful when Cantwell spoke up.

"Look, Chief," Cantwell said. "We went to a bunch of bars, in the village and outside the village. There's a makeshift bar in the basement of the old bank building. They call it the Bloody Bucket. They never got a license for it. You could shut them down if you wanted. Might think twice, though. A friend of the mayor is running it. Point is, no one saw a woman, alone or drinking with a man. These bars were filled with men, that's all. The people in the Alcove don't speak English. The bartender wasn't the most helpful, either. Claimed in a heavy accent he didn't know what we were talking about and pointed to the door for us to get out."

Doc drove up. He sat in his car with the engine running for several minutes, looking over the scene. Paul felt a measure of relief at Doc's presence that quickly faded as he sensed Doc's hesitation to step outside his car. Laying off the beer the night before had been a good idea, and he felt controlling his drinking would be key to moving forward with his investigation. But, beyond that, he needed someone he could talk to candidly and who would have suggestions for what he should be doing. Someone levelheaded, a problem solver. Neither Cantwell nor Evans could fill that role.

"Morning, Paul," Doc said after exiting the car, but standing a distance away as he surveyed the scene and smelled the smoky air. He stepped towards the front of the house to see the damage inside.

"Morning," Paul said. "Glad to see you."

When Doc saw the charred body, he stiffened. His right hand rushed to cover his nose and mouth. He took an awkward half step backward, nearly stumbling, staring at McKay's remains, the skin black and in places burned to the bone. The dead man's fingers, toes, and the features on his face, had burned off. The lower jaw hung down from a blackened, skeletal face.

Doc's face registered a horror Paul could not put into words. He reached out with one arm to try to calm him. Turning, Doc took giant steps to reach his car.

"What do you want me to do?" Paul called after him.

Doc breathed loudly, pulling air into his lungs by the mouthful. Doc said, "I can't . . ."

"What should I do?" Paul asked.

"Someone will come and pick up the body and bring it to the funeral home."

"Why are you leaving?" Paul called out.

Doc got in his car, floored the gas pedal, and sped down the street. An hour later, two men arrived in the funeral home's black station wagon. Along with three firemen, they pulled the corpse out of the debris and placed it into a plastic bag. They carried the bag to the porch, and the two men went back to pick through the debris, looking for body parts. One came out with a forearm and slipped that into the bag.

When Doc arrived at Paul's office in the basement of Village Hall, Paul told him he wanted to visit the three bars within walking distance of the McKay house himself. Doc agreed to come along. In the car, Doc sat mute, his head cocked off to the side so he was staring out the window. It seemed wise not to bring up Doc's reaction to the burned corpse.

Not one to make small talk, Paul said, "I don't know what we have so far."

Doc turned towards Paul.

"I mean," Paul said, "both McKays were murdered." He waited for Doc to say something, perhaps add some insight into the conversation. When he didn't, he went on. "And there's the guy run over by the train."

Finally, Doc said, "You have your hands full." He turned away again.

They went to the Dead Mallard first. The bartender was getting ready for the evening and the next game of the World Series. He was adamant that no woman had been alone in the bar the night of the murder. Same story at the Hungry Cod.

Before ten P.M., Paul and Doc arrived at the Alcove. Just a few feet away were the railroad tracks, on either side of which were the dark stains left by the crushed body. Paul made a mental note to ask the highway crew to clean it up. Inside the bar, a cloud of cigarette smoke enveloped them like toxic fog. The radio was on at a high volume. A dozen or more men sat or stood at the bar. The bartender walked to the far end of the bar and said to two men, "*Seien Sie vorsichtig, das ist ein Cop.*"

Doc translated. "'Be careful, that's a cop.'"

Paul shouted at the bartender, "Turn down the radio!"

The bartender, a thickly built man with a hairless head, held one hand cupped at his left ear. Paul shouted it again, louder and with an edge of impatience.

"Don't play dumb with me, pal. Just do it."

Taking his time, the bartender reached to a top shelf and turned down the radio. Shouts and boos erupted. Then he leaned up against the bar and said, "What do you want?"

"I'm Chief Beirne of the village police department. This is my associate, Doc Liebmann. Were you here on the night of the twenty-ninth?"

"What?"

"Were you working on Saturday the twenty-ninth? That's not a difficult question."

The two men at the far end got up, noisily tossed coins on the bar, and walked past Paul to the door. They veered towards Doc, bumping him so hard he struggled to keep his balance. Paul grabbed one of the men by his coat and shoved him into the edge of the bar. Shouts erupted, and the bartender gestured for the men to leave.

Paul said, "A woman was in here that night, probably alone at first. Would have sat at the bar. She left with a man who was also here."

"You mean the dead broad?" the bartender said.

Doc put his hands on the bar. The bartender glared at him. He turned to the others at the bar and said, "*Schau dir dieses Arschloch an, oder?*"

"Enough of this Kraut shit!" Paul said.

He pulled his badge off his belt and pushed it into the bartender's face. He pulled back his coat to reveal his revolver. More men threw coins on the bar, stools scraping the floor, pulled on oil-stained work coats, and walked out.

Paul was surprised at his own bluster. Pulling back his coat to show his gun was not in his playbook. It felt like he was playacting. He resolved to tone down the anger, something he'd had a hard time with since he returned from Asia. His ex-wife said it came in hot bursts, most often over something petty, but knowing it was a problem and doing something about it were far apart. Beyond the bartender's attitude, he was pissing Paul off.

"Was there a woman in here by herself? Drinking alone?" he asked once more.

Doc took a full step away from the bar. The bartender turned his gaze on Paul. "You are killing off my business."

Someone shouted, "Turn the radio back on!"

"Once again, was there a woman in here drinking, who may have left with one of your customers?"

"Not that I can recall," the bartender said.

"What's your name, anyway?" Paul asked, pulling a notepad and pen out of his coat pocket.

"Gunther," he said.

"Gunther what?"

"Gunther is enough."

"Are you the owner?"

"Sort of."

"How long have you owned it?"

"Since 1948," he said.

"Why in this village? What brought you here?"

"My cousin has lived here since '31. I came to live with him."

"What's your cousin's name?"

"Why do you need to know?"

Paul said, "Where did you live before you came here?"

"In a prisoner of war camp."

The answer caught Paul by surprise. They had something in common.

"Where?" Paul asked.

"Colorado," he said. "Camp Hale. In the mountains."

"Where were you captured?" Doc asked.

"I was on the *U-521*. We were sunk on June 2, 1943, near Cape Hatteras. Two of us survived, me and the engineer. When the war ended, my hometown was in East Germany. I had nowhere to go."

"Did you have family there?" Doc asked.

"They were incinerated in the bombing of Dresden," Gunther said. "What's the word I read in your newspapers about the Jews? Genocide? What would you call firebombing a beautiful city and burning everyone alive?"

"We aren't here to argue history," Paul said.

"One day you'll have to," Gunther said.

Paul turned to look at Doc and wondered what was going through his mind. It was the first time they were together where someone in their presence spoke German. Doc appeared desperate to get out of the building.

The bartender said, "I don't know anything about a woman in here. I was in and out that night. I am asking you to leave before the rest of my business is lost tonight."

After a few minutes standing in the smoky silence, Paul and Doc stepped outside. In spite of the cool night air, sweat had beaded up on Doc's forehead. He buried his hands in his coat pockets. He shivered badly. Two men who had been in the bar but had slinked out once things got heated stood by Paul's truck.

Stepping towards them, Paul said, "How you boys doing?"

"You the police chief?" the older man said.

"I don't recall seeing you around the village."

"We're from Brooklyn," the man said. "There's work out here. A lot of houses are being built. Look, we don't want to get involved, but my friend, he was in the bar the other night. He come in around midnight or so. A woman was talking to one man off in the corner. It got loud. They were arguing about something."

"Did you hear any of it?"

"All I heard was her saying something like, 'I will rat you out if I have to. Your secret isn't safe with me anymore. Not after what you did.' And something about an agreement they had they never intended to keep. She said she was lied to. Then she was up on one of the tables dancing. Pulling her dress up. This guy shouted as he left. '*Du hältst besser die Klappe!*'"

Paul looked at Doc for help. "'You better keep your mouth shut,'" Doc translated.

"How about your names?" Paul said.

Both backed down the street and stopped at a black 1953 Ford Crestline parked against the curb. Paul followed them, making a mental note of the car make and model. As they drove away, Doc walked to the car.

"Can you take me home?" he said. He stared at Paul. "Please."

FIVE

After dropping off Doc, Paul returned to the Alcove. The two men he'd seen outside were seated back at the bar. He was surprised to see they had returned, and assumed they wanted to tell Gunther about their conversation outside. One was leaning over a jar of pickled herring, the sight of which reminded Paul of his father eating the same thing out of a mayonnaise jar and licking the goo off his fingers. Another horrible memory of the old man. Gunther was huddled over the bar talking to them. All the stools were occupied.

"I want to ask you again about two nights ago," he said to Gunther.

"I told you. Nothing happened."

"You're lying," Paul said.

Gunther pointed to the door. "Get out!"

A man in stained work clothes stood up at the bar and stepped towards Paul, who jerked the pistol from its holster.

"Stay there," Paul said.

"I told you to get out," the bartender said. "You have no right to come in here and harass my customers."

"I will come in anytime I want," Paul said. "There was a woman in here, and she left with someone. Is that person in the bar right now?" He shouted, "Is it one of you?"

He walked the length of the bar, his pistol pointed at the floor. Everyone turned away from him. When he reached the last man, Paul stood behind him, staring at his back. The man turned to face Paul, cleared his throat, and sent spit sailing onto Paul's coat. He shoved the pistol back into the holster and, with both hands on top of the man's head, slammed his face onto the bar. Pulling his head back by the hair, he slammed it a second time, and the man's nose flattened and spewed blood. Gunther vaulted over the bar as the others surrounded Paul. The man with the broken, bloody nose pushed off the barstool and took a wild swing towards Paul's head. As Paul dodged the fist, Gunther grabbed him by the back of his coat and shoved him towards the door to the street.

When he woke early in the morning—the sun had yet to reveal itself on the east side of the bungalow—he was surprised to see he was on the couch. He had not changed his clothes or taken off his shoes. Still, he was relieved to see the table in front of him empty of beer bottles. He went to the bathroom to relieve himself.

Standing over the sink, waiting on the hot water, he stared at himself in the mirror. Washing hot water over his face, he saw in front of him several Japanese officers standing on wooden crates, ropes around their necks, hands tied behind their backs. He saw himself walk across the dirt yard to one of the men, kick out the box, and watch the body drop. The neck snapped. Loudly. For several years after that day, he had felt he did the right thing. This morning, staring at himself in the mirror, regret overtook him.

I should take this mirror down, too, he thought.

When he got out of the shower his task was to start the coffee. One of the few things he had of his mother's was the silver coffeepot that had sat on the stove in their house. He did not remember why he had taken it with him, but assumed his father, who had cleaned out the house after she was gone, throwing out piles of her belongings, did not want it.

As the coffee percolated, he stood by the front windows. He saw the figure of a man standing in the wooded lot across the street from his bungalow. Sometimes people parked at the dead end of his street and walked to the creek to go fishing or crabbing. This man, who stood in the thicket a good fifty feet from the road, obscured by trees and brush, did not look like someone eyeing a place to fish. Nor was there a car nearby.

He went to the front door and stepped outside towards the street. He shouted, "Hey!" and ran across the street. No one was there.

Back inside, the phone rang. It was Cantwell, speaking in his usual rapid-fire way of talking when he was overwhelmed by events. Paul told him to calm down. They agreed to meet at headquarters at seven A.M.

"We got two dead, Chief," Cantwell said as Paul arrived and sat at his desk. "Actually three, but the first one was an accident. My question is, what does one have to do with the other?"

"Well, that's the big question, isn't it?" Paul said.

"That's not terribly helpful," Cantwell said. He stared at Paul. "What's the matter with you? You're either hungover, angry—you got a temper—or wallowing in your own misery, and that isn't helping us get to the bottom of this. Without Liebmann you'd be walking in circles talking to yourself."

Paul just nodded.

"I can't take this kind of indecision, the lack of any plan to get ahead of this thing," Cantwell said. His voice was beginning to break as stammering took over. "I don't know what to do and you don't know what to do."

"Roger, you know that patch of woods across the street from my house?"

"What about it?"

"This morning, I saw a man standing there. Well back into the trees. I think he was watching me."

"You don't know that, Paul. Could have been someone looking for something. Could be anyone. You're chasing shadows."

Evans bounded down the stairs.

"You talked to Gunther?" he asked.

Paul nodded. "How do you know him?"

"I know the bartenders in the village."

"He wasn't helpful," Paul said.

"You must have pissed him off," Evan laughed. "He's not the owner. He says he is, but he's not. It got sold to a guy named Muller. Mueller. Something like that."

"Where does he live?"

"He's been fixing up one of them summer bungalows near Great Neck Creek."

Paul said, "Split up and hit all the tire stores, in the village and in Babylon Town as well."

"Tire stores?" Evans said.

"See if you find someone coming in the day after the murder to get new tires. Let's meet back up here early afternoon."

"What are you saying?" Evans asked.

"Do I really have to explain this to you? You can't honestly be that stupid."

Cantwell raised both hands. "Hey, Chief. Come on. Billy's just asking for some direction. We're political appointees. None of us has any training. You kiss your political leader's ass, you get a government job. But that don't mean we can solve two murders."

"Maybe this guy is smart enough to assume he left tire marks, and traded in his tires to be on the safe side," Paul said.

"Oh, shit," Evans said. "This psycho wouldn't think of that in a million years. Besides, whoever did this is back in the city somewhere."

"Well, he might, and I want to check it out," Paul said.

"Makes sense to me," Cantwell said.

"Well, not to me," Evans said.

"The first thing we have to do is find out who killed the woman," Paul said. "We have to crack that one first. Hopefully, once that's out of the way, McKay's murder becomes obvious. What I can't square in my head is, was the first murder random, and the second one not? Or were both planned—part of something else?"

"Don't sound like you are thinking clearly," Evans said.

"You have a better idea?" he asked.

"Not right now."

"Then I'd suggest you shut your mouth."

Paul found Mueller's house at the end of Seacrest Avenue. He remembered coming to this part of the village with his mother in the aftermath of the 1938 hurricane and finding blocks of bungalows had washed away. Mueller's house was halfway through a remodeling into a Craftsman-style home with an added-on porch wrapped around the front. A stack of plywood leaned against the outside wall, next to a pallet of roof shingles. As Paul parked in the sandy driveway, Mueller came around from the back of the house.

"Mr. Mueller?" he called out. "I'm Paul Beirne. Chief of the village police department."

Mueller stepped closer to Paul but did not stick out his hand.

"You've been to my establishment," he said.

Paul could see Mueller's back was already up and all he'd done was introduce himself.

"You should have called first before you came over and pushed people around. How can you behave like that and expect anyone to go out of their way to help you? Beating up people when they don't answer your questions is not the road to success."

There was the hint of a German accent, but slight enough that Paul concluded he had been in this country for decades. Paul guessed Mueller was nearly sixty years old, with prematurely snow-white hair and a well-maintained mustache of the sort that requires careful attention and daily maintenance.

"The woman who was murdered—you know about that?"

"Who doesn't in this village? Someone sneezes in the post office and within an hour everyone knows about it."

"She may have been in your place in the hours before she was killed," Paul said.

"I doubt that," Mueller said.

"Why do you doubt it?" Paul asked.

In an awkward, rocking gait, Mueller turned and walked around the side of the house to the back, Paul in tow. Two-by-fours were stacked along the back of the house. He went to a table with four chairs overlooking the creek. He picked up the stub of a cigar from a clamshell ashtray, put a match to it, and fell into a chair.

Mueller said, "Your father—Helmuth Baer? Everyone calls him Howard?"

Paul moved closer to the table. "What about it?" he said.

"We have a poker group. Meets every other Monday night. I'm curious. He is Baer, and you are Beirne? He said you changed your name at some point and took your mother's maiden name. You have a young son who also has the Beirne name. Is that right? What are you running from, anyway?"

"What business is that of yours?" Paul asked.

"Clearly, you are running from something. You hate him. That's quite a burden to carry around with you, Chief Beirne."

Paul took an instant dislike to the man. He resisted the urge to turn around and walk away.

"Look, Mr. Mueller. A woman was dancing on a table in the Alcove. Were you there?"

"I would hate to think she was in my place, left with one of my customers, and was murdered and dumped by the side of the road," he said, his voice taking on a more conciliatory tone. "We attract a mixed crowd, but hopefully over time the heavy drinkers will find somewhere else to go. But I don't think anyone who would come into my bar could do something like that. The animals in the city rip women up. That's not anyone I am acquainted with. We Germans, we don't commit that kind of cruelty. We are a cultured people. Bach, Beethoven, Goethe, you know. Civilized."

"Civilized?" Paul said. "I assume you read the accounts at the Nuremberg trials. I don't think I'd apply that word to your kind."

Mueller stared at Paul, his eyes flashing, his head shaking side to side. "That history will be argued over for decades," he said. "And in the end, thoroughly denied."

"History isn't what you pretend it to be," Paul said. After nearly a minute of awkward silence, Paul said, "Were you there?"

"I was in and out that night, yes. But I didn't see that, nor did anyone tell me this had happened."

"How did you meet my father?"

"I will answer that if you answer my earlier point: Why do you use your mother's maiden name?"

"Is that what he told you?"

"You blame him for your mother walking out on you both, and in response you took her name over your birth name. You were Baer when you enlisted in the Navy, and Beirne when you returned. Is that right?"

Paul ignored him.

"Sounds to me like one of your goals in life is to punish your father, make him guilty of some sin you've invented in your head. I find it hard to believe you could be a normal man, doing normal police work, Chief Beirne, after your time in a Jap camp. Barbarians, those people."

Paul fell silent as disgust for the man gripped him. That his old man would talk about personal family matters with this man was grotesque.

Mueller said, "How we know each other is a long story. We were both born in a town in southern Germany. I came here after the Great War ended, your father after that. All three of my brothers were killed on the Western Front. Your father has a brother. He tell you that?"

This was news to Paul.

"That would be your uncle." When Paul did not respond, he said, "You know anything about the history there at that time?"

Paul shook his head.

"You and your father don't talk?"

"Don't lecture me, Mueller," Paul said. "I don't give a shit what you think."

Mueller waited a moment. "Your father and I, we were in First Company, Sixth Bavarian Reserve Division. That's where we met for the first time. Did your father ever tell you about the battle at Ypres? Forty thousand men were killed in less than three weeks. What do you think that kind of human slaughter does to a survivor? Huh? Perhaps you should take that into consideration."

"Whatever happened to you, and to Baer—in a war your country started—"

"You can't even say 'father'? You hate him that much?"

"I don't know what I am doing here with people like you," Paul said. "I find all of you thoroughly sickening. Your ilk marched up and down Wellwood Avenue in the thirties with your flags and your uniforms singing your bullshit songs. You thought you were in Germany instead of the Village of Lindenhurst. America didn't suit you—you wanted to import your horror here."

Mueller put both hands on the arms of the chair and awkwardly pushed himself up. As he did, Paul saw the lower part of a wooden leg. A crutch lay on the grass. Unable to hold himself up, Mueller fell back into the chair.

"In our company was a corporal who became famous a few years later. Did your father ever tell you this?"

"Tell me what?"

"About this corporal?"

He shook his head.

"You are not aware of your father's biography? That's a shame. You must be reading all the claptrap in your American newspapers about trials and the like in Germany. Get off my property, or I will call the state troopers and have you removed. You are a sick man, Chief Beirne. It will catch up to you."

"Are you threatening me?"

"Giving you some advice."

SIX

He parked behind Village Hall. Doc was waiting on him. He was glad to see him, if only to help him push Mueller out of his thoughts. Mueller was the voice of the past his ilk wanted to hold on to as a point of pride and to tie the facts up with so many lies that the past would reinvent itself. On the other hand, Doc was the voice of common sense, the voice of *this is what happened*. They walked to the funeral home and down the stairs into the basement. When they reached the last step, Doc flipped a switch and the bright ceiling lights turned on. On the stainless steel table lay the burned remains of Mr. McKay. The arms, legs, and torso were black. The remaining skin on the top of his head was curdled. Paul found the sight too horrific even to stare at for a few seconds.

"The fire, of course, erased so much of what I would need to look at," Doc said. "It's certain he died from the hanging. His throat was crushed. The second vertebrae, C2, was broken. The hangman's fracture, I think they call that. There were pieces of cord that bound his hands behind his back. His ankles were also tied together. We can't return to the house and examine what took place. We can't recreate anything. It's all destroyed."

"Is it possible it's a suicide?" Paul said.

"No," Doc said. "He'd have to tie his own hands and ankles and then wrap the rope around his neck. Not possible. The remains of his clothing also had the faint smell of gasoline. But I did find something interesting."

He pointed to the table in the corner. Some loose change, a belt buckle, and a charred wallet sat in a porcelain bowl.

"His wallet was in the back pocket of his trousers. I opened it with some tweezers. Inside was a tightly folded postcard."

Paul walked to the table. He held the postcard between his thumb and forefinger. On one side was a picture of the Statue of Liberty, on the upper right a one-cent stamp. He turned it over. One word had been written on the back: *VERRATERIN?* It was addressed to the McKay house and postmarked in Manhattan.

Paul stumbled on the pronunciation. "What does that mean?"

"Traitor," Doc said. "There are two ways to spell it, feminine and masculine. This is the feminine version of the word. It's interesting that there is a question mark after it."

"How do you interpret that?"

"It was a warning: don't betray us. Keep a secret," Doc said. "But directed at Mrs. McKay. Or more likely, both of them."

"Would she know a German word like that?" Paul said.

"Maybe that word," Doc said. "Probably not the first time she heard them, either. By the way, no one has claimed the remains."

Paul wasn't surprised. "What will you do, then?" he asked.

"Keep them here for a week or so, then put them in a cheap box and bury them in the village cemetery, in the back where the paupers and the unclaimed go," Doc said. "That's where both of them will end up."

"That night we were outside the Alcove with those men," Paul said. "One of them said Mrs. McKay was arguing with a German-speaking man, threatening to blow the whistle on something. Now this." Looking around, Paul said, "What happened to the body run over by the train?"

Doc walked to the metal desk in the corner. "It was claimed," he said.

Paul was surprised.

"I got a call from a funeral home in Yorkville. The Upper East Side of Manhattan. The man said someone would come out and claim the body. The remains were picked up late yesterday afternoon."

"Who was the dead guy? Did this man say?"

Doc picked up a file folder. "I asked him. He was reluctant to give a name. He acted like he didn't know, then changed his tune that they—whoever 'they' are—wouldn't tell him. I said I could not turn over the body to the funeral home without a name, and he hung up. When the attendant from the funeral home came to pick up the remains, I tried again."

"Did he tell you?"

"The dead man was one Hermann W. Lang. He also made an odd comment: Lang just got out of federal prison and was to be deported to Germany in the coming days."

"What was he doing in Lindenhurst at the Alcove? He was going to go back to New York City and be deported? Where's the sense in that?"

"Before the man came out, I went over the remains again," Doc said. "The two-hundred-ton locomotive crushed the body. It would be impossible to try and figure out what was there that was not caused by the train itself. But there was a break in the skull, in the back, about three inches above the neck. A horizontal break about four inches in length. It split the skull. I found it when I turned a bright light directly on the back of the skull and combed up the hair. I missed it before because the man's hair covered it. When I used a comb to lift the hair this time, I could see it under the bright light. I kicked myself for not seeing it before, but then everything pointed to a drunk man falling on the tracks and being run over. Besides, I am a medical doctor. Educated in the classical style in Vienna. I am not a medical examiner trained to look for evidence of a crime."

"It wasn't an accident?" Paul asked.

"Oh, the train ran over him. The question is, was he dead before it happened, or unconscious and someone put him on the tracks so the train would run him over and it would look like an accident?"

"What caused the head wound? Could it be connected to the train hitting him?" Paul said.

"Based on the damage, my guess is he was face up when he got run over. That action cut the body in half and pushed both halves to either side of the train. I don't see how or where the back of his head would have come into contact, either with the train or the surface of the road, hard enough to cause a very clean split in the back of his head that is no wider than the width of a hair."

"What caused it?"

"A thin metal rod," Doc said. "Not something wide like a baseball bat. That would cave in the head. More like a steel pipe. The skull itself was not pushed in. Brain matter didn't seep out. Certainly, it knocked him out completely, which then would have allowed whoever did this to lay him out on the tracks and get away. He was probably alive when the train ran over him."

Paul sat down at Doc's desk. Once again that feeling of being overwhelmed with details swept through him. Looking up at Doc, he said, "The night before the McKay woman was killed—were both in the bar?"

"I think you should assume she was. Which then begs the question: What does Lang have to do with her? Or, to turn it around, what does she have to do with him?"

He looked at Doc, hoping he would say something brilliant that would clear up the whole thing.

"I don't know how to do this, Doc. I need another set of eyes and another mind thinking about all of this."

"I know the dead, Paul," Doc said. "The rest is your job."

"I can't do this by myself," Paul said.

"You will have to," Doc said. *"Man muss innere Stärke finden und diese lösen."*

"What does that mean?"

"You have to find your inner strength." He walked to his desk. "There was the medal I found covered with blood inside his shirt." He picked it up and handed it to Paul. On one side was a date: 9 November 1923. On the opposite side was a swastika. A red ribbon hung from one end.

"What is it?"

"That month and year something called the 'Beer Hall Putsch' occurred in Munich. We read about it when I was growing up in Vienna. Hitler and a small group of men tried to take over the government. The coup failed. Some went to jail, and that's when Hitler wrote that great piece of trash, *Mein Kampf.* Everyone in that group was given this medal as heroes. It's called a Blood Order medal. It's very interesting that this man was in that small group. It makes him not just a Nazi, but a very special Nazi."

Nearly every time Paul talked with Doc he felt out of his depth. He was embarrassed for his lack of knowledge and his shallow view of history. He didn't know what Doc had been through. He could guess.

Still, somehow, Doc could go about his day with a sense of purpose. He remained levelheaded while Paul struggled with the everyday. Some days he was embarrassed to be around such a learned man.

❖

Cantwell found Paul's truck parked in front of the Dead Mallard. It was a few minutes past midnight. Paul was sitting alone at the far end of the bar, a half-filled whisky glass in front of him. The Dead Mallard was a notch above dive, with more beer choices, a higher class of hard liquor, and several food items for sale prepared in a back kitchen. Sandwiches, oysters, and clams on the half shell, a halfway decent clam chowder, fried squid. Bowls of peanuts sat on the bar along with a jar of loose cigarettes. The clientele was different as well. Several better-dressed men seated at the bar looked like office workers.

The bartender looked at Cantwell as he approached, and jerked his right hand towards the door to indicate he wanted Paul out of the bar.

"Chief, we found a tire place down on the highway," Cantwell said.

When Paul did not look back over his shoulder at his deputy, Cantwell said, louder, "We found a tire place down on the highway. Are you hearing me?"

He looked up, wiping his face with a napkin and pushing away a tray of oysters, the shells empty. He picked up the whisky glass, eyed it for a moment, then returned it to the bar. The bartender quickly grabbed it and dropped it in the sink.

"Yes, I heard you, Roger," he said.

"Allen's Tire Repair. I went to high school with Richie. Fought in France before his tank got blown up. Came home in a hospital ship. Had to learn how to walk again. He said a guy came in the morning after the murder. Early, before Richie opened. He drove a 1949 Plymouth DeLuxe. Bright blue. Mud and dirt all over the sides. Empty beer and whisky bottles on the floor in the back. Inside smelled like puke. The driver wanted four new tires. Richie put the car up on the rack and went outside and told the guy the tires were fine; they didn't need to be replaced."

Paul stood up. "What happened next?"

"He put on four new tires like the guy said."

"And the old ones?"

"Well, normally, Richie waits until the end of each week and then loads up a pickup and takes the tires to the town dump, where they get burned. That's that rubber smell that floats over the village on Friday afternoons. He said this guy wanted to take them."

"You get a name?"

Cantwell reached in his coat pocket and pulled out a receipt. He handed it to Paul, who read the words out loud: "Wouldn't give name." Below it was a license plate number.

"Call the trooper barracks and see if they can help us with the plate number," Paul said. "And where is Evans?"

"He dropped me off. He said he had some other places he wanted to try," Cantwell said. "I think he's already talking to the troopers about the plate number."

In the morning, Paul read the note on his desk: *Rudolf Haase, age 47, six feet, four inches in height, 230 pounds, no criminal record, lives on Fulton Avenue near the intersection of Hamilton Avenue.* Paul knew the house: two-story with a wide porch in the front and garage on the side that was used to store lumber. He recalled it had a wood-working shop in the back. He called the funeral home and asked Doc to go along with him and Cantwell in case Haase did not speak English.

In the car, Cantwell said, "I don't know about this, Chief. Don't we need to talk to a judge first? Seriously. We don't know nothing about this guy other than he was looking for new tires. I don't know what to say to him. Do you?"

When they arrived, a tall, long-armed man with short, steel-gray hair wearing worn jeans and a white undershirt under a denim jacket stood in the driveway hosing down a blue Plymouth DeLuxe. The number on the license plate matched the one on the receipt. A vacuum cleaner, its cord running into the back door of the house, sat next to the car. They got out and walked up the driveway.

Haase turned towards them, stared for a moment, then went back to hosing down the car.

"Mr. Haase?" Paul called out. The Plymouth was running and the radio on. "Can we talk to you?"

Haase twisted the nozzle on the hose, turned, and faced the three men. He reached into his denim jacket and pulled out a pack of Camel cigarettes. One went in his mouth, which he lit with a silver lighter.

Paul looked him over, struck by the man's enormous hands and mile-long fingers. His bulging chest and upper arms stretched the jacket. A woman, over six feet tall, with dyed-black hair pulled back into a tight knot, stood in the backyard in the remains of a vegetable garden. She was holding a shovel and staring at Haase. Two teenage boys stood with her. The woman dropped the shovel to the ground. She yelled in German at the boys to go inside the house.

"Good afternoon. I'm Paul Beirne, chief of the village police department. These are my associates, Deputy Cantwell and Doc Liebmann. I can see you have new tires on your car."

Haase stood still. Paul looked to Doc for help.

"Guten tag, Herr Haase. Haben sie ein paar Minuten, um mit uns zu sprechen?"

Haase turned to the woman, who was walking towards him. He shouted, *"Du gehst jetzt rein."* She retreated into the house.

"We need you to speak in our language, Mr. Haase," Paul said.

"Yes. I speak English okay," Haase said.

Walking past the vacuum cleaner, Doc peered into the car. The front seat was wet. The floor mats had been removed and hosed down and were draped over the rusting fence that enclosed the backyard.

Paul lifted the car's trunk.

"Where do you work, Mr. Haase?" Paul asked.

"Huh?"

"He is asking where you work?" Cantwell said.

"I'm a carpenter."

"A carpenter?" Paul asked. "What exactly do you do?"

"Carpentry," he said.

"Yes, I get that. Could you be more specific?"

"I do my own jobs. Kitchen cabinets are my specialty. Some remodeling. I also work for contractors in the area. Mr. Levitt is building a lot of houses to the west. I'm getting a lot of work now."

"Good for you," Paul said. "How long have you done that?"

"A few years," he said.

"What did you do before that?" Paul asked.

He walked around the far side of the car, looking through the glass to see what Doc had seen. He stopped, looked at Haase, and repeated the question.

"The Republic plant," he said. "Other odd jobs. Whatever they asked me to do. Mostly carpentry."

"What other odd jobs?"

"A lab up in Cold Spring Harbor."

"What did you do there?" Paul asked.

"The scientists needed shelving and cabinets."

"How did you get that job?"

"Through a friend of mine. He recommended me."

"Who would that be?"

"I don't remember."

"What kind of lab work is done there?" Paul said.

"They study the human body," Haase said. "Eugenics is the word in English. The differences between people, that sort of thing. Why the *zerstörte Menschen* in society should be disposed of."

"Damaged people?" Doc said. "That's what you said? Damaged people should be disposed of? Like trash?"

"I'm just saying that's what they did," Haase said.

Doc stared at Haase's hands, which were six or eight inches across the wide part of the palm, and nearly a foot from his wrist to the tip of his longest finger. This caught Cantwell's attention, too, which caused Haase to cross his arms over his chest and step away from the car. He threw the cigarette on the driveway and stepped on it.

"Do you know about the woman found dead by the side of Wellwood Avenue?" Paul asked.

He looked up and saw the woman from the backyard looking at them from the kitchen window.

"I don't know about that," he said.

"Sie mussan gehort haben," Doc said. *"Es ist das Gerede des dorfes. Worum spielst du dumm?"*

"I'm not playing dumb," Haase said. "I work late some days and I don't have many friends, and when I am not working, I come home."

"You're a family man—is that what you are saying?" Doc asked.

Haase looked at Doc. "What is this accent you have? Austrian? Viennese?"

Doc ignored him.

"High class? Is that what you are?" Haase said. He pinched his nose with his right thumb and forefinger as if warding off a foul odor.

Paul said, "Do you go to bars in the village? When your work for Mr. Levitt is done? Do you have a bar or two you like to visit and have a few drinks before you go home?"

"I work. I come home."

"You really don't look like a man who goes to work and then comes home for dinner with the family, and you all sit on the couch listening to Jack Benny or the Lone Ranger on the radio. You look like a man who enjoys his alcohol. The night of September 29, Mr. Haase. Tell us about that day. Where you were."

"I was installing kitchen cabinets for Mr. Levitt," he said.

"That was a Saturday. You worked then?"

"There's a lot of work to be done," Haase said.

"Where did you go from there?"

Haase's face twisted and his eyes squinted.

"Come on," Paul said. "You can remember a few days ago, can't you? You left work—where did you go?"

"I go to Baloney John's," he said. "I wanted to listen to the baseball game since my wife, she don't know nothing about baseball."

"Your wife?" Paul asked.

"Charlotte."

"Maybe we should talk to her, Mr. Haase."

"She doesn't speak good English," he said. He stepped sideways to block anyone from trying to get through the gate towards the back door.

"Ich kann helfen," Doc said. He turned to Paul. "I told him I can help with that."

"It's not necessary," Haase said. "She keeps to herself."

"Are you saying you keep secrets from her?" Paul asked.

"I went to Baloney John's. I had a few drinks, and it was too loud to hear the game. I went home."

"Straight home?"

"I wasn't there when that boy caught the ball the way he did," Haase said.

"Did you go to the Alcove? That's your kind of low-class place."

"I didn't go there, no."

"What time did you get home?" Paul asked.

"I can't remember."

"Take your best guess."

"Around ten." He looked puzzled for a moment. "Yes. Ten."

"You remember it exactly?" Paul asked. "Exactly ten o'clock?"

He nodded.

"Your wife was up? She can vouch for that?"

"No," he said. "She's asleep by nine most nights."

"Very convenient," Paul said.

"So," Doc said. "Describe the moment you came home. You say it was around ten? You drove up this driveway in this car. Parked. Then what?"

Haase stammered, raised his hands, tried to say something but pulled back. After he had collected himself, he said, "I went in the house." He pointed to the back door.

"What happened then?" Doc said.

"Who are you?" Haase said. "Some Jew from Vienna?"

Paul had heard about "the Jews" from his father since childhood. His long-winded, boozy rants of conspiracies about cabals and secret

Jewish groups manipulating the world to their advantage while the hard-working man struggled to put two pennies together was heard at a hundred dinner tables. Paul's mother tried to get him to stop, but the more she brought it up, the more he spit it out.

Doc ignored him and stepped towards the gate. When he looked up, an ancient woman was staring at him through a window. Her deeply wrinkled face and snow-white hair filled the window. Doc looked away and towards Paul. When he caught his eye, he jerked his thumb up over his shoulder, pointing to the woman.

"I went inside," Haase said.

"We've established that," Paul said. "Let's try and move ahead, will you? Don't talk like you don't know anything. You got inside. What next?"

Doc looked again and the old woman was gone.

"I went in the kitchen."

"Were you drunk by the time you got home?"

"I am never drunk."

"But you drink a lot," Paul said. "Looking at you, I can tell you can really put it away. What did you do when you got into the kitchen?"

"I took a beer from the refrigerator. There's a radio in the living room and I turned it on, and I listened to the game. I don't know, maybe it was over. I can't remember. I was tired and went to bed."

Haase glared at Doc. *"Die Juden ziehen alle Fäden. Du weißt, dass,"* he said.

"The Jews pull all the strings?" Doc said. "That's your excuse about why your life is so worthless?"

"They manipulated everything in Germany."

"Shut up!" Doc shouted. "What were the German Jews, Haase? One percent of the population? They did all that? If you were in the gutter, it's because you're stupid and lazy."

"That's bullshit," Haase said.

"You are a lover of conspiracies, Haase," Doc said. "You need them to explain your own failures in life." Doc turned to Paul. "I can't believe I come to this country and encounter people like Haase."

"What time did you go to bed?" Paul asked, trying to keep the questioning on track.

"I don't know," Haase said.

Paul pushed open the gate and took a step towards the back door. Standing on the bottom step, a piece of plywood set atop two cinder blocks, he peered through the glass when the door suddenly jerked open and he was face-to-face with the old woman.

"Geh weg von meinem Sohn," she shouted, waving a knobby, arthritic hand in Paul's face. *"Du horst mich?"*

Stepping closer to the fence, Doc said, "She's telling us to stay away from her son."

"She can say anything she wants," Paul said.

Haase put his arm across the old woman's shoulder and tried to steer her back into the house. She wouldn't have it.

"Du willst meinen Sohn einrahmen," she shouted. *"Deshalb bist du heir. Um meinen Sohn zu rahmen."*

"What the hell is she going on about?" Paul asked.

"'You want to frame my son. That's why you are here. To frame my son.'"

"She is interfering with official police work. Tell her I can arrest her."

"She must know something," Cantwell said. "It might be a better approach, Chief, to make nice with her."

Paul shouted, "Haase. Tell me. Why are you cleaning your car today? Why are there new tires on your car?"

"It's my day off. I always wash the car on my day off."

"You didn't need four new tires, but you bought them anyway. Where are the old ones?"

"I take care of my car. I don't let it go downhill."

"You are a liar. Are you going to let us in the house?"

"No," he said. "There is no reason for you to go in the house. You've upset my wife and my two sons and my mother, and I don't appreciate what you are doing."

With three fast steps Paul stood in Haase's face, his right hand on Haase's chest, pushing against him. Doc put his hand on Paul's arm to pull him back.

"Paul," he said. "Let's not go there." He pulled harder, and Paul retreated.

Paul turned to Cantwell. "Roger, check out the garage. See what's there."

"Don't we need a search warrant?"

"Just do it," Paul said.

The old woman grabbed her son by the arm and pulled him towards the house. With her right hand pointed at Paul, she said, *"Ich habe Leute wie dich gekannt. Sehen sie, was sie mit Frau Hauptmann gemacht haben. Sie alle liegen Morder."*

"What the hell is she going on about, for God's sake?" Paul said.

Doc said, "'I've known people like you. Look what they did to Frau Hauptmann. Lying murderers, all of you.'"

"Frau who?" Paul said. "What is she talking about?"

"Wer ist Frau Hauptmann?" Doc asked.

That name—Hauptmann. Paul heard his mother say it in one of the many arguments he overheard between his parents when he was hiding in his bedroom out of fear of his father.

Before she could answer, Paul shouted, "What did you do with the tires you took off the car, Haase?"

"Nothing in the garage, Chief," Cantwell said.

Haase's head spun to the right. A state police car pulled up in front of the house and stopped in the middle of the street. Jack Homestead, in his uniform as the superintendent of the barracks, and Trooper Schmidt stepped out of the car.

"Hello," shouted Homestead. "Hello, Paul." Both men walked up the driveway.

Paul stepped towards him. "What the hell are you doing here, Jack? Someone call you?"

Homestead said, "I thought we'd come by and see if we can help out."

As the two men reached the top of the driveway, Haase and his mother retreated through the gate and into the house.

"You have no business being here," Paul said.

"Hey. Come on," Homestead said, both hands up in front of his face as if surrendering to Paul. "We are on the same side, aren't we? You are always so angry, Paul. What's with you? This is a heinous crime, and we are here to assist and help you reach a resolution—"

"Assist? Who asked you to assist, Homestead?"

"That's Superintendent Homestead," Schmidt said.

"Hey, Paul, let's go," Doc said.

"What are you doing here, Homestead?"

"You want to be reasonable? Huh? You want to act like a professional?" When Paul said nothing, Homestead said, "I have important information to pass on to you. If you can climb off your high horse."

When Paul turned towards him, Homestead said, "We got a call last night and again this morning from one of the supervisors up at the Pilgrim State lunatic asylum. She said one of the people there has been talking about the dead McKay woman."

Paul said, "He used her name?"

"That's what we're told, yes," Homestead said. "This is the nursing supervisor if you want to talk to her."

He pulled a slip of paper out of his coat pocket and handed it to Paul.

"Why didn't you just call me?" Paul said. "Why did you come here? How did you know we were at Haase's house, Homestead?"

Schmidt jumped between Homestead and Paul. "You will show him some respect, Beirne. Who the hell do you think you are?"

"You are a real problem, Beirne, you know that?" Homestead said. "A real problem. You don't seem to understand. Besides, I don't answer to you."

The two men turned and walked to the car.

SEVEN

The next morning, after a fitful night without sleep, Paul walked outside and across the street to the woods. He walked fifty feet into the trees, looking down at the ground for anything that might have been dropped there. He found a pile of oyster shells, some rusty soup cans, spent cigarette butts, and an oily rag. He picked up one of the butts: a Camel. Haase's brand.

At his office, he told Cantwell to contact Lindsay Henry and ask him to get a court order to put a tap on Haase's phone. He told Evans to go to the town dump and look for tires bound for the incinerator. Paul drove east on Montauk Highway until he turned north on Fifth Avenue and then to Crooked Hill Road towards Brentwood.

Everything about Haase had kept him up all night. For well over an hour he sat by the back door looking out at the creek, glowing pale in the light of a nearly full moon. He watched the tide come in. At one point he filled a whisky glass, then poured it back into the bottle.

Haase had become a mirror image of Paul's father—oversized, loud, abrasive, brutish, overly aggressive, easily enraged into a fight. They were cut from the same cloth. Hearing Haase and his mother going on in German brought back memories of his own mother and father, before she left, with his father shouting at her in German and his mother, cowed, unable to respond. Haase's German, and the German of Paul's father, had become the oppressor's language.

He veered west towards the massive complex of Pilgrim State, a monolith of how one state treated its mentally ill and criminally insane. The brick high-rise buildings sat on one thousand acres, a city unto itself, with its own electrical plant, water- and sewage-treatment plant, carpentry shop, cemetery, four greenhouses, a farm field to grow food for the inmates, and its own police and fire departments. Paul had read recently in the *Star* an announcement from the state that the facility was the largest of its kind in the world, with over thirteen thousand "patients."

The road took him to the front of the cluster of buildings. He removed the revolver from under his shoulder and locked it in the glove box, got out of the car, and walked up to the front entrance. He had been here on official business a dozen or more times on missing persons cases, and each time it made him physically sick. The sight of the patients, the stale air in the building, the hopelessness of people waiting to die—it all sickened him. They were no better off than he was trapped in a pitch-black, airless submarine on the ocean floor. He recalled his first visit when a wave of panic rippled through him. His mind seized on the fear that he would be locked inside, banging on the doors, screaming his lungs out, all the while surrounded by men and women in hospital gowns.

As he passed through the entrance doors into the main lobby, his stomach turned over. Groups of men and women in white shirts and white pants sat in clusters, some bound tightly in straitjackets. Others were chained to chairs or to metal rings set in long rows along the wall. The smell of urine-soaked clothes, cigarette smoke, and disinfectant filled Paul's nose. Shouts erupted down a hallway. He stepped towards a group of men and women in wheelchairs. One of them jumped up from his chair and was jerked back by a chain.

"You! You!" the man shouted.

Paul's attention was drawn to the man's forehead. His right eye appeared smaller than the left, and the skull above the right eye was slightly dented. Stepping backward toward the entrance, Paul bumped into a uniformed security guard.

"Are you here for a purpose?" the guard said.

He pulled his badge out of a coat pocket. He handed the man the slip of paper with the supervisor's name on it.

"Do you know how I can find her?" he said.

The man went to the desk by the front door, opened a binder, and read through the names.

"Supervisor O'Donnell is on the fourth floor. I will have someone take you up there. Or you can wait until she can leave her duties and come down to meet you. It could be a long wait; she's very busy."

"Well," Paul said. He had no intention of sitting here waiting. "I guess I should go up there."

"Okay," the man said. "I'll get someone to take you up."

"I can't go up on my own?"

"Believe me, you wouldn't want to," the guard said.

Five minutes later, a young man in a white coat escorted Paul to the elevators but veered towards a door leading to a staircase. Halfway up they passed a woman in a floor-length coat seated on a step. They climbed another floor to a locked door. The escort removed a ring of skeleton keys from his belt and tried several before he found the right one.

Pulling open the heavy door, he turned to Paul and said, "Stay close to me as we walk. It's best not to make eye contact with the patients. They see you looking at them, you'll never get out of here."

A long hallway flooded with overhead lights ran from one end of the building to the other. Men and women in white coats and gowns scurried about. They passed two men walking with an elderly woman hovered over a walker. As they got closer, Paul noticed her forehead, which had that same disfigured look as the person in the lobby. Loud voices and shouts echoed down the hallway.

"There's one thing you never want to do here," the escort said. "And I mean ever. Don't get into a conversation with these people. You start talking to them and you might as well jump out the first open window."

They crossed a room full of seated people and entered a small office. The escort closed the door behind them.

"Dr. O'Donnell will be here shortly," the escort said.

"Where is she now?"

"In the operating room."

"You do surgeries here?"

"Oh, yes," the escort said with a measure of pride. "That's our specialty. Prefrontal lobotomies."

He pointed to his forehead with the index finger of his right hand.

"You drill a hole in the skull or go in just under the eyelid with a long needle and scramble the connections to the front of the brain. Cutting the wiring, essentially. It's simple, really. I've watched. Hell, I could do it. Doesn't take a half hour. One after another, like an assembly line. They used to drill a hole in the skull with a power drill and pour acid into it, but they stopped that a while ago."

As the escort left the office, Paul was relieved to see a woman holding a clipboard coming towards him. She took a chair and, looking up at Paul, said, "Are you okay? Don't pass out on me."

Her name tag read: DR. KAREN O'DONNELL.

"I want to get this over with," he said, falling back into one of the chairs.

The confinement, the wretched smell that permeated everything, the scratchy voices of patients shouting for attention, the narrowness of her office, rattled him. Claustrophobia gripped him. He took a handkerchief out of his back pocket and wiped sweat off his forehead.

"You called the state police to say someone here was talking as if he knew something about the murder I'm investigating?" Paul said.

"August Lothar Hagar," she said. "Auggie for short. He was first brought here in the spring of 1939. He stayed a little over a year and then was released. I also heard he was living with a man in the village he knew from the old country. He was readmitted later, and he's been here ever since."

"Why was he admitted the first time?"

She looked through the papers on her clipboard. "It was after he was questioned by state police for the murder in November 1938 of a woman found dead in a lake on the South Shore." She flipped up some pages. "November 10, 1938. A young Jewish woman."

"I believe that's an open case," Paul said.

"I doubt any authority cares enough to take another look at it. I doubt they cared then. That date has some significance in Germany if you know your history. It's called the 'Night of the Broken Glass.' If Hagar did it, he got himself in here to avoid being arrested. Or maybe someone wanted to shut him up and had him admitted. In those days, it was easy. It's still easy. The way the law works, a husband can bring his wife in and, on his signature, have her admitted. Once she's in, it takes quite an effort to get her out. I asked him once if he was involved, just to see how he would respond, and he said something like, 'It wasn't me, but I know who did it.'"

"How is that relevant to my case now?" he asked.

"Someone carved a swastika on her forehead with a pocketknife," she said. "Before that was done, her attacker shoved his hand up her vagina and ripped out her insides."

He was surprised at the details. "How do you know that? I doubt the newspapers back then had that kind of information."

"Hagar told me that's what happened to the young woman. He was very specific about what happened to her."

"When?"

"I've heard it on a number of occasions, but again two nights ago. He does talk about a lot of things. He is approaching insanity. So whatever he says has to be taken with a grain of salt. He also goes on about a dead boy, a toddler. I've heard that one several times. I have no idea what that refers to."

On her desk she picked up a copy of that week's Lindenhurst *Star* and a thick binder under it. She unfolded the newspaper, with the large headline: WOMAN FOUND DEAD OFF WELLWOOD. The photograph on the cover was taken from the road and showed a fleshy mound on the ground in the distance, Doc Liebmann and Paul standing over it.

"You've seen this, I'm sure," she said. "It quotes Trooper Schmidt as saying her insides were pulled out. When I read that, I thought of Hagar and what he talked about the other night."

She reached out with the newspaper, but Paul didn't look at it.

"There are newspapers all over the facility for our patients to read," she said.

"As I said, there was no conviction in the 1938 murder," Paul said.

"You will see in the binder that Hagar had an alibi when police questioned him. He said he was in Germany burning down synagogues. He rambles a lot when he's sitting with other patients. I can't reconcile that with his telling me he knows who killed the girl."

"You say 'patients.' Is that what they are?"

"What would you call them?"

"Inmates. Prisoners. This is little more than a POW camp."

"This isn't a prison, sir."

"Yes, it is," Paul said. "These people can't be on the outside. I assume most will never get out and will die here."

"Well, there is some truth to that. We do have a cemetery. In the southwest corner by the farm field. If no one claims them, which is most often the case, they end up there."

"A mass grave?" Paul said.

"Yes, something like that."

"You bother to write down the names of the people who get dumped there?"

"I doubt it," she said. "What would be the point?"

"My God," Paul said. "So someone could spend a lifetime here, sitting in a chair in a straitjacket, staring out the window. And when it all comes to an end, they're dumped in a hole in the ground out back?"

"Yes," she said. "That's right. If you have a better idea what to do with these people, you should write the governor and tell him. Otherwise, I'd suggest you withhold your criticism."

"Are there gravestones?"

"No, the state wouldn't pay for that. Sometimes a plaque with a number on it. Most often, though, there's nothing at all."

"You said he rambles when he sits with people here? About what?"

"Killing a toddler. Bashing his head in. Also, he was in the German American Bund chapter in Lindenhurst. He loves talking about that. Nazis in uniform marching up and down Wellwood Avenue in the village."

She got up from the chair. "Follow me," she said.

They walked through the room, which exploded in shouts. When they reached the elevator in the center of the building, O'Donnell pressed the button to go up.

"Mr. Hagar is in his own room on the fifth floor," she said. "Be prepared. The fifth floor is different than the fourth floor."

The air inside of the elevator reeked of body odor and urine. The walls looked like a pack of dogs had crowded into the elevator and lifted their legs to piss. Paul's legs went weak and he reached out to touch the wall and steady himself. Along the walls were metal rings. Dizziness from the stale air and smell overwhelmed him, and when the door finally opened on the fifth floor, Paul jumped out, breathing deeply. The hallway along both sides was lined with locked rooms, with bars on small windows and little doors an attendant could open and slide a meal tray through.

"This is mostly a no-human-contact floor," O'Donnell pointed out, as if she were giving a tour to a group of curious Rotarians. "Our patients are in their rooms, and there is no contact with the staff, other than a hello or goodnight through the thick glass window. But I want to make sure you understand they are like family to us."

She stared at Paul, waiting for his reaction.

"Family? Drilling into someone's brain and cutting the connections doesn't sound like 'family' to me," Paul said. "No, I don't understand. Twenty-four hours a day? No contact at all? In a locked cage? Who gets to decide that?"

"I am going to ignore your statements and, due to your position, make an exception to our rules. We are going to enter Mr. Hagar's room, so you can hear him for yourself and make up your own mind. Then you will leave."

They moved down the well-lit hallway, past a dozen or more cell-like doors, stopping at the second to last one on the right. She removed a set of keys from her coat pocket, fumbled through a dozen, and unlocked the door. Inside, Hagar, wearing a white smock-like shirt and white pants, lay on his back on his bed, eyes wide open, staring at the ceiling.

Paul stepped inside. On one wall was a toilet and a sink; the bed was pushed up against the other wall. A pair of slippers sat neatly on the floor under the bed. There was no window to the outside. The only light for the room came from a single bulb hanging from the concrete ceiling. Hanging next to it was an insect strip covered with dead bugs.

"Mr. Hagar?" she called out.

He turned his head to make eye contact with her. Then he cast a confused look at Paul. Sitting up, he said, "Who's that? Did someone finally come to get me out of this hole?"

"This is Chief Paul Beirne of the Lindenhurst Village police department. He wants to talk to you."

Hagar beamed. "Oh, that's wonderful," he said. "He came to see me? Oh, dear, what made me so important?"

There was nowhere to sit but the thin mattress atop the bed or the toilet seat, which was black with mold. Paul stood in the middle of the room facing Hagar, who was no more than five feet in height, at most 130 pounds. His face was flat, his nose pushed into his skull. His hair was longer on the top and brushed straight back; the hair on the sides of his head was shaved to the skin. Paul fought back a rising panic. Claustrophobia clawed at his chest.

"What do you want, sir?" Hagar swept his right arm in front of him and dipped his head in an attempt to mimic a formal bow. "How can I be of service?"

"There was a murder in the village," Paul said. "A woman was killed in a particularly horrific way."

"I know all about it."

"What do you know about it?"

A laugh tumbled out of Hagar's mouth. "Her insides were pulled out through her pussy," he said, smiling. He giggled.

O'Donnell gently pushed Hagar down on the bed and away from Paul, who breathed deeply through his nose. His hands went into his pockets.

Staring intently at Paul, Hagar waited on him to lead the conversation.

Paul said, "How do you know that a woman was murdered in the village and killed that way?"

"Very simply: I was there."

"What are you talking about? What am I doing in this hellhole listening to this nonsense?"

"I was there," Hagar said. "Yes, sir, I was! With her. The lovely Mrs. Constance McKay. Are you listening? You have come to my home in the crazy capital of America, Long Island, New York, and you must pay attention to every word I say. What I say, when I talk, it's wisdom from the mountaintop."

He jerked up, pushing off the bed with both hands and rolling his tongue over his lips. Paul, disgusted, stepped back and collided with the door.

"Let me begin: We had a lovely night at the theater in Manhattan. *Portrait of a Lady.* Dinner at Sardi's. Drinks at the 21 Club. Dominick, my favorite bartender, was on that night. He treated us exceedingly well. Known him for years! That's how the evening went. We drove back out in my brand-new Buick. Clean and shiny and ready for what lay ahead. I was going to drop her off at her house, but we decided to park somewhere. It was her idea."

"Park where?"

"Off Wellwood. By the new cemeteries."

"You were going to drop her off at her house? What was the address?" Paul asked.

"Oh, please. We didn't go to her home. Her husband was there. So, because it was her idea, well, my thought was, here we go, Auggie. That's my nickname, by the way. But you call me Mr. Hagar."

He waited for a response from Paul. "The door was wide open for me. Lay back and enjoy the ride. But she didn't give me what I wanted, and I was drunk as shit, and so was she. I threw her on her back and forced her knees apart and reached inside of her as far as my hand could go."

He held up his right hand in front of Paul's face to show him the murder weapon.

"That's what you did to the Jewish girl in '38," Paul said.

Hagar shook his head. "Why do you bring that up?"

"Answer me, Hagar."

"Mr. Hagar."

"Answer me."

"That was not me. No, sir. I was in the New Germany doing what had to be done to the pestilence corrupting our race. But if you can get me out of here, I will tell you who did that one."

"You're truly disgusting. No wonder they locked you up in here."

Hagar shouted, "They can't hold me. I come and go as I please. The missus here will confirm that."

"So—a night at the theater? That's your story?" Paul said.

"Oh. Chief. You are not—listening to me. No one has ever listened to me. All my life, I bring them the truth on a silver platter, and they don't listen to me. No matter what I do. Even when they execute the wrong man, they don't listen to me."

"What are you talking about?" Paul asked.

Turning to O'Donnell, Hagar said, "Tell him, my good doctor. Go ahead. Tell him everything I have told you over the years."

She said, "He's been locked in this room. He hasn't escaped and gone to Lindenhurst and killed that woman."

"Oh, dear God," Hagar said. "That is nonsense. I can leave here anytime I want."

Turning to O'Donnell, Paul said, "How does he know about it? I assume he's reading the papers?"

"Are you talking around me, Chief?" Hagar said, waving his right hand between Paul and O'Donnell. "Don't look at her and ask about me. Don't treat me like I'm not here. Understood?"

She said, "People talk. He picked it up from his attendant, or someone brought him the paper. But I can assure you he didn't unlock the door, walk down the hallway, down the elevator, and out the front door for an evening of theater in New York City."

"You don't know shit," Hagar said. "Nobody in here knows shit. You're all crazy!"

On a shelf over the sink was a framed photograph of a younger Hagar in black boots, black pants, a brown shirt with a leather belt that ran from his waist to over his left shoulder, and a swastika armband. He was in a long line of people marching down Wellwood Avenue in front of hundreds of people. Paul focused on one of the men in the front of the parade of uniformed Nazis: his father.

"See something you find interesting?" Hagar asked.

He pointed to one of the men in the photograph.

"Yes," Hagar said. "That's me. You recognize anyone else?"

"When was this taken?" Paul asked.

"Nineteen thirty-seven, if memory serves. Then, a few years later, the federal people rounded up some of us who'd been in the German Bund and put us in prison."

"You were arrested?"

"No, Chief. No, sir. They questioned me. I told them I had every right to join my countrymen in a parade through the village or in the big rally we had in Madison Square Garden. I'm sure you read about that, Chief. And there was another big one in Iowa with the great Lindbergh! He supported us, you know. He knew the truth everyone else wants to suppress. The death of his little boy didn't change his view of the people he loved."

Paul stared at the ceiling, blocking out Hagar's voice, doing all he could to stay focused. The only conclusion he could come to was that he was wasting his time, that this trip to the asylum was well off what he was doing. Homestead had sent him on a wild-goose chase to get him away from the Haase house.

He stepped to the door and reached for the handle. He jerked hard on it, but the door would not open. Hagar laughed, softly at first, then building into a roar. O'Donnell fumbled with her keys. When the door opened, Paul pushed past her and out into the hallway. He sprinted towards the center of the building. The doctor caught up with him at her office. Paul fell into a chair, putting both hands over his ears to drown out the shouts of the people behind him. She said something about getting him water and an escort out of the building.

"Hagar—he didn't get a lobotomy?" Paul asked.

"Not yet," she said.

"Who decides such things?"

"A family member approaches a committee here, makes the case, and the committee decides," she said. "Without a family recommendation, it's entirely our call. All very proper."

He bolted out of her office. The elevator wasn't there, so he darted down the stairs and emerged into the sunlight. For nearly thirty minutes he sat in his car before driving away.

EIGHT

You know the Giants won the World Series, right?" When Paul didn't look up, Doc said, "Willie Mays is a great player, don't you think? Not that I know a thing about baseball, mind you."

"Someone told me, yes," Paul said.

"America is such an interesting country," Doc said. "Very conflicted, it seems to me. The fans love Mays because he is a great player but hate him because he's a Negro. They love him on the field but wouldn't allow him to live in a house on their street. They'd burn the house down before they'd let him live there. It feels like a uniquely American issue: you love him as an athlete but don't want anything to do with him as a human being."

When Paul did not reply, Doc said, "You know, it's right in the deeds to each of the lots in the big Levitt development. All written out. Only Caucasians allowed. They are not playing games and pretending. They just come right out and say it. It doesn't say 'no Jews allowed,' but if I showed up, there'd suddenly be nothing to buy."

"How do you know this?"

"My brother and I asked to see one of the models," Doc said. "The salesman was uncomfortable with us, as my brother was wearing a yarmulke. Plus, the accents. At one point, the salesman said, with disdain, 'Are you foreigners?' He showed us the language in the deeds. He thought that would make us go away."

Connie, Paul's part-time secretary, placed a folder on his desk.

"I think this is what you are looking for," she said.

Paul handed Doc the file. He opened it to find three onionskin sheets of paper with some typed notes and a pencil drawing of the crime scene. There were coffee stains on the drawing. Underneath were photographs. One showed the woman's body, her legs spread wide to show the wound, lying on the grass by the edge of the water. Uniformed cops stood around the body. Another showed the swastika carved on her forehead.

"She was Jewish and she was killed on November 10, 1938," Paul said.

Doc didn't answer.

Cantwell walked in and stood by Paul's desk.

"Did you talk to Lindsay Henry about the wiretap on Haase's phone?" Paul asked.

"He said it would be up by tonight."

"I want you to arrange to go to his office and pick up a file, if he has one, on the 1938 murder of a Carol Berkowitz. Bludgeoned and dumped in Argyle Lake, where it turns into a creek and runs into the bay by Montauk Highway. She was alive when she was thrown in the water: there was water in her lungs. Last known address was Floral Park. All that was put together here was so cursory it's worthless."

He handed Cantwell the file. "That's all there is," he said. "I'm hoping Lindsay has a file somewhere with a lot more in it. And find out if she has family anywhere. We will want to talk to them."

Cantwell, puzzled, said, "What's the point now? That was sixteen years ago."

"There are similarities," Paul said. "How she was killed, how the McKay woman was killed. Dear God. You can't see that? The past is creeping up on us. All these Nazis crawling around the place."

"I'm not stupid, Chief," Cantwell said.

"Then don't act stupid," Paul said.

The following evening Cantwell found Paul sitting at the bar at Baloney John's, a plate of fried squid and a dozen bluepoint oysters half gone before him. He placed a manila envelope on the bar.

"This is what Henry had, Chief," Cantwell said.

To Paul's surprise, the file was several inches thick. He paid his bar tab, walked Cantwell to his car, and drove to Doc's house. Walking to the front door, he heard music. Doc and two other men were seated in a corner of the living room. Doc was playing a cello. He guessed one of the men was his brother. He was playing a violin, as was the other man. Doc nodded at Paul and the three men continued to play. He picked up some sheet music from the top of the piano, which filled nearly a third of the room, and read the name on the cover: Frederic Chopin.

A few minutes later Doc said, *"Lass uns ein paar Minuten unterbrechen."* He stood up. "Paul, I don't think you have met my brother, Heinrich," he said, pushing his cello forward and leaning it against the side of the piano.

Heinrich said, "And this is our friend Richard. We were playing Haydn's *String Quartet Opus 76* when you walked in."

He looked down at Heinrich's arm. There was the tattooed number on the left forearm. Richard surely had the same. Heinrich was thin to the point of sickly, gaunt, his skin pale, sad-eyed, his shoulders stooped over. His wrists were no wider than two of his fingers. He was shorter than his brother, his eyes set deep in his head as if they had retreated and couldn't bear to see what was in front of them. Dark smudges lined the skin under his eyes and on both sides of his nose.

Richard, silent, distracted, picked up his sheet music and, with his violin and bow, walked into the kitchen without making eye contact with anyone. Paul watched him lay his violin on the kitchen table and stare out the back door to the yard beyond like a man lost. He seemed to be enveloped by an invisible shroud.

"In case you didn't know, Paul," Doc said. "I was playing the cello, my brother the violin, and Richard the viola. Next, I will be playing Chopin on the piano."

He showed Doc the file from the district attorney's office. "I'm sorry to interrupt, but I'd like to go over this with you," Paul said.

Doc placed it on the kitchen table.

"The three of us, we try and meet a couple times a month," Doc said, ignoring the file. "Sometimes in Queens, but often here, too. It is important to all of us that we continue to play this music."

"How long have you been doing this?" Paul said.

"We met up to play ten years ago."

"In Vienna?"

"Poland," Doc said. The word escaped Doc's mouth thickly, pushed out with a measure of reluctance but in a way as to cut off any further questions.

From a side table, Paul poured whisky into a glass and sat at the kitchen table with the file from the district attorney's office. He stared at the glass and pushed it away.

"Our father was a concert pianist," Heinrich said, in a voice so low it was barely audible. He, too, seemed to have trouble making eye contact. "He once was in demand all over Europe. My brother and I played Chopin before we were five years of age."

Heinrich's accent was thicker than his brother's, and Paul had to focus to suss out the words. Heinrich and Richard gathered their instruments and walked into the living room to take their seats. Heinrich looked at his brother, his lips moving silently as he followed the notes on the sheets. Richard stared at the wall.

Doc took his seat at the piano, his fingers gracefully suspended above the keys. The music began softly, slowly, a gentle touching of the piano keys. The others held the instruments on their laps as Doc played. There was a mystery to the music, a grandness, a beauty that seemed beyond the notes themselves. The feeling it instilled in Paul was the same as when he was in his boat on the bay on a day when the sky glowed and wet light reflected off the salt water.

He slid a sheaf of papers onto the table. The onionskins were frayed and discolored. A clip held a stack of carbon copies. He tore open an envelope, and a dozen photographs of the dead girl fell out onto the table. Her pale skin and soft features gave her the appearance of a child. Her brown hair—tied with a pink ribbon that deepened her childlike appearance—was in thick wads and knots, tangled with seaweed and sand. One photo, from her groin looking up towards her damaged face, showed the same wound Paul had seen on Constance McKay. He looked through the rest of the contents of the folder. Their slimness and lack of detail and any follow up investigation suggested the police did very little to find out who was responsible for the death. There was an account of the funeral in Floral Park, but nothing pointed to why the young woman was in Lindenhurst at the time of her death.

When the music ended, Heinrich and Richard packed up their instruments and Doc walked them to their car. When he returned, Doc sat at the kitchen table and picked up the file.

"Your friend Richard," Paul said. "He's very quiet. Is he okay?"

Ignoring the question, Doc put down the file. "No, no, no. I don't want to read this," he said. "Why are you showing me this?"

"I need you to tell me what it means," Paul said.

"I don't want to tell you what it means," he said.

"Why?"

Doc stood up and stared out the back door. "I don't want to be associated with anything like this," he said. "We—my brother . . ." His voice trailed off. "Now you show me these pictures? Besides, I don't understand what you are doing, Paul."

Paul sat at the table. "What do you mean?"

"You have unsettled issues that haunt you," Doc said. "You want answers to your own mysteries more than you want to solve these murders. When we first met, you told me your mother was gone. I recall the word you used: *disappeared*. You want to find some way to explain your father. You changed your surname to escape him, so your feelings must be very deep. Going back to a 1938 murder is fine if you have nothing else to do. But you need to focus on the here and now if you are going to make any progress at all."

"Lecturing me on what I need to do with my life isn't going to help me," Paul said.

"You asked about Richard. He's lost, Paul. Overwhelmed and damaged beyond repair. You have more than a slight resemblance to him."

NINE

I t was nine in the evening when Paul called the funeral home in Floral Park. The man who answered the phone said his father would have handled a death in 1938.

"Could I speak with your father?" Paul asked.

"Perhaps if we go together, he might open up to you. He's forgetful. We had to put him in a nursing home in Manhasset. If it is important to you, we can try."

After Paul hung up, he made a liverwurst sandwich, grabbed a Rheingold from the refrigerator, and walked outside. The night was calm and cool. The cold of autumn had not yet arrived. He could smell the tide was out in the creek. A noisy flock of geese passed overhead. Although he could not see them, he could hear their honks as they moved southeast towards the bay. When he went back inside, he put the unopened Rheingold on the counter. He took a bottle opener from the drawer and opened it, took a big swig that emptied half of it, and then poured the rest down the sink.

❖

He was up early and went to the diner on Montauk Highway. Seated at the counter, he ordered black coffee, scrambled eggs and bacon, and a toasted corn muffin. In a nearby booth, two men talked of their fishing trip on the bay the day before. He pushed the plate away, put a one-dollar bill and three quarters on the counter, and walked to his car.

When he reached Floral Park, the man with whom he'd spoken the night before greeted him at the door of a Victorian home. He was dressed in a dark suit, white shirt and dark tie, the uniform of people who deal with the dead. Inside, the air smelled of an abundance of flowers. Paul found the smell somewhat sickening. They exchanged pleasantries and got in Paul's truck for the drive to the nursing home. This was Paul's first time in Floral Park, where the streets were lined with small houses on quarter-acre lots.

"I read the papers, Chief Beirne. You have had two murders in the last week or so. A husband and wife. Don't you have your hands full enough now? Why are you worrying about the murder of this girl sixteen years ago?"

When they arrived at the nursing home, Paul followed the man through the lobby, down a corridor, and into a room with a curtain that separated two beds, both of which were occupied. A nurse stood by one of the beds.

"Hello, Mr. DiPietro," the nurse said. "Your father ate a good breakfast this morning. He asked if you would be coming today. He's been unusually talkative."

She picked up the bedpan and took it into the bathroom, where she splashed the contents into the toilet. The old man's eyes opened, and his son propped up the pillow under his head. He stared at Paul.

"Who are you, sir? Other than my son, I don't recall receiving visitors."

In a slow voice, frequently interrupted with the old man saying, "Speak up, please," Paul said the name Carol Berkowitz. He repeated it, louder. The man's eyes widened. He tried to push up on his elbows.

"I remember her," he said. "A beautiful girl. So horrible."

"Was she murdered because she was Jewish?" Paul asked.

DiPietro's head rocked back and forth. He raised his right hand, his index finger wagging up and down.

"Do you know about the German American Bund out east on Long Island during the 1930s? Your village had a large chapter. Nazi parades marched down your main street."

A memory formed of seeing his father with his right hand stuck straight out as uniformed men carrying swastika flags marched down Wellwood Avenue.

"She was an only child," DiPietro said. "Her mother and an aunt came to the funeral home. I knew her mother very well, which is why she came to my place. Otherwise, they would have gone to a different funeral home more attuned to their customs."

"How did you know her mother?"

"She was my bookkeeper. Her husband before her had also been our bookkeeper. A marvelous couple. Very smart, well-read and informed. They were particularly interested in events in Europe where they had relatives. He died and she took over the accounting practice."

"Is the mother dead?"

"She died after her daughter's death. She couldn't survive the horror of it."

"Did Carol have a job?" Paul asked.

"She had many jobs, but the one her mother told me about lasted only a few weeks. Early in 1932, she went for a job interview at the Lindbergh mansion in New Jersey. An agency in New York referred her. They had built a big house out in the woods, away from everything, and they needed staff. Mrs. Lindbergh hired her to help in the kitchen. She was there when Mr. Lindbergh returned from one of his trips to Europe and abruptly fired her."

"Why did he fire her?"

"Simple—he didn't like Jews," the old man said. "He certainly didn't hide it. He, Mrs. Lindbergh, and Carol were standing in the kitchen. Lindbergh said, right in front of the girl, 'Anne, I don't want her here.' He wouldn't even look at her. He was disgusted that she was in the house, and his wife had hired her in his absence. He was horrified his toddler son would be around a Jewish woman. Surely you remember his comments at the big rallies around the country before the war? His view was that the Jews would push America into a war with Germany. He was also a supporter of the idea that some people are superior and others are inferior. The so-called science of eugenics. Once you settle on that belief, what do you think comes next?"

"When was she fired?"

"A few days before the Lindbergh child was kidnapped and murdered. Otherwise, she would have been in the house that night. Someone put up a ladder against the side of the house right at the nursery window, which was unlocked, and climbed inside."

A ladder next to an open window to a child's bedroom, Paul thought. He heard his mother's voice again.

"Do you know if Carol was interviewed by the police about that?"

"It was entirely a New Jersey State Police case, Mr. Beirne. As for the kidnapping of the child, the FBI wanted to get involved but Lindbergh refused their assistance. He even rebuffed Mr. Hoover's attempts to assign agents to the case. That's all in the newspaper accounts. The FBI was the most experienced at that sort of crime, but Lindbergh kept them out of it. That has never been properly explained. Your child is gone, don't you want all the help you can get? I do remember Carol's mother told me her daughter was going to be interviewed by the local state police in Lindenhurst, as a courtesy to New Jersey."

"When was that?" he said.

"A few days before she was murdered. Carol was staying with her mother in Nassau County. The state police in Lindenhurst wanted to talk to her. After Carol's murder, her mother fell into a deep depression. She told me, 'I can't escape from this. It follows me.' One day she was walking her little dog, a dachshund. It was late at night. Odd for her to be out so late. She was found dead the next morning in a building lot. The authorities said she had a stroke. The dachshund was never found. I saved all the newspapers about the Lindbergh case, Mr. Beirne. My son can show them to you. The *New York Times*, the *Daily News*, *Journal-American*, the *Daily Mirror*. Those are the ones I would buy when something big happened. Armistice Day in 1918. The stock market crash. The Lindbergh kidnapping."

When Paul arrived back in Lindenhurst, he went to the police department and spread the newspapers out on his desk. The first was the *New York Times*, with a headline on the right-hand side of the front page: LINDBERGH BABY KIDNAPPED FROM HOME OF PARENTS ON FARM NEAR PRINCETON; TAKEN FROM HIS CRIB, WIDE SEARCH ON. The *Daily News* headline read LINDY'S BABY KIDNAPPED. A photograph showed a ladder leaning up against the side of the house next to a second-floor window. A second *Daily News* front page: LINDY BABY FOUND DEAD. The last front page was the *New York Times*: HAUPTMANN PUT TO DEATH FOR THE KILLING OF LINDBERGH BABY; REMAINS SILENT TO THE END.

The photograph of the ladder up against the side of the house, to the right of a window the story said was the Lindbergh nursery, caused Paul to get up and walk around the small office. The picture was familiar to him. His father had left a copy of a newspaper on the kitchen table and Paul had seen it when he got up to get ready for school. He knew it.

Two hours of reading left Paul with a strong sense that the case against Hauptmann was illogical. The pieces used to convict Hauptmann did not fit together. The prosecution's case had a made-up feel to it, as if they were pulling it out of thin air as they went along, inventing what they needed to fill any gaps. It was preposterous to conclude that one person—the "lone wolf" described in the stories—pulled off the stealing of the child of the most famous man in America from a fully occupied house.

Paul wondered how Hauptmann would have known the family was staying in the house that night. How would the kidnapper know how to enter the house? Reading further, he learned that the child was taken from a second-floor nursery, out the window with the broken shutter, and down a crudely fashioned ladder that was broken at the bottom. The Lindberghs and their staff were all downstairs. There was a dog with them.

He compiled a series of questions in his mind:

How would Hauptmann have known which window to go through? How would he have known what time the child was alone in the nursery? The ladder, shown in photographs in the newspapers leaning against the side of the house, looked more like a prop than a tool in a notorious kidnapping. Did someone inside the house hand the child out the window to the person standing on the ladder? How would the kidnapper, holding a toddler, back down the ladder, and exit the property?

Richard Hauptmann was arrested in the Bronx because he had some of the ransom money in his possession. Other people did, too. Paul could not picture this man, a German immigrant described as a skilled carpenter, constructing a crude ladder, leaning it up against the correct second-floor window, climbing up and through the window, stealing the child, leaving the scene somehow, and then extorting the family for the ransom money. All by himself.

No fingerprints were found in the nursery. The entire room appeared to have been wiped clean. No dirt from outside on the nursery floor.

The official story, Paul thought.

Connie returned with her lunch in a brown paper bag. She saw the headlines on the old newspapers. She said, "I am considerably older than you, and those days are something I will never forget. My Fred, he followed every story from the kidnapping to the electric chair."

"The man they executed," Paul said. "He was guilty?"

"Dear Lord, yes. The wood that made up the ladder came from his own house. He had the ransom money. He killed a toddler. The child's head was crushed. You can't get more evil than that, Chief. He deserved to be strapped into that chair and fried. Your parents surely talked about it, like everyone else did. Just before he was executed, Hauptmann said something along the lines of the 'case would never go away.' It would never go away because he was innocent. That was his big lie, right up until they threw the lever."

Late in the afternoon, Lindsay Henry called the police department looking for Paul. Evans answered the phone.

"Tell the chief that the wiretap on Haase's phone isn't working out, but we will keep it on another few days before we have to return to the judge," Henry said.

"What are you learning?" Evans asked.

"Nothing," Henry said.

TEN

Paul came in on a Saturday morning and sat at his desk, drinking coffee out of a thermos. His mother had given it to him as a gift on his ninth birthday when he was going camping on the barrier beach with the Boy Scouts. He remembered the morning of the Scout trip, and how his mother looked when she was preparing food for him and putting it in his backpack.

"You have a great time over there," she said.

Bologna and cheese on white bread, cookies she made the night before while he did his homework at the kitchen table. She was happy that morning. His father was working somewhere and had not come home in several days.

The basement office was quiet. The day was cool, as fall had begun to present itself with its colors and soft light, and sunny, and he considered taking the boat out onto the bay. Morning temperatures were cooler now and nightfall presented itself sooner. By all rights at this time of the year, when the water temperature in the bay was dropping and large schools of bass arrived to feast on bait, he would be out there as often as he could. But there was nothing typical about this fall.

Connie left a note on his desk that Mayor Madden was looking for him and he was expected at Tuesday's village board meeting. There was also a note from Evans taped to the telephone about the wiretap: "Lindsay Henry called. They got nothing."

It occurred to Paul that he had not spoken to Doc in several days since he barged in on their music night, nor had he seen Doc's car parked by the funeral home. He picked up the phone and called. No answer. Paul then called his uncle out east on the North Fork. The phone rang and rang. He called back several times, until his aunt picked up the phone at lunchtime.

"I am glad you called," Anna said. "Martin has not been well again. He gets up every day and works in the barn, but he has little endurance for it anymore. Is there any way you could come out? I know you are busy. We get the papers out here. You are dealing with a lot. But if you can come, it will help Martin."

Before she hung up, she said, "And he wants to sell the *Predator* for scrap. He can't handle it anymore. He loves that boat and all the years he was a commercial fisherman on the side. If you want Pauli to see it before it's gone, you should bring him out."

Paul went home and packed some clothes. Before ten A.M., he was driving east on Montauk Highway. When he got to Riverhead, the county seat, he went north, crossing a bridge over the Peconic River where it empties into the bay. He continued north until he hit a farm road. In the hamlet of Northville, he stopped at the Grange Hall, where he thought he saw his uncle's pickup truck parked. A farmers' meeting was going on, but Martin wasn't there, so he proceeded east until he reached Mattituck. There, he turned north to Oregon Road, and east again, passing by farms that had been harvested of potatoes and cauliflower, by hay barns used for potato storage, and by houses occupied by Irish and Polish immigrants.

Since childhood, he had known every stretch of this road—every barn, every big tree, all the old houses. When he closed his eyes he could see his mother as a child on the farm, in the barn, and later as a grown-up in the kitchen preparing dinner. Paul knew every part of his uncle's house, the barns and work sheds, and the layouts of the four bungalows—more like crudely constructed shacks—that the Negro workers lived in. Paul knew how his uncle organized his tools in the various racks and drawers in the different sheds. Wooden crates held drills; drawers perfectly organized held screwdrivers, wrenches, and chisels. Axes, hatchets, and crowbars hung on hooks on pegboard. An anvil sat on a tree stump in the metal shop. As a child, Paul had loved opening the drawers, holding the tools, putting them back as he found them.

Inside the house, he knew the photographs on the wall in the parlor—there were several of Martin and Paul's mother as school children, on their first communions, and two of the Irish grandfather who had bought the land in the weeks after the battle at Gettysburg, when he was a soldier with the Fighting 69th. He knew how his uncle organized his paperwork and farm journal on the desk in the living room, which sat next to the radio.

Tacked to the wall over his uncle's desk was a nautical chart showing water depths in Gardiners Bay. Circled with a black pen was the spit of land north of Gardiners Island called The Ruins. He knew it as his uncle's favorite place when he went out on the *Predator*.

Under the circle, he had drawn the coordinates of The Ruins on the chart: 41 08'29" N/72 08'46" W.

Work clothes hung on the clothesline attached to the south-facing wall of the barn, drying in the southwest breeze. Walking around to the back of the house, he could see no one was in the kitchen, so he walked first to the shed where his uncle kept a workshop. Seeing no one there, he proceeded to the big barn, but before he got there he stood at the foot of the broad, flat farm field. Great white clouds floated across the northern sky. His uncle had in recent weeks dug up the potatoes and brought them to the barn for washing, sorting, and bagging, and the land lay open, waiting on winter to arrive.

Men's voices from the barn drew his attention. Inside, dust clouds floated above the equipment. A familiar smell: wet topsoil washed off potatoes. At the back end of the barn, a conveyor belt brought potatoes in from the truck parked outside. There, one of the Negro workers pushed the potatoes out of the back of the V-shaped truck and onto the conveyor belt, which carried them inside through a window in the barn.

Anna waved to Paul. She shouted above the din of the clanking equipment to Martin, who was loading bags of potatoes onto a pallet. He turned to see Paul, waved, and walked over to a steel column that held up the roof. He flipped a switch, and the connected series of belts, scales, and machinery ground to a halt.

Tall and broad, his thick hair black as shoe polish, Martin had done nothing but farmwork since childhood. Hard work had given him a stout chest, strong hands, and muscular arms. Today his uncle looked weaker, tired, thinner. His strength seemed to be leaving him. His right leg appeared to have given up being useful. His ability to keep antiquated potato-sorting equipment running each fall was a marvel to Paul. But looking around now, Paul could see the motors and conveyor belts were rusty and neglected.

Inside the house, Anna made cheese sandwiches and a pitcher of lemonade. Martin, huddled over a cane, washed up at the sink and went to his desk in a corner of the living room to make notes in his farm journal. He recorded the temperature, rain totals in recent days, and how many bags of potatoes he had loaded onto the pallets for the trucks to pick up. On the wall over his desk was the photograph of a white-haired man in a Union army uniform.

Paul walked into the living room and stood behind his uncle. He saw his uncle had put a framed photograph of his sister on the side of the desk.

"I have not seen that photograph of my mother before," Paul said when he walked back into the kitchen.

"I found that in a drawer in Martin's dresser," Anna said. "He got it framed and put it on his desk a few days ago. He's been talking more about his sister in recent weeks than in the last few years."

Work in the barn stopped late in the afternoon. Paul walked the farm road up to the woods overlooking the Sound. He followed a path to a bluff where his aunt and uncle had set up a bench. As the sun set in the west, the sky turned a deep blue. He could see across the Sound to the gray line of the coast of Connecticut.

Dinner was roast chicken, baked potatoes, string beans, and corn bread with fresh butter at the kitchen table. Martin erupted in a fit of coughing. When it was under control, he said, "Have you seen your father?"

"Not in many months," Paul said.

"Do you know how he's doing?"

"Not really, no," Paul said.

"We'd love to see your boy again," Anna said. "Is he okay? We miss him."

"I see him whenever I can," Paul said. "It's become very difficult now that his mother has a boyfriend. He seems to think he has a voice in how much time I get to spend with Pauli."

"We wanted you to come out so we could talk with you, Paul," Anna said.

"If there is a way for you to help me out, I'd appreciate it," Martin said.

Paul leaned back in the chair. "I don't know if I can, Martin."

"We know what your work involves, Paul," Anna said.

"Yes, but I still need your help," Martin said. His voice took on an insisting tone. "This place—all of it—was to be your mother's one day. In recent weeks, I've been thinking a lot about my sister. I don't know what became of her. The not knowing is so difficult. What will become of this farm after we pass?"

The question hung in the air, unanswered. Anna got up from the table to put the kettle on the stove. After the dishes were cleaned up, Paul walked outside into the fading light and around the barn. When he walked back to the house, he saw that the light was on in Martin's metal shop. He found him filing the blade on a mower. Paul sat on a chair by the workbench.

After a moment of silence, Paul said, "Do you know anything that can help me understand what happened to my mother?"

"For several years, I thought she got away from your father and went off with someone else," Martin said. "In recent days, the thought occurred to me something else happened."

"But what?" Paul asked.

The bulb hanging from a wire over his head swayed, casting Martin's face in shadow, and then light, and back again.

"You ever ask your father that question?" Martin asked.

"From when I was a teenager on, yes. I gave up at some point before I enlisted."

"What did he say?"

"He'd get angry. Told me to get over it."

"Whatever he tells you, you can be sure he's lying," Martin said. He put down the tool and leaned against the workbench. "His story doesn't make any sense to me. It's never made any sense, Paul."

ELEVEN

Paul knew before getting out of bed in the morning he was in the wrong place. He was anxious to return to Lindenhurst but knew his uncle needed his help. After changing into work clothes, he walked to the kitchen. A different photograph of his mother was on the kitchen table. On the back of the photograph: *This was also in Martin's drawer. He brought it out this morning. Joyce's senior year in high school in Cutchogue.*

Next to it was a note: *We will be in the barn when you get up. Coffee is on the stove. We will have a nice breakfast when we get back from eight o'clock Mass at Sacred Heart. Please come with us. Martin and I hope you can stay till tonight. The Haggartys and the Polish family that bought the farm next to them are doing a cookout.*

They left the farm in Martin's truck at 7:45 A.M. and arrived at the Sacred Heart church a few minutes later. Parking behind the church, they walked around to the front and entered through wide doors. On both the east and west sides of the building were stained glass windows with the names of early members. The name BEIRNE adorned one handsome, brightly colored window. They sat in the front right-hand pew next to the window dedicated to the Haggarty family.

His mother always wore white gloves when she came here. The softness of the leather gloves was so familiar, and it came to him now. He never remembered his father being in this church. A photograph his mother had of her wedding day showed the only time his father had set foot in the church. She always held her rosary in her gloved hands. The smell of her perfume stuck with him for years, and this morning as they sat down—in the very same pew where he sat with his mother—he smelled it again.

After church, Paul changed his clothes and joined Martin in the barn, where they swapped out the clutch in one of the 1939 Farmall tractors.

Late in the day, Paul showered and dressed and waited outside by the road. When Martin and Anna came around with the truck, he climbed in, and a minute later they turned onto the Haggarty farm a quarter mile east on Oregon Road. Around the back of the farmhouse, Haggarty was tending a wood fire in an oil drum cut in half lengthwise and set on concrete blocks. On top of a grill lay a pig cut in half. Blue smoke curled skyward. Festive lights hung from ropes strung between the porch behind the house and the barn. As Paul climbed out of the truck, Haggarty came over with a short, bulky man whose face was brown from working outside.

"This is Mr. Kiloski," Haggarty said. His accent held tightly to his Irish birth. "His family worked on different farms around here after coming over from the old country. Last summer, they bought the Hannaberry place after the old man died. An Irish family departs, a Polish family moves in."

Kiloski extended his right hand. *"Przykro mi, że mój angielski nie jest zbyt dobry. Bardzo miło Cię poznać,"* he said with a broad smile.

"I think that means he is glad to meet you," Martin said.

When the pig was cooked, Haggarty cut slices, and everyone sat at wooden tables set alongside the western side of the barn to catch the last light of the evening. Bowls of potato salad sat on each table, along with trays of the last of the summer tomatoes and corn. When the dinner was finished, Haggarty and Martin sat on fold-up seats facing each other. Haggarty removed a fiddle from a case and began to play. After a few minutes, Martin sang softly:

> *"Mavourneen, Mavourneen, my sad tears are falling*
> *To think that from Erin and thee I must part*
> *It may be for years and it may be forever;*
> *Then why are you silent thou voice of my heart*
> *It may be for years, and it may be forever;*
> *Then why are you silent, Kathleen Mavourneen."*

Early in the morning, the sun peeking over the line of oak trees on the eastern edge of the farm, Paul and Anna walked outside to his car. She leaned against Paul's chest and wept.

TWELVE

When he pulled up alongside his bungalow, he saw that a light glowed in the kitchen. After removing his pistol from the glove box of his truck, he walked down the driveway, looking through the side windows into the living room. The sofa had been overturned, the chairs thrown aside. Coming through the sliding door from the deck into the kitchen, he saw the cabinets had been emptied, their contents thrown on the floor. He raised the pistol in front of his face and walked down the hallway to his bedroom. All the drawers in his dresser were pulled out.

He backed down the hallway, went through the kitchen and into the living room. On the far wall by the front door was a painted swastika big enough to run from floor to ceiling. To the right of the swastika, in bright red letters: WE ARE STILL HERE.

Turning the couch upright, he fell onto the cushion. His breathing had become difficult. He was panting. His first thought was to call Cantwell and ask him to come with the camera. Bringing in his deputy would accomplish little more than to frighten him. His next thought was Doc. But he couldn't show him what was painted on the wall. He had done his friend enough harm.

After an hour he got up, drove to the hardware store in the village and bought two gallons of white paint, a brush, and a roller. At home, he poured paint into a tray and covered the swastika and the words. An hour later the paint was dry. He carried the cans to his garage. Instead of going inside the house, he walked to the creek and waited for sunset.

❖

The next day, Tuesday, after another night of hardly sleeping, Paul walked upstairs to the village board meeting at one P.M. and took a seat in the back. The seats were filled with the usual gadflies. The five board members filed in through a rear door and took their seats at the table on the dais, and a few minutes later the mayor arrived and ceremoniously stood behind his high-backed chair, smiling at the crowd. An assistant pulled out the chair and Madden sat down. As he did, he blew kisses to women in the back row, then banged the gavel on the table.

"This meeting of the Lindenhurst Village board will come to order," he said.

Before the mayor read the first item on the agenda, Marvin Kloss walked to the front of the room.

"Mr. Mayor," he said. "I was born in the village sixty-five years ago this week and in all that time, going back all them years, I don't remember there ever being two murders within days of each other. You know why we are all out here, on Long Island, Mr. Mayor. And you know, just a few weeks back, a colored man was looking to buy a house in this village. He talked to several of our real estate people. He was even shown a house, Mr. Mayor. On my street! We can't protect our neighbors and the value of our homes if that kind of thing is going to happen. And we all know, Mr. Mayor, what Mr. Levitt is doing not far from here and how with the paperwork he is making sure the wrong elements can't live there. And we need that kind of protection here. I am asking, Mr. Mayor, if our police department is up to this challenge, and what can be done if they aren't, and why aren't we asking for help from the state police? Should we all be worried that the wrong element is involved in these killings?"

The room erupted in applause as Kloss took his seat in the front row. Madden leaned back in his chair and crossed his arms.

"Let me say this: I doubt very much if our police department under the current chief is up to the challenge it is now facing," he said.

He pointed to the back of the room and, with a broad gesture of both hands, waved for Paul to come up to the front. Heads turned as Paul walked to the first row and stood in front of Madden's position on the dais. Jimmy McGregor, the editor of the *Star*, sat in the first seat scribbling notes on a legal pad. When he finished that task, McGregor jumped up, picked up a camera, and moved closer to Paul to take a picture. Paul recoiled, as if retreating from a bad odor.

"Well, Chief, you heard the question?" Madden said.

"Yes, I heard it. And your comment as well."

"What do you have to say?" Madden said.

Paul turned to Kloss. "The Negro who was looking for a home to buy? What would you want me to do?"

"Put a stop to it," he said.

"By what law?"

"Laws don't matter. What we want matters. Nothing else. Make it clear to this Negro to look somewhere else. Simple as that." The room erupted in applause.

"As for the murder investigations, I am conducting them. When the day comes that I can't do my job, I will let you know."

Madden raised his right hand and waved to someone in the back of the room. Paul turned to see Brady Whitener waving back at Madden. Whitener held a leather case in his right hand. He was dressed in a three-piece suit, brightly colored tie, and black bowler hat. A cane of carved wood hung from his right forearm. Paul regarded the man as an unprincipled grifter. He'd encountered him several times in recent years and seeing him now was too much to bear.

"Hello, Mr. Mayor," Whitener called out.

He brushed past Paul and took a seat in the front row. As he sat down, he straightened his pants and ran both hands over his two-toned shoes as if to preserve the perfect shine. Paul regarded him as the height of pompous arrogance.

"Always nice to see you, Brady," Madden said. "Are you here to speak to the board?"

Whitener stood up. "I have important business to discuss with the board, either here in public, which is fine with me, or in a more private setting."

Paul returned to the back of the room. McGregor took a series of photographs of Whitener.

"Mr. Mayor," he began. "My law office in our village has been retained by the Haase family. You may not know them, or even heard of them, but when I am finished speaking about the treatment afforded them by an official of this village, you will know them well and, I am certain, be as outraged as I am about the events of recent days."

He turned to make sure Paul was still in the room.

"I was brought in as their counsel when it became clear to them, Mr. Mayor, that the village police chief was out to frame Mr. Haase and deny him his rights. Charlotte and Rudolf Haase have lived in our village for two decades since their arrival from Germany. Mr. Haase has been a hardworking man who has provided for his family. He took the time to become a citizen of our democracy."

He removed his bowler and placed it on his chair. With both hands he scraped the side of his head to push down his gray hair. He pulled down on his suit coat.

"Chief Beirne is a village employee," Whitener said. "He has been since his return from service in the South Pacific. He came home to this village, where he was raised by his mother and father, and where, I think we can all agree, he once did a competent job. He was certainly told to play by our rules. But, Mr. Mayor, his behavior in recent days has been dishonorable and illegal. He has confronted my client Mr. Haase in a rough way, questioning him about the horrific murder of the poor woman found ripped apart off Wellwood Avenue. Without an ounce of evidence, Chief Beirne has laid the blame on my client, bullied and insulted him. We all know no white man committed that crime."

He turned to Paul. "Stay away from my clients. Do not approach them again, or I will file a very impressive lawsuit against this village."

Whitener took his seat, and Madden waved Paul to the front of the room. "What is your response?" Madden said.

"I have no response, Mr. Mayor. I am conducting a murder investigation. That won't be carried out in a public setting."

"As you heard, Chief," Madden said, "you have been accused of harassing this family. Any response?"

"None." He turned and walked towards the double doors at the back of the meeting room.

❖

Paul called Lindsay Henry's office when he returned to his desk. The woman on the phone said Henry was with the county coroner and would be back later in the afternoon. An hour later, walking out the back door of Village Hall, he saw Madden, McGregor, and Whitener huddled in a corner of the parking lot like criminals plotting their next robbery.

He drove to Doc's house. No one was home. He looked in the front windows. The house was dark. Back in his car, as he pulled away from the house, he saw a late-model Ford truck parked a half block away, a man behind the wheel. The truck gunned forward and sped down the road, turned a corner, and was out of sight.

Checking the glove box, he was reassured his pistol was there. He drove along the creek towards the bay. When he was a half block from his father's house, he stopped the car. A Cadillac was parked in front of his father's bungalow. Mueller was chatting with his father by the front door. Paul backed up, turned around, and returned to his office in Village Hall. As he entered the room, the phone rang.

"Paul, this wiretap has been a bust," Henry said. "We have to go back to the judge to either end it or extend it. I told that to your deputy before."

"Haase isn't saying anything about the dead woman?"

"He's not even on the phone. His wife is on, speaking German. I had a guy in the office listen to that, and he said it's all meaningless small talk."

THIRTEEN

At the diner, Paul ordered coffee and two fried eggs. When he was done, he put two silver dollars on the counter and drove to Haase's house. The same late-model Ford he saw near Doc's sat at the curb in front of the house. The driver was talking to Mrs. Haase, who was standing on the curb, her head bent down towards the driver's side window.

Paul pulled to the side of the street, concealing his presence behind a line of cars. From the glove box he removed a pair of binoculars. He focused on Mrs. Haase, who seemed animated, pleading. Then he aimed his sight on the truck and, on a grocery receipt from King Kullen, wrote down the license plate number. Ten minutes later, Paul proceeded down the street. He parked in front of Haase's house and walked up the driveway. Mrs. Haase was standing by the gate to the backyard.

"*Was willst du? Mein Mann ist nicht zu Hause,*" she said.

"Stop with that!" Paul said.

"You don't know German? Your father is German. Why don't you know the language?"

"It's none of your business," he said. "Where's your husband? I want to talk to him."

"Ich habe es dir schon gesagt. Er ist nicht zu Hause."

"Speak English."

"He's not home," she said.

He walked closer to her. She retreated to the other side of the gate and closed it behind her.

"Who was that you were just talking to?" he said.

"Entschuldigen Sie mich? What do you want?"

"You were talking to a man at the curb. Who was that?"

"I don't answer to you."

"When I was here last time you were in the backyard. What were you doing?"

"I have a garden."

"Pretty late in the season to be tending to your garden," he said.

"Not really," she said.

"You're afraid of your husband? He ever beat you? Get drunk and go nuts on you?"

"I'm going inside."

"You read how that woman was killed? He ripped her insides out. She bled to death on the grass. That's the man you're married to."

"You are desperate to make an arrest. You're scared you will fail. Don't come back here again."

"I don't need your permission to come back," Paul said. "Who is paying your lawyer's legal fees? You certainly can't afford him."

She disappeared into the house.

He pushed open the gate and walked into the backyard to a strip of soil where the remains of a garden lay on overturned soil. He walked the length of the yard to see where she was standing with her shovel when they had arrived to confront Haase as he cleaned his car. He kicked the ground with his foot. She was staring at him from the kitchen window. He walked back through the gate to the driveway. She watched him from the side door. He walked down the driveway to his car. She was now at the front window. He walked up a brick path to the front door. She opened it as he arrived on the top step.

"I have no beef with you, Mrs. Haase. If there comes a time when you might want to talk, or get away yourself, you can contact me, and I will help you."

"I don't need your help," she said, closing the door.

❖

Not having a clear investigative path in mind, Paul proceeded to Sunrise Highway and west towards New York City. He was picking up loose threads. In Queens, he cut north towards the Midtown Highway and into the tunnel to Murray Hill. He found his way downtown and, driving up and down street after street, stopped at 80 Lafayette Street when he saw the Norden Industries sign on the side of the building. He parked and walked inside. A uniformed man at a desk by the elevators stood up to greet Paul. He showed the man his badge.

"Is there someone I could speak with? I'm trying to learn about people who worked here during the war years."

"Mr. Norden isn't here," the guard said. "He's in Switzerland."

"Is there someone else who could help me?"

A few minutes later, a middle-aged man in a dark, tailored suit and polished black shoes stepped out of the elevator and introduced himself as Mr. Davidson, assistant to Mr. Norden. Davidson removed a pipe from his mouth and tapped it against an ashtray by the elevator doors.

"I understand you're looking for information on our employees," he said. "You are a police officer?"

"I'm the chief of the Lindenhurst Village Police Department out on Long Island," he said. "Two people were murdered in my village. Both worked here at one time. Their last name was McKay."

"Constance McKay was Mr. Norden's private secretary," Davidson said. "Her husband was an inspector on the assembly line. I believe he had another job out on Long Island before he was hired here at his wife's insistence."

"Did he work in this building?"

"Here and in our plant on Varick Street in Brooklyn. What is this about, Mr. Beirne? I do read the papers, and was certainly struck when I saw both had been murdered."

Davidson steered Paul out the door. They walked a half block to a coffee shop and took a corner table away from office workers out on a break.

"Do you know what the Norden Mark 15 bombsight was, Mr. Beirne? Have you read anything about the Duquesne spy ring?"

"I remember there was a trial in federal court here in Manhattan."

"A very big trial, Mr. Beirne. Its secrets may have something to do with what you are investigating. That was my first thought when I read in the papers that the McKays had been murdered. If you know any recent history, you can see the connections. The Norden bombsight was a brilliant design. It helped American forces drop a bomb from thousands of feet into a very specific area. Precision bombing, Mr. Beirne. It was invented, designed, and built in our building and in the Brooklyn building. Mr. Norden is the genius behind it. Only a small number of Americans knew about it. It was very top secret—at least we all thought it was."

"Mr. McKay worked on it?"

"He was an inspector on the assembly line. Like the others, he worked on a part of the overall design. Through his wife, he certainly had access to the specs and the entire blueprints, which were kept in a wall safe in Mr. Norden's office. As Mr. Norden's private secretary, she had access to everything."

"Are you saying she stole them?"

"Neither of them were charged. The whole truth of what happened has never been revealed. Somehow an assembly line inspector made copies of the entire Norden blueprints and all the technical specs. Exactly how he got them is not known. Someone gave him the plans, and they were smuggled to a man on one of the German liners that was going back and forth between Hamburg and New York before the American entry into the war."

"What was the name of the man who stole the drawings and gave them to the Germans?"

"Hermann W. Lang," Davidson said. "He was also a supervisor here. The timing of all this, of your inquiries today, seems rather curious, Mr. Beirne. We were formally notified just a few days ago that Lang got out of federal prison in Kansas and was being deported to Germany."

"Did he and Mr. or Mrs. McKay know each other?"

"During the spy trial, a federal agent came here and looked at personnel records for the McKays. Why, exactly, he wanted to see them, he would not say. But when Mr. Norden looked at them, it was clear that Lang knew the McKays from years before. We don't know what that was, how they met, but the thought was it was something that took place well before the war."

A waitress brought two coffees to the table.

"In fact, it was Mrs. McKay who recommended Hermann Lang for the job here. Understand, she was with Mr. Norden every day. They took several trips to Washington together. Mr. Norden trusted her completely. During a typical day the complete plans were in his office, spread out on a conference table. The full set of plans were never in any other part of the building. It was curious to Mr. Norden that neither Mrs. nor Mr. McKay were called as a witness at the spy trial. Mr. Lang was convicted, and that was that. The case was then closed."

He looked towards the street, then down at his coffee cup.

"There was something else between the three of them, Mr. Beirne. Something personal. I heard her talking in the cafeteria about something she was promised, but it never came through."

"Do you have any idea what that might have been?"

"As I said, Mr. Beirne, so much about these people is a mystery."

❖

At The New York Public Library on Fifth Avenue, Paul walked into a large, high-ceilinged room filled with microfiche machines. He approached a desk and told the man with a name tag on his shirt that he wanted to find clips from the *New York Times* or the other newspapers about the Duquesne spy ring.

The man returned with several tins of film and showed Paul how to thread the reel into the microfiche machine. Soon he was looking at the front page of the *Times*. Dozens of mug shots were spread across the screen: grim-faced men and a woman named Lily Stein. Her face sparked a memory about his father. He tapped the print button to make a copy of the page.

It was late in the afternoon when Paul finished with the last reel of microfiche. When he returned them to the desk, the man said, "Can I help you with anything else? You're researching the German spy ring?"

"I don't remember the headlines at the time. I was away then," Paul said.

"Do you know about the German spies who landed from a submarine out on eastern Long Island?" the man said. "Four of them landed on the beach in Amagansett, in East Hampton, in 1943. They took the night train into New York City. My parents have a home near that beach, and every time I walk there, I imagine what had happened."

"Why do you bring that up? Is that connected to the spy ring?"

"I mention it because a man was in here the other day. He started off speaking in German, then switched to decent English. He wanted to see the newspaper accounts of both the spy ring and what was written at the time about the Germans on the submarine."

"What were these spies here for?" Paul asked.

"Well, very little was known at the time, and, quite honestly, very little is still known about what their mission was. The government said it was about sabotage, creating havoc, you know, blowing up Jewish-owned businesses, but that never made sense. All the way here for that? Most were caught, tried, and executed; two were deported to Germany. What drew my attention was that this man specifically wanted to know about a spy named Burger, who was one of the lucky ones who was deported."

He regretted not taking a photograph of Lang when he lay on the table in Doc's funeral home.

"Did this man sign anything or give his name?" Paul asked. "Can you describe him?"

"Average height, gray hair, heavy accent. Seemed eager to see what had been written. But that one name—Burger—he repeated a few times. He wanted to know what happened to him. He made some sort of comment, as if he and Burger had been friends, if he could find him in Germany. After he left, I looked at the newspaper accounts. In addition to being on that submarine, Burger was one of the small group of Nazis involved in the Beer Hall Putsch in 1923. They were regarded as early heroes of the Nazi movement, very special people."

FOURTEEN

It was after dark when Paul approached his father's house. On the passenger seat next to him was the copy he made of the front page of the *Times* showing all the faces, a circle around the photograph of the familiar Lily Stein. He picked up the copy, stared at the faces, put it down again. In his rearview mirror he saw his father and Mueller climbing into his father's car. He waited fifteen minutes, turned around, and parked on the grass on the north side of his father's property. The house was dark. He walked around the back and stepped up onto the deck. The back door was unlocked. It was a safe bet he'd find a flashlight in the kitchen drawer next to the stove.

Reluctant to turn on any lights, he located the flashlight, looked around the kitchen, and proceeded into the living room. On the coffee table were issues of the Lindenhurst *Star*, with the headlines about the murder and the fire at the McKay house. An earlier edition of the paper featured the headline: UNIDENTIFIED MAN RUN OVER BY TRAIN. He had believed his father only read the German-language newspaper from New York City.

Two cardboard boxes filled with mail sat on the couch, along with a box of blue-backed legal papers. He picked up the first set. They referred to an action in Suffolk County Surrogate's Court filed in late August. His father had gone to court to have his wife declared legally dead "for the purpose of ending a long period of not knowing her fate, so the petitioner could one day remarry and collect on a life insurance policy taken out on his wife in 1938."

The words "legally dead" slapped him in the face. She wasn't "missing" or "ran off with another man" or anything else as descriptive. The story he held in his memory of his mother, the never knowing, took a sharp turn. Now these words: *legally dead.*

He folded the document and stuffed it into his coat pocket. From the letter box he pulled out the first pile, which was held together with a rubber band. Four of the letters had the stamp of a federal prison in Kansas on the upper-left corner of the envelope, along with an inmate number. Underneath the letters was a stack of old copies of the *New Yorker Staats-Zeitung.* One showed a photograph of a Bund parade in Yorkville on the Upper East Side of Manhattan in the fall of 1937. A copy of the New York *Daily News* from February 1939 showed a photograph of a massive rally in Madison Square Garden of pro-Nazi Americans. He put the letters and the copy of the *Staats-Zeitung* in his coat pocket.

As he reached the bottom of the box, he saw a tattered copy of the *New York Times* with the headline: HAUPTMANN PUT TO DEATH FOR THE KILLING OF LINDBERGH BABY; REMAINS SILENT TO THE END. He had seen it before, on the kitchen table of the family home. All these years, his father had kept this one copy out of hundreds about the trial, declaring Hauptmann had been executed.

Before returning the flashlight to the kitchen drawer, he walked down the hallway to his father's bedroom. Two suitcases lay open on the bed, half packed with clothes and shoes.

❖

Back home, he spread the German-language newspaper on the kitchen table. He rummaged through drawers in the kitchen and in his bedroom until he found a magnifying glass. Starting at the upper right corner of the photograph, he looked closely at the page. He was halfway across it when he stopped, lowered the glass closer to the paper, and stared at his father's face. He wore a black uniform. He was carrying a swastika flag.

Paul's face heated up, his eyes widened. He fell back into a kitchen chair, nearly knocking it over. He muttered, "Dear God." A banner held by the man next to him read AMERIKDEUTSCHER VOLKSBUND. Paul looked closely at everyone around his father, as well as the crowd lined up along the sidewalk on First Avenue.

The next morning, he called the district attorney's office and gave an investigator the license plate number of the truck he'd seen at the Haase house. An hour later, the investigator called back and said it was registered to Schmidt. He drove by Doc's house and then back to the funeral home. Doc was at his desk.

Paul pulled out the letters he had taken from his father's house and the copy of the spy ring story from the *Times* and handed them to Doc.

"Can you tell me what these say?" he said.

Doc looked at each of the letters, then up at Paul. "These are addressed to your father," he said. "Where did you get them?"

"From his house."

"He gave them to you?"

"No."

"You stole them?"

"I wouldn't say that."

"Then how would you characterize it?"

"The door was open. I went in. I saw some material that pertained to my mother, and a German-language newspaper published in New York City and an old copy of the *New York Times*."

"I'm confused, Paul."

"What are you confused about?"

"You are investigating murders in this village, right?"

"Yes, obviously."

"So why are you breaking into your father's house?'

"I didn't break in. The door was open," Paul said. He waved an arm at Doc to discourage any more questions.

"I'd suggest you stay on one investigation before branching off into the grievances you have against your father."

Paul said, "There was a document in his house saying that he's trying to declare my mother legally dead. I have to know, for myself, for my mother's brother, what happened to her."

"Put that aside for now," Doc said. He opened the first envelope. "This is from the federal prison in Leavenworth, Kansas. Federal inmate number 167089. 'Dear Howard: I will be released mid-August and flown to New York City. I will be driven to a halfway house in Midtown. Deportation to Germany is scheduled for October 5. We need to meet to discuss certain matters before I return to Germany. *Geheimnisse müssen gewahrt bleiben.*' It's signed Hermann W. Lang."

"What does that mean in English?"

"'Secrets must be kept.'"

He opened the second and third envelopes. "Lang is telling your father that 'our friend Burger' is now back in Germany."

"I was in The New York Public Library looking at clips, and the man at the desk said someone came in and asked specifically about that name," Paul said. "My father knew Lang?"

"He's been in prison, he's being deported, and there's something between Lang and your father he wants to settle before October 5, which was a few days after he was killed. Whatever it is, it also involves this man Burger."

"Lang and a group of others, including a woman named Lily Stein, were rounded up in a big German spy trial and convicted. He worked at the same factory with Mr. and Mrs. McKay."

"Stein?"

"Yes. Lily Stein."

"What was she doing with those people?"

"I have a memory of my father introducing me to a German woman named Stein in Lindenhurst at the beginning of the war. She came to the house, and he introduced her to my mother. They never spoke English. I heard my mother say, 'What is she doing here?'"

He handed Doc the front page of the German-language newspaper. He pointed to one of the faces in the crowd.

"Doc," Paul said. "That's my father."

"This happened in New York City?" he said.

"I know my father took my mother to a big rally in Madison Square Garden in 1939," Paul said. "He came home and told me about it in his breathless way what a great night it was. He called President Roosevelt 'that Jew Rosenfeld.' After that night I never saw my mother again."

Doc walked in a circle around his desk and sat down.

"Someone went into my house," Paul said, "and painted a swastika on the wall. Next to it were the words WE ARE STILL HERE."

Doc looked up at Paul. "You are just now telling me this?"

Paul nodded.

"The last two nights, I was here late," Doc said. "Each night when I left, there was a car in the rear of the lot with a man sitting in it. I walked towards the car. The driver was staring at me. He started up the engine, and as he passed by my car, he held his hand out of the driver's side window and mimicked shooting a gun at me. I wasn't close enough to see his face."

Doc picked up a scrap of paper off his desk. "This was taped to the office door when I came in this morning," he said. He handed it to Paul.

On it was written: *Die Endlösung ist noch nicht vorbei.*

"What does that mean?

"The Final Solution is not over."

FIFTEEN

As Paul opened the back door to Village Hall, there was Madden standing at the top of the stairs.

"You are just in time, Chief Beirne," Madden said. "Come to my office immediately."

Loud voices spilled out of the mayor's office. Brady Whitener and Mr. and Mrs. Haase were seated in chairs set in a half circle in front of the mayor's desk. Madden sat in his high-backed chair. Whitener jumped up and stuck his hand out to Paul, who ignored it. Leaning against the paneled wall next to Madden's desk stood McGregor, his arms folded, his camera draped over his right shoulder.

"The issue this morning is your recent visit to the Haase house," Madden said. "Mr. Haase was away tending to his ill mother. You were told to leave and not come back."

"I am conducting a murder investigation," Paul said.

"You were told to stay away, yet you walked into the backyard, where you had no business, poked around, then walked to the front of the house, where you banged on the front door to confront Mrs. Haase. She could not have been clearer with you. Yet you persisted. I can only conclude from this that you are determined to frame Mr. Haase for the murder of the McKay woman. Mrs. Haase will fully back him up that he was home and not off somewhere killing that poor woman."

Mrs. Haase leaned towards her husband and said, *"Das haben sie Richard Hauptmann—"*

Whitener cut her off. "Stop that. We have nothing to hide."

Madden stood up. McGregor moved closer to the desk.

"Are you some sort of advisor to the mayor, McGregor?" Paul asked.

"You are the last person to be throwing insults around," McGregor said.

"Let's stay focused," Madden said. "That the editor of the local newspaper is dating your ex-wife—I use that word loosely—is not part of the discussion today. Here is how we move forward, Mr. Beirne. You will turn over the McKay investigation to the state police barracks. Trooper Schmidt will lead the investigation from here forward. You will refrain from confronting Rudolf or Charlotte Haase. If you comply with these instructions, you will not be fired by the village board."

An hour later Schmidt stood by the door to the village police department, along with Madden and McGregor. As Paul walked towards them, McGregor snapped pictures.

"Hello, Chief," Madden called out. "Trooper Schmidt is here to pick up your files on the murder investigation, as well as the death of Mr. McKay."

Paul pushed McGregor's camera away from his face. McGregor let out a dramatic scream as if his rights had been violated. Schmidt and Madden followed Paul down the stairs to his office. On Paul's desk were the photographs Cantwell had taken at the crime scene. Schmidt gathered them up and tucked them under his arm. He opened file cabinet drawers. On top of one of the cabinets was the file on the Jewish girl murdered in 1938. He picked it up, looked it over, and put it back where he found it. McGregor took photographs of Schmidt going through the cabinets.

"If you want to keep your job, you will stay out of the way," Madden said. "Do you understand? I won't get the board to fire you now, but if you interfere with the state police, you will be gone immediately."

❖

Paul woke up on the couch in the clothes he'd worn the night before. Three empty beer bottles sat on the floor. He shook his head in disgust. He would have to try harder. He found his watch on the floor and was relieved to see that it was a few minutes before six A.M.

For a moment he thought about Doc and the threatening note he found. He wanted to do something for Doc. No obvious answer came to him. Between the two of them, Doc was the most vulnerable. He could not offer him a gun. Nor would Doc have accepted it. Paul felt a keen sense of shame for having brought Doc into this case.

He was out of the house by 7:30 A.M. He found Cantwell at his desk.

"Hey, Chief," he said as Paul took his seat. "I saw Billy last night. He was with the mayor and that clubby entourage of his at Baloney John's. Schmidt from the state trooper barracks. The whole lot of those hangers-on. I thought it was odd."

"How so?"

"With them was Mueller." He paused for a moment. "I've only seen him around the village a few times. Your father was there, too."

"Did you hear anything?"

"He, Schmidt, Mueller, and your father were speaking Kraut. Billy was loaded, Chief. At one point he came over to me and said, 'Meet your new police chief.'"

For the rest of the morning, Paul sat at his desk doing paperwork. Cantwell left to make his rounds and to get lunch. Later in the afternoon, Paul looked up from his desk to see Madden and Evans.

"The village attorney has drawn up papers for you to sign," Madden said. "You have been suspended without pay for the next three months. You are to stay away from your office. If you return or try to return, you will be arrested and prosecuted for trespassing. At the end of the three months, the village board will take up the question of whether to fire you or return you to the chief's job. As of now, Billy Evans is the acting chief of the Lindenhurst Village Police Department."

"Your nephew. You must be pleased," Paul asked. "Politics to you is nothing but a racket. What's the cause?"

"You have failed to make an ounce of progress in murders that occurred in our village, you have been insubordinate to me and the village board," he said. "You have gone so far as to try and frame an innocent man."

"Everyone has to kiss your ass," Paul said.

"I am going to ignore that, Beirne," the mayor said. "We made a terrible mistake making you the chief in the first place. Some of us had reservations. But out of respect for your father, and your experience during the war, we gave you that job. And today we know what a huge mistake that was."

"What about my father?"

"Deputy Evans is now the acting chief. Don't think about coming back here for three months."

Paul bounded up the stairs and into the parking lot. Climbing into his truck, he revved the engine and pulled out, turning south on Wellwood, barely avoiding a woman crossing the street. Two minutes later, he arrived in his father's driveway. The lights in the kitchen were on. He pushed the pistol under the belt of his pants, in the front so it would be visible to his father. When he reached the front door, he slammed both fists against it. The door swung open.

"What do you want?" Baer said.

He put his right hand on his father's chest and pushed past him into the living room.

"Was willst du? Du warst seit Monaten nicht mehr hier."

"Shut up, old man."

"I am asking you, why are you here? What do you want?"

Paul could smell alcohol on his father's breath. He passed through the living room and into the kitchen. Mueller and Schmidt were seated in Adirondack chairs in the backyard along the edge of the creek, cans of beer in both of their hands. Baer grabbed his son's shoulder and spun him around to face him.

"You will show me respect," he said. Mueller and Schmidt were now standing by their chairs looking into the house.

"Du bist nicht länger mein Sohn!"

Paul pulled out his revolver. He pushed him back with his left hand and his father fell into a kitchen chair, which slid out from under him. He landed hard on the linoleum floor. Mueller and Schmidt stepped towards the kitchen door and Paul waved the gun to keep them away.

"You paid off the mayor?" Paul shouted.

"What are you talking about? *Du bist verdammt verrückt, genau wie deine Mutter.*"

Paul knew 'mutter' meant mother. "You bribed the mayor because you thought when I came back from the Pacific, I was a basket case. You played his game."

"Everyone does it, so what?" Baer said.

Paul raised the pistol over his head intending to whip it across his father's face.

"You drank every day and had nightmares. You couldn't stop asking about your mother. You never got over that she walked out on both of us."

Paul thought of mentioning the legal document his father had filed in Surrogate's Court, but Baer would know he'd been in the house.

The door opened and the two men walked in. Mueller reached out to touch Baer's arm.

"*Sagen Sie ihm, er soll Ihr Haus verlassen, sonst rufen wir die Polizei und lassen ihn verhaften.*"

"I don't want him arrested," Baer said. "He's in enough trouble. He's screwed up his life. His family, his son, the job I got for him."

Paul stuffed the pistol back under his belt. "What did you pay these thieves?"

Schmidt reached under his right arm and pulled out a .45-caliber pistol. He let his arm drop so that the gun was pointed at the floor. Paul stepped away from him.

"There will be no jobs anywhere for you, Beirne, without my approval," Schmidt said. "Do you understand that?"

Mueller steered Baer into the living room.

"*Wo bewahren Sie die Schrotflinte für Enten und Kaninchen auf?*"

"It's in the closet in my bedroom," Baer said. "I used all the twelve-gauge shells during duck season."

"I'll get you more," Mueller said.

SIXTEEN

At six A.M. the following morning, the phone woke him.

"Paul, we need to meet somewhere," Cantwell said.

For a moment Paul was confused by the comment. He sat up on the bed. *What now?* he thought.

"I don't think that's a good idea, Roger," Paul said.

"Remember where the McKay woman's body was found? Go a bit north of there, over the railroad tracks. There's a dirt road on the west side of Wellwood where hundreds of new houses are going up. Let's meet there."

"Wait—what for?"

Cantwell hung up.

A half hour later, Paul pulled down the dirt road, passed through a grove of apple trees, and parked by a hay barn, its roof half collapsed.

"Evans gave all the McKay files to the mayor," Cantwell said. "The investigation is dead."

Paul climbed out of the truck. "What do you mean 'dead'?"

"I mean dead. No more. The mayor's burying it."

"Who said that?"

"I was in the office with Evans. Connie was there. She can back this up. I said something about the murders, and Billy said the mayor told him the investigation was over. Billy said that Madden told him Mrs. Haase was a friend of his. He wanted it to go no further."

"What does that mean, a 'friend'? And not Mr. Haase, but Mrs. Haase?"

"That's what he said, yes."

"They have a relationship?" Paul asked.

"I don't know what it means," Cantwell said. His voice rose in frustration. "Are you listening to me? The investigation into these murders is dead, Paul. You have to understand this."

Back at his house, Paul threw the latest edition of the *Star* on the kitchen table. His face was on the cover. It went into the trash.

Lost on how to fill the hours, he spent a cold afternoon on the bay looking for bass. It was after dark when he got home. On the floor by the front door was a letter from his aunt the postman had pushed through the slot. The first sentence read: *Can you come out?*

Paul called his ex-wife's house. He told her he was going to drive out east. He asked if Pauli could come with him. After a brief back-and-forth, Phyliss agreed Paul could pick up their son Saturday morning. She insisted the boy be back by the end of the afternoon.

His son was waiting for him in front of the house when Paul pulled up. Phyliss was inside, standing by the front door.

"You are no longer the police chief," she said as she stepped towards Paul.

He said nothing. The worried look on her face caught his attention.

"It has happened twice now. Someone has been following Pauli when he walks home from school in the afternoon," she said. "A different car each time, but the same man. Why would someone do this?"

When he didn't answer, she said, "What's going on, Paul?"

He turned away.

"I don't know," he said.

"What have you gotten into?" She repeated, as they walked to his truck.

❖

When they arrived at the farm, Pauli jumped out of the car to marvel at the farmland that spread north towards the Sound. He went into the barn while Paul went into the house through the kitchen door. On the table he found a note: *Come to the Greenport dock with Pauli. Martin and I are meeting the scrap dealer.*

Twenty minutes later, Paul pulled up at the dock in Stirling Harbor. Both sides of the narrow harbor were lined with large boathouses that had been used during the war and were now empty. Some were falling down, the long docks in front of them ripped up in places by storms. The *Predator* was tied off to its dock, a line of trawlers tight to the dock in front of it, their nets rolled up on giant wheels on their transoms. The hull of the *Predator* was partly covered in rust, the glass that enclosed the wheelhouse broken.

Pauli ran to the dock to greet Anna. Martin, leaning over his cane, was on the boat, talking to two men. With encouragement from Anna, Pauli climbed up the plank to the deck of the trawler.

"Can you stay tonight, Paul?" Anna said.

"No, we can't," he said.

Paul climbed up the plank. He waved at Martin and followed Pauli into the wheelhouse. The boy stood at the big wheel, looking out the broken windows towards the opening of the harbor into the bay. Beyond that was Shelter Island, where sailboats bobbed at their moorings.

"These men are offering a lousy price for the boat," Anna said. "If Martin can agree on a price, crews will start cutting it down, from top to hull, and selling off the scrap."

Her voice caught. "This is how it ends," she said.

Near the end of the day, he dropped off his son at his mother's. He didn't go inside, nor did Phyliss come out to greet him. At home he stood in the kitchen, staring out the window towards the creek. He felt as lost as he had in the first days after he had moved out of the family home, hoping Phyliss would call and invite him back.

His father's house was dark when he arrived. After sitting in the car for a few minutes, he got out and stood by the side of the house. He went to the unlocked back door and slipped inside. The flashlight was where it was before.

In a corner in the living room sat a radio, and next to it the desk. At the desk, he opened the top drawer and found a stack of bills held together with a rubber band. In the bottom drawer was a folder which contained dozens of letters, some typed but most handwritten. All were written in German, many with the name of the German town, Kamenz. They seemed to be in chronological order; most were postmarked in the early and mid-1920s. Many were signed "Richard." Some had the initials "RH."

Some letters were written by Baer's mother, Paul's German grandmother. He knew nothing about her. His mother had told him that Blobel was the grandmother's maiden name. She wrote on stationary, with her name—Pauline Blobel—embossed on the top. There were a half dozen other envelopes, and he opened one to see a letter written in German. At the bottom of the third page was a name: Karl Egon Neumann. Near the top of the pile was a Western Union telegram from New York City to Baer.

Paul held it close to the flashlight and read out loud: "The tourists have arrived. Staying in the Hotel Martinique. Let's get together as old friends. Burger." The date across the top: June 14, 1942.

On top of the telegram were more letters from Pauline Blobel to her son on Long Island from the winter and spring of 1951. In a folded-up envelope he pulled out a clipping from a German newspaper, which had the headline: SIEBEN WURDEN WEGEN KRIEGSVERBRECHEN DER NAZIS GEHÄNGT.

He pulled out some of the "Richard" and "RH" and Blobel letters, and the clipping. He slipped the Western Union telegram into his coat pocket. Looking at his watch, he figured it was safe to remain in the house a little bit longer. He shined his light around the room and approached the hallway towards his father's bedroom in the back of the house. The suitcases he had seen earlier were packed, sitting on the floor by the bed. The closets had been emptied.

Pulling open the top drawer of the bedside table, Paul pushed aside a bottle of Aspirin and two medical prescriptions signed by a local doctor. Underneath them was a Luger pistol and a box of bullets. He lifted the pistol out of the drawer, looked it over, and as he put it back saw a small, wallet-sized piece of embossed leather. He assumed it was a billfold of some sort. Inside was the same German medal—9 November 1923—that Doc had found on Lang's body.

He put everything back as he found it. In the hallway, a rope knotted at the end hung from a panel in the ceiling. Pulling on it, the panel, hinged at one end, dropped down. Shining his light into the space, he saw the rafters that held up the roof. He found a ladder in the closet by the front door that fit together in sections with dowel rods. He assembled the sections, carried it to the hallway, and tilted it up so that it extended into the attic.

When his head rose above the ceiling, he shined the light all around. At one end of the attic was a wooden trunk. A padlock hung from a brass latch on the front of it. Swinging the light around, he saw that against the far wall on the north side of the house was a metal box with a handle on the top and a glass window in the front, with two black dials below the glass. As he stared at the box, a bright light flashed on the hallway walls, and he heard a car's engine in front of the house.

He scurried down the ladder, pulled it down, and pushed up the panel so that it merged with the ceiling. He went to the living room and pulled apart the sections of the ladder, pushing them into the closet. The back door slid open, and the kitchen lights turned on. He stepped into the closet and pulled the door shut. Footsteps arrived in the living room. They proceeded down the hallway. Paul heard his father pissing into the toilet.

He opened the closet door and stuck his head out, listened again, then walked through the living room to the hallway. His father was standing over the sink. Paul walked into the kitchen and out the back door. He broke into a hard run, tripping in the darkness on a tree branch and landing on his face. Pushing off the ground, he felt warm blood under his nose. He fumbled for the keys in his coat pocket.

❖

In the morning, he saw his face in the mirror: a bruise stained the skin under his right eye, and dried blood dotted the side of his face like pinpricks. He waited for the water to get hot and took a washcloth, soaked it, and placed it on his face as he sat on the edge of the bed. When he was through, he filled a plastic bag with ice and held it against his face.

He went to the kitchen and called Lindsay Henry's office: no answer. He placed the letters he had taken from his father's house on the kitchen table and arranged them until they were lined up in columns chronologically.

There were more than twenty: the ones from Kamenz, Germany, ran from the summer of 1921 to the first week of November 1923. On the last one, dated November 3, 1923, the writer had drawn in pencil the image of an ocean liner. Over it the person wrote: *Nach Amerika kommen*. One column contained a half dozen letters from his father's mother and five from the man named Neumann.

When Paul arrived at Doc's house, he spread the letters on the kitchen table, arranging them in the same columns. Doc looked at Paul's bruised face, shook his head, but said nothing. Paul guessed Doc's silence was an indication he thought Paul had been drunk and had a bad fall.

"You broke into your father's house again?"

Paul ignored him.

Doc said, "These letters are from the city of Kamenz, from 'Richard' and 'RH.' Kamenz is in the east, south of Berlin. The Russians occupy it now."

Holding one up, Doc read, "'Helmuth, I am leaving shortly. I have plans to stow away on the ship to New York. I have a place to live when I get there. I will look you up after I settle in. We remain a family in grieving, with both Max and Herman dead in the Great War.'"

He read the letters signed by Neumann. "Whoever this is, he is working as a forester on the old Bismark estate," Doc said. He held up one letter and read it slowly. "In this one, he asks if your father is in touch with 'our mother.' He says, 'make sure you give her my name for future correspondence.'"

"Why wouldn't their mother know his name?"

"Did you know your father had a brother?" Doc asked.

"Mueller told me; that's the first I heard of it."

Doc picked up the Western Union telegram, with the name Burger at the bottom.

"Any idea what this is?" Doc said. He handed it to Paul.

"He's arrived at a hotel in Manhattan and is telling my father he's here. I guess my father was expecting him."

"What strikes me, Paul, is that it is in English and not German. That date—it's the middle of the war. Whoever this is, wrote in English so as not to draw attention to himself. My guess would be a German who had lived here and went back to Germany, and for some reason had returned."

Doc turned over the telegram.

"Did you see the penciled note written on the back?" He handed it to Paul. He had not seen this in the darkness of his father's house. He handed it back to Doc.

"'I will meet you at the H and H on Broadway.'"

"Horn and Hardart," Paul said. "Can you read the name?"

"Hermann Lang." He stared at Paul. Doc read through the rest of the letters. "Your father's mother is not a Baer, but a Blobel?" he said.

Doc picked up the German-language newspaper. "The headline says, SEVEN HANGED FOR NAZI WAR CRIMES." He read into the story. "Including one Paul Blobel."

He looked up at Paul. "She is writing her son, your father, to tell him her brother was executed. She must be using her maiden name in post-war Germany as a point of pride."

Late in the afternoon, Doc went to King Kullen to buy groceries. When he arrived at Paul's house, he unpacked everything on the counter while he spoke.

"It's very curious to me why your father, whose surname is Baer, is receiving letters from his own brother, who is using the surname Neumann," Doc said. "My brother and I, we encountered a German man with the Baer surname in Poland."

He removed chicken cutlets from the packet and placed them on a dry towel on the counter by the sink. He took three small bowls from the cupboard. In one he put flour, the second one three cracked eggs, and in the third one breadcrumbs he fashioned from a half loaf of stale white bread atop the bread box.

Using Paul's iron skillet, he pounded the three cutlets until they were thin, then dredged them in the flour, followed by the beaten eggs and breadcrumbs. He put the skillet on the stove and turned up the flame. In a pot of boiling water, he sprinkled salt and emptied a bag of noodles. As the skillet heated, he turned to Paul, who had brought boxes from the living room and put them on the kitchen table.

"I do like to drink while I am cooking. But it would be better if you didn't join me," Doc said.

Paul retrieved the whisky bottle from the back of the cupboard and poured an inch of liquid in a glass and handed it to Doc, who placed the cutlets into the hot skillet. From childhood memories of being in the kitchen with his mother, the sizzling sound of cutlets cooking was familiar to Paul.

"Wiener schnitzel," Doc said. "Only with chicken instead of veal. You can debate for hours whether veal is kosher, about how the animal is killed and the blood removed. But tonight the issue is settled. We are having chicken."

"I don't know what you are talking about."

"Rules and customs are important," Doc said.

"Did you follow the rules growing up?"

"As my brother and I got older, we were not as fastidious with the rules. I have regrets about that. The world around us in Vienna had no regard for observant Jews. We went along with it. Shame on us. We were both prominent surgeons, mind you. When the Germans arrived in March 1938, my brother and I went into hiding. One day a man found us and said his wife was giving birth and was close to death. We came out of hiding and went to the hospital. We saved her. She was the wife of a prominent American journalist. We were just the sort of smart, successful people the lower class of uneducated Nazis could not tolerate. They wanted what we worked for. Funny how, when I look at their extraordinary hatred for Jews, I see jealousy of our successes, our educations, and accomplishments. How do you hate such a small percentage of the population if not out of jealousy?"

He turned to Paul. "Your father must have eaten wiener schnitzel."

"He ate sausage, morning, noon, and night," Paul said. "My mother was frying it all the time."

"You didn't like it?"

"I became sick of it. Plus that fish in a jar. He liked that, too."

"Did your father have any sort of education?"

"He was in the First World War. That much I know."

"Why did he emigrate?"

"I don't know."

"Did you ever have a serious conversation with him?"

"Never."

Doc said, "Your own father, he's a stranger to you?"

"Completely."

Paul pulled out the boxes he had gotten at the funeral home. In it were the copies of New York City newspapers that covered the Lindbergh kidnapping case. As the chicken cooked, Paul stared at the whisky bottle but did not fill his own glass. Doc sat at the table and went through the clippings.

"Paul, on the letters from Germany to your father, the initials were RH or the name Richard. Richard Hauptmann was the man put on trial for kidnapping and murdering the Lindbergh baby. Some of the stories say his name was Bruno Richard Hauptmann. He was from Kamenz, Germany, and smuggled himself onboard an ocean liner and landed in New York City."

SEVENTEEN

He barely left the house. Most days he sat on the couch or walked around the living room, aimless, lost in his own place. If he needed anything, he went out at night, minutes before the market closed, so he'd be the last one in and the last one out. Avoiding people and unpleasant conversations was his mission. Some days he had no food in the house, but he stayed home, the shades drawn. At night he sat in his bungalow, reading and rereading all the material he had collected, going through the boxes. He wrote lists of names on legal pads; on index cards he wrote down areas where he needed to go to the library for research. He stayed away from whisky, flirted with a beer or two, but that was it.

Some afternoons he drove by his son's elementary school, parked the car, and waited for recess so he could see Pauli on the playground. Once he caught the boy's eye and waved to him. After the fourth day of this, he was parked by the school when Evans came by in a police car and stopped, angling his vehicle in front of Paul's to block him in.

"Your wife should get an order of protection, then I could arrest you," Evans said.

Paul backed up the car and drove away.

❖

When another Monday night arrived, Paul parked at the wooded dead end near his father's house and watched the old man come out the back door, get in his car, and drive off. He waited thirty minutes, then walked from his car along the street to the bungalow. The last light of day shimmered on the surface of the salt creek. He came around the house, walked up to the deck to the back door, and slid it open.

The smell—fried sausage, unwashed beer glasses, the odor an old man gives off who no longer cares about anything—caused him to seize up. His first thought was to turn back. Retrieving the flashlight from the kitchen drawer, he went back to the desk in the living room, opening and closing each drawer. He thought he should have brought the paperwork he had taken before and returned it, but he convinced himself that the old man would never see that it was missing.

From the desk, he went to the closet by the front door. There were boxes on the top shelf that contained nothing of interest. He walked down the hallway to his father's bedroom. He opened the drawer on the side table. The Luger took up the drawer, along with two new boxes of bullets. Pulling out the magazine, he could see it was fully loaded. The bedroom closet and dresser were empty.

He turned to leave the room, when he spotted an envelope from a travel agency on the bed, partially sticking out from under the pillow. His father had booked passage to Hamburg for the third week in

October, first class. He placed it back just as he had found it. Standing in the hallway, he pulled on the rope that lowered the trapdoor to the attic. He reassembled the ladder from the closet, and with the flashlight illuminating his way, climbed up the stairs and this time went all the way up.

The ceiling was five feet from the floor at the center ridge, with the roof sloping down steeply to the walls of the house. He pulled on a string and the room lit up. At the far end under the window were stacks of cardboard boxes. In some he found Christmas decorations; in another, books on the history of Ireland. He picked up a book of Yeats's poetry, opened it, and there was an inscription in his mother's handwriting: *I recite his poems by memory, as the Beatitudes from the Gospel of Matthew are forever etched on my heart.*

A third box held rolls of yarn—yellows, greens, blues, and browns. His mother loved bright colors. At the bottom of the trunk, he found a manila envelope containing two postcards from his mother to his father. They were postmarked February 21, 1939. The images on the top of the postcards featured Fire Island beach scenes and a lighthouse. His mother's signature—Joyce Beirne—was on both. Other than the name, one postcard was blank, and the other, once he held it up to the light bulb, he could read part of a word written in pencil. He could make out *grim*. He placed them on the floor by his feet. In a second envelope was a three-ring binder that contained legal documents from Germany. Several pages had been torn out of it.

He gathered up the postcards, pulled on the string, and the room went dark. As it did, he noticed another trunk at the opposite end of the attic, by the big box with the dials on the front of it. He pulled on the string again. His back bent over as the height in the room narrowed towards the eaves. He dropped to his knees and crawled.

An unlocked padlock hung from the clasp. He thought of the empty dresser drawers and closet. Inside was his father's Bund uniform, the swastika armband on the shirt sleeve. Under it were black pants and belt and knee-high black boots.

Under the boots was a leather photo album of the sort families use to collect holiday pictures. In marker on the cover was written *Glückliche Tage.* Opening the cover, he saw a note on a torn piece of stationary with writing on it, with that name he had seen before in his father's correspondence: Karl Neumann. Handwriting on the note read: *Helmuth, ich dachte, das würde dir gefallen.*

Looking at the dozens of photographs, carefully, even lovingly, preserved like a rare family treasure, brought on a sickening revulsion. He had long grown numb to everything about his father, but now, seeing the photographs, anger and disgust ran over him, crushing him. His stomach pushed up into the back of his throat. He swallowed over and over.

Before him were photographs of uniformed Nazis, some of them women, and groups of people singing happily in front of a man playing the accordion. Some photographs had writing below them: *Hier gibt es Blaubeeren.*

That word—*blaubeeren*—he knew. Some summers when all three of them went to the Cutchogue farm, his father collected blueberries in a patch Martin kept on the west side of the barn where the afternoon sun was the brightest. The photographs of these men and some uniformed women were vulgar in their ordinariness. There was an obscenity to the normalness of them happily posing for photographs. He pushed down the top of the trunk and, with the postcards and the photo album, climbed down the ladder. A few minutes later, he walked down the street to where he had hidden his car.

Leaning against it, he stared up into the dark sky, momentarily unable to get in and drive off. He didn't feel rushed. It didn't matter if his father drove down the street and saw him. He would deal with it. Every horrible thought he ever had about his old man came back to him in an onslaught. He slammed his right hand on the hood of the truck and screamed an obscenity he didn't care if a neighbor heard.

At the stationary store, he purchased a sheaf of white paper fixed to a cardboard backing, three feet by two feet, an artist's easel, four black markers and four red ones, tape, and thumbtacks. Back at home, he made a pot of coffee and, as it percolated on the stove, set up the easel.

For the next two hours, he went through all the material he had collected, the newspaper clipping, what he had taken from his father's house, and the printout he made of the front page of the *New York Times* showing all the faces caught in the spy ring. He returned to the easel and began writing dates on the first sheet of white paper in large black letters.

March 1, 1932—Lindbergh baby kidnapped and murdered.
April 3, 1936—Hauptmann executed in the electric chair. Offered clemency if he confessed. He refused.
November 1938—Carol Berkowitz murdered.
Monday, February 20, 1939—Madison Square Garden.

In black marker he circled the date and wrote: **the last day I saw my mother.**

February 21, 1939—My mother sends two postcards to my father.

September 1954—Hermann Lang murdered at Alcove Bar. Lang part of spy group convicted in the city. Writes my father—they know each other. Knows the McKays.
Next night—Mrs. McKay murdered after a night in the Alcove. Body found north of village near LIRR tracks.
One night later—Mr. McKay murdered in his house.

He spent the afternoon and into the evening at the Lindenhurst Public Library going through reference books and writing down dates. He read more copies of the New York newspapers' coverage of the Lindbergh trial. The trial testimony gave him dozens more pieces of information. It was after dark when he returned home. His timeline was getting longer as he filled in the gaps.

January 30, 1933—Hitler comes to power.
December 1933—Trial coverage shows Isidore Fisch leaves for Germany from NYC. He gave Hauptmann the ransom money. Approximately $35,000 Lindbergh ransom money unaccounted for.

Paul was grateful he had enough to put together a meal of fried onions and ground beef. He popped the cap off a beer bottle and tipped the bottle up to his mouth. He took two deep swigs and put it down. Alcohol would offer him no assistance now. Before he went to bed, he rooted through the kitchen drawers to find the key to the front and back doors of the bungalow.

EIGHTEEN

He stared at the wall for long periods. There were so many boxes of papers and old newspapers stacked on the kitchen table and spread out on the linoleum floor, he had a hard time navigating a path. His collection began to take on the look of obsession. There was too much information, too many names. He could hear Doc telling him he was mired on too many side trails. That was fine for him to say. Paul no longer believed that.

In one of the boxes he found the telegram with Lang's writing on the back. In his head he wrote a brief bio: *Hermann Lang. German spy. Convicted felon. Friend of my father. Lang is murdered in Lindenhurst, body thrown on the tracks, before Mrs. McKay's death. She was likely with him at the bar.*

From another box, he pulled out the New York *Daily News* accounts of the Lindbergh trial. He was struck by a close-up picture of the ransom note found in the toddler's second-floor nursery. On the bottom edge were circles, horizontal holes, and wavy lines. It was a strange symbol—but of what?

He spent the following afternoon, a Saturday, at Lindsay Henry's home in Babylon Village. He was grateful for the company, as Henry was the only politician he had talked to who had been helpful. He had become—even if Henry didn't see it this way—a mentor to Paul. He knew Henry as a serious prosecutor and also someone who liked to sit on a barstool in a favorite pub and if he drank too much would begin singing Irish songs popular during the Easter Rising of 1916, where his grandfather played some sort of role before he emigrated to America. Henry was both jovial and serious, contemptuous of politicians and the political system. They sat outside at his bayfront home until nearly nightfall. Over the course of several hours, Henry refilled his whisky glass three times. No water and no ice.

They went over what Henry knew about the trial in New York City of the Duquesne spy ring and Lang's appearance in Lindenhurst after being released from federal prison.

"Why would he come here?" Paul said. "Okay, he knows my father. Is he here to say goodbye to him? That's no reason to risk being put back in prison. Why was he killed?"

"It seems more likely he was there to see the McKays, since they worked together in Manhattan," Henry said.

"Why would he need to see them before he's deported?"

"Maybe he was afraid of what they knew," Henry said.

"Knew about what?"

"I don't know. But I was once taught to focus on the simplest explanations first, then work outward from there. Detective work is one part science, two parts logic. In the end, after all other explanations have been discarded, go back to the simplest one."

The following morning, Paul returned to the Lindenhurst Public Library and began the process of going through the microfiche of the *Star* and the Babylon *Beacon*. The first thing that caught his attention was a photograph with a short story below it. The date on the photograph was 1946. The caption read: *The old Miller boat storage barn was headquarters of the Lindenhurst chapter of the German American Bund from 1933 to 1941. Village fathers have been asked to have it demolished but say they have no authority to do so. The barn is owned by the estate of the Miller family, which also owned the boat-building operation on the site.*

After hours of scrolling through page after page of the *Star*, he found a first-person account of a reporter who traveled to a Bund rally in Yaphank in the summer of 1937, an hour east of Lindenhurst, that the Nazi sympathizers called Camp Siegfried. There was a series of photographs on accompanying pages. On the last page, he saw a photograph of a line of men dressed in uniforms, parading in front of an enormous swastika hanging from a stage.

He went to the reference desk and asked for a magnifying glass. When he returned to the machine, he went over the photograph, stopping at the men in the middle of a long line passing in front of the stage. He saw his father's face first, and behind him, a tall, thick-set man who looked like a younger version of Haase. Behind him was August Hagar. Standing behind Hagar were two men, one of whom could have been Lang. He had no idea who the second person was. He tapped the print button and the page scrolled out of the machine.

At home he took his black marker and in big letters wrote BAER, HAASE, HAGAR and drew a circle around the names. He added LANG and ??? to it. He was organizing the files and newspapers in the boxes in some sort of order when the phone rang. It was Lindsay Henry.

"Lily Stein was another in that Lang spy ring," he said. "She is out of prison and awaiting deportation in a federal halfway house off Times

Square. Same deportation date as Lang had. If you want to see her, that's where she is."

Paul drove to Doc's house and then to the funeral home, where he found him seated at his desk doing busy work and sipping tea. WQXR played classical music on a radio behind the desk. He placed the photo album from his father's house on the desk.

"What's this?" Doc asked. He reached behind him and, reluctantly, turned off the radio. "That was Bach, by the way, Paul. You should get to know him. He, too, can answer many of life's mysteries."

"I was hoping you could help me," Paul said. "My father had it in a trunk in his attic."

Doc looked at the cover. "Those words mean 'happy days.'" He opened the cover and picked up the note written on stationary. "It says, 'Helmuth, I thought you'd like this.'"

"The name again," Paul said. "Karl Egon Neumann."

Doc muttered something as he turned the pages. His hands rushed to cover his face. He made a gagging sound and with both hands pushed off the desk.

"No, no, no."

Paul looked down at the album, the page open to a photo of four uniformed men smiling at the camera. Doc stumbled backward, nearly falling over the chair.

"Who is that, Doc?" Paul asked, dreading the answer.

Doc retreated to a chair in the corner. "That's Josef Kramer, a doctor named Mengele, Richard Baer, and Karl Hocker."

Seated at the desk, Paul stared at the photo. "Richard Baer?"

"He was in charge when the 440,000 Jews from Hungary arrived at Auschwitz. This was May to July 1944. My mother, my brother, and I were in one of the transports. Our father had died of a heart attack before we were deported from Vienna. He was spared this madness. The day we arrived, Mengele was on the platform making selections as to who would be gassed. Because we were doctors, my brother and I were separated from the rest. Mengele seemed fascinated with us. He pointed in one direction for us and another for our mother. We pleaded with him. Begged him. That was the last time we saw her. We learned an hour later she was gassed and cremated. They turned her into ash and smoke." He sat up. "Take that away, Paul."

"Baer is hiding in Germany under the name Neumann." Paul choked out the words. "He's my father's brother."

He could not look Doc in the eye. His regret at pulling Doc into this investigation sickened him as he saw Doc come undone looking at the album.

"His crimes are too big even for the imagination," Doc said. "How do you kill 440,000 people in a matter of weeks?"

Doc sank in the chair, his head dropped, his mouth halfway open as if breathing had suddenly become impossible and oxygen was scarce. Paul was speechless. Doc pushed the album away.

All Paul could think of to say was a weak, "I'm sorry."

After a few minutes of silence, with Doc staring at the floor, Paul picked up the album and drove home. There, he put it on a shelf in the closet by the front door. He waited two hours for Doc to compose himself before he went back to get him. He knew he was exposing his friend to far too much personal pain. But because of his own inadequacy, he needed him. He couldn't leave him out.

Soon they were on their way to Manhattan. Doc sank low in the passenger seat, his head leaning against the car window, his eyes closed. His face was pale, shiny with perspiration. The fingers on both hands were tightly laced together. He was the picture of a man holding on.

They found the address of a four-story brownstone on West 47th Street. There was no plaque on the wall by the door indicating it was a government facility. They rang a bell. A uniformed guard let them in. He escorted them to a sitting area and left to get Stein from her room on the top floor. It was nearly a half hour before Paul heard awkward footsteps on the stairs and a white-haired woman, feeble to the point of helplessness and hunched over a cane, entered the sitting room.

"*Sprechen Sie Englisch? Oder sprechen Sie lieber Deutsch?*" Doc asked.

She navigated towards a chair, all the while staring at Doc. Paul remembered her photograph in the newspaper he had seen at The New York Public Library. The paper with all the photographs of the spy ring was tacked to Paul's living room wall like a wanted poster on the bulletin board of the post office. She looked young, with dark, curly hair and a pretty face. The woman before him was the picture of a failed life collapsing towards the end.

"I've been in this country for many years," she said. "My English is quite good. Prison can do that." To Doc, she said, "Are you German?" When he didn't answer, she said, "Viennese?"

He nodded.

"What is your surname?"

"Liebmann."

"The family that makes the Rheingold Beer?"

"Not me, no," Doc said.

"You're Jewish?"

He glared at her. "As are you—and yet you worked for the murderers. How can you explain that?"

"I didn't know what they would do," she said. Her answer had a practiced feel to it, as if she had repeated it countless times.

"You didn't know? From 1933 on, you saw what they were doing. November 1938—you saw what the mobs did. Yet you worked for them."

"You came here to berate me?"

She sank in her seat, her head bowed towards the floor.

She was silent for nearly a minute before Doc said, "This is Paul Beirne. We need to talk to you."

Her eyes stayed on Doc. "So—you got away? How did you manage that?"

"And you served them," he said. "Maybe you could explain that to me."

"Don't lecture me, Herr Liebmann. Don't look down your nose at me. I know you find me thoroughly disgusting, but after a decade in a federal prison, and about to be shipped to the human ash heap that is Europe, I really don't care what you think."

She leaned back in the chair, draping the cane over her legs. Doc stepped towards the door to leave, but Paul reached out to restrain him.

"I don't want to hear your story, lady," Doc said. "Being in the same room with you makes me sick. You were a collaborator—"

She screamed, "How dare you! You can have your opinions of me, Herr Liebmann. That is your right. I came to this country before the madness began. I didn't believe Germany was capable of wholesale extermination. Admiral Canaris, whom I knew quite well, assured me the Nazis would not do what they said they would do. You know what they did to Canaris? Do you know?"

"Oh, the excuses," Doc said. "'We didn't know.' 'How could we know?' 'Yes, the Jews disappeared, and we took their homes and businesses, but we didn't know they were being killed.' 'Hitler made the autobahn, didn't he?' They pile up so easily. You are truly sickening."

"They hanged him from a meat hook," she said. "You don't know what you are talking about—"

Doc cut her off, shouting a stream of angry German obscenities. He stormed out of the building, slamming the door behind him. The noise brought the guard back in, who assisted Stein as she tried to navigate her way back to the stairs.

"I don't want any part of this," Stein said. "You tell that friend of yours he can go to hell."

Paul had no idea of the history the two were arguing over. Doc's accusation that she was a "collaborator" threw him. He stared at Stein for several minutes.

"Miss Stein, please, I need your help," Paul said. "Give me a few minutes of your time."

"You don't understand me, do you? You are the same as your friend." She looked at Paul. "Perhaps I don't understand myself, if that makes any sense to you. A collaborator? My God. An accidental spy is the most you can call me. But tell me, what do you want?"

"I've had three murders in my village on Long Island. The McKays. They worked at the Norden plant, where the bombsight plans were stolen and given to Hermann Lang."

"Lang was convicted along with me," she said. "We sat at the same defendant's table for several months listening to the evidence against us."

"Did he tell you who gave him the plans to the bombsight?"

"I know who it was, but there is no point in naming names today," she said. "I had dinner with this person and her husband one evening in New York City. Lovely people as far as I could tell. Professionally Irish with all its stereotypes and anger at the English enemy."

Paul said, "In Lang's circle was a man named Helmuth Baer."

"He called himself Howard. I met him at the Little Casino restaurant in Yorkville," she said. "And I went to his home once. Out on Long Island. He had a little bungalow by the bay. Nineteen forty-one,

I believe. He lived alone. He told me his wife had left him. In the attic of his house he had a shortwave radio that was important to our effort."

Paul said, "I need to understand what you did together."

"We had common interests," she said. "It does no good talking about it now. I've served my time. This Howard Baer, he escaped American justice for his role. Germany was defeated. I must live with my sins. Your friend would have me executed if he could. To the extent that I passed information on to Germany, that makes me a collaborator. But I knew nothing about the horror that was unleashed. I had no part in that. Sitting in a prison cell I went over my life a thousand times. I guess all I can offer are excuses."

"I need to know more about Baer and the others," Paul said. "What did they do?"

"Why? What's the point now?"

"What do you know?"

"I was introduced to Baer by Lang. They had known each other for quite some time. My group, we had another wireless station on the north shore of Long Island. These were vital links back to Germany for the passing of information."

"Baer was a member of the spy ring?"

"I don't understand, Mr. Beirne. You said a moment ago you are investigating three murders. Now you ask me about Helmuth Baer. What does he have to do with anything?"

"There isn't a simple answer to that question," Paul said. "You knew Hermann Lang?"

"I never trusted the man. He was hiding something. So was Baer, Mr. Beirne. Lang had money that was well-used in our effort. Where he got it, I have no idea. I suspected he was robbing banks. He used to write to me often when I was in prison. One of his last letters said, 'We have our secrets and we must keep them.' He is to be deported with me, Mr. Beirne. I don't know why you are asking about him."

"He's dead," Paul said. "He came out to Long Island to see someone, and he was killed. I believe he was with the McKay woman the night before he was killed."

"Lang was murdered?"

"Beaten and laid out on the railroad tracks to be run over."

She shook her head. "That is . . . extraordinary. It sounds like someone is getting even. Shutting people up. As for Constance McKay, she and Lang were quite close." She fell silent for a moment. "And Baer? Other than he was in our spy group, and was never arrested, why do you care about him now?"

"He's my father."

Staring at Paul, she shook her head. "Let me tell you something I learned sitting in a prison cell, Mr. Beirne. The less you know, the better off you will be. When I first read about the testimony in Nuremberg, I tried to hang myself in my cell."

She pulled down the collar of her blouse to show scars circling her neck. "I tried the sleeve of a sweater. I couldn't make it work. I tried a bedsheet. A guard stopped me. Your friend can rightfully condemn me. But he doesn't know the truth of my life."

Standing up, she said, "In a matter of days, I will be back in the very country that murdered my parents, sisters, nieces, and nephews. Two of them were four-year-old twins. Gassed at an extermination factory in Poland. Belzec was the name of it. Perhaps you can understand how I will feel when I set down in that place."

NINETEEN

Paul walked up and down the street, peering into store fronts and bars. He walked to where he had parked his truck. When he returned to the halfway house, Doc was seated on the stoop, his head hung over. His face was wet, his eyes small red orbs. His bow tie had been pulled loose and hung around his neck. When he stood up, he reached for the railing to steady himself, but fell back onto the step.

As he sat next to Doc, Paul looked up to see Stein staring at them through the window on the top floor.

"I'm sorry you came along," Paul said. "I didn't know what this was. I've put you in a terrible place, Doc."

"Maybe one day I will find a way to understand history," Doc said. "And human behavior. But I don't know if that will ever be possible. The path of human history has been forever broken. It will never be the same." Standing up again, he said, "What will you do with that photo album? It's a view of hell in the form of uniformed men out having a good time."

"I don't know," he said.

"You understand its significance?"

"I don't know that I do, Doc."

"Under one of the pictures someone wrote, 'Here there are blueberries.' They are slaughtering tens of thousands every single day in their industrial-scale factory, and these people take a day off to relax and listen to music and collect blueberries. So vulgar in its banality. Behind the happy faces are gas chambers and ovens working full-time. You understand any of this?"

He didn't wait for an answer. "And you bring me to this place. This woman. My God. What a pathetic human being. How can she live with herself?" He rubbed both hands over his face as if to erase her memory.

"You may not understand how important that album is. It must be preserved. The doctor in the photograph. Mengele. He's hiding somewhere. My brother and I, we knew him, saw him do his cruelties. He was curious about our surgical skills. He wanted us to teach him. The obscenity of it, my God! Understand this: we lived. We both should have died along with our mother. We survived, Paul. What does that say about us?"

"I don't understand. You are punishing yourself for surviving?"

He turned to face Paul, who could see Doc wasn't going to answer that question.

"I saw Baer dozens of times. He's in hiding. You now know the name he is using. And you need to come to terms with the fact that this barbarian is a member of your family. Paul—you are his nephew. What does that make you?"

❖

For the next few days, Paul stayed close to home. He went to his bank and rented a safe deposit box. In it, he put the photo album and the letters signed by Neumann.

At the end of the week, he walked into the lobby at the Pilgrim State psychiatric hospital. As he passed by the men and women in their wheelchairs staring out the front windows, his stomach turned over and the feeling of revulsion came over him again. A half hour later, he was escorted down the hallway to Hagar's cell. He found him standing at the door staring out through the bars.

"I knew you'd come back," Hagar said as Paul stepped into the room. "I told myself over and over, he will come back. And here you are. Back to see me. How can I be of assistance?"

Hagar stood too close to Paul. He could smell his breath. He shoved Hagar hard enough that he fell backward onto the bed.

"Were you often in attendance at the big Bund camp in Yaphank?" Paul asked.

Hagar affected the pose of a deep thinker, one hand on his chin, his eyes raised to the concrete ceiling. "I want out of here," Hagar said. "You don't understand. They will turn me into a vegetable."

"I don't care," Paul said. "Answer my question."

"Yes, several times. Thousands went. The railroad ran a special train from the city just for Bund members and their families. We were a privileged lot in this country. This was a wonderful, festive time to celebrate our great heritage, our race, and our leader. What does that have to do with the murders you're investigating?"

"Did you go with friends? Or by yourself?"

"Why does this matter to you?"

Paul pulled the printout of the newspaper out of his coat pocket. "I saw in the local paper a feature story on the camp. In one of the photo spreads, I could see a picture of you and Rudolf Haase. You were marching by the grandstand."

"Haase?"

"Do me a very big favor this time, and don't act like you're an idiot."

"Ah, yes, him. Freakishly big hands. Greatly disturbed. Molested by his parents. Both of them. Mother and father. Raped his sister regularly. An oversized brute. A drunk. Would stick his dick into a hole in the ground, or a cow or a child or God knows anything. He could pour gallons of booze down his gullet. But, yes, to your question: we went there together."

Paul pointed to the photograph of the men marching. His finger stopped on one of the men. "Who is that?"

Reaching for eyeglasses by the bed, he wrapped the wire around his ears and stared at the photo. "That's a man who used to work at the camp on rally weekends," Hagar said.

"What's his name?"

"Burger. Ernst Burger."

"You knew him?"

"Yes, of course. He was a man of distinction."

"Carol Berkowitz? You killed her? Or was it Haase?"

"I don't know what you're talking about. We've gone over that. I told you I was in Germany."

"Haase killed her? You could tell me that."

"Yes, I could tell you. But you have done nothing for me. I sit in here day after day, year after year. Waiting for them to scramble my brain. You could change that. Besides, you assume too much and then try to fit pieces together that don't fit together. I get it. Besides, I read the local rag. I know you got suspended as police chief. Why are you asking me this?"

"How did you meet Haase?"

"We were charter members of the Lindenhurst Bund."

Paul pointed to Baer in the photo in the newspaper.

"Oh, yes, one of my heroes. His history is quite amazing. Another member of an elite group."

"When did you meet Haase?"

"I don't know."

"Try and remember. Was there some event that brought you together? Spying for Germany? Something else?"

"You have that angry, perpetually-the-victim Irish DNA in you. Maybe one day your people will get over their grievances, but I wouldn't bet on it. You will milk it for another one hundred years."

"What event brought you together?"

"There were several events, early in 1932 and later. The German elections that October. As I recall, they were somewhat disappointing for our cause and our leader, but that didn't stop us. We came together again, in late January 1933. At a party at the Washington Hotel in Lindenhurst."

"What were you celebrating?"

"Hitler's appointment as chancellor. Lang was the featured speaker. He had recently come into a great deal of money."

"How did he come by that money?"

"I didn't ask."

"In Lindenhurst, Long Island—you were celebrating Hitler?"

"That's right. And 1945 doesn't change anything. We are still here."

"Was Baer there that night?"

"Baer was our banker. He kept the money Lang brought in. He was rather greedy about it. Myself and some of the others, we wanted him to divide it up. He refused. Far as I know, he still has the money. How do you know that name?"

"He's my father," Paul said.

He whistled. "Now, isn't this an interesting development!"

"Burger? Was he there?"

"He catered the evening at the Washington Hotel. And years later, Lang and other patriots were framed by your government. He went to prison, along with the others. Burger was deported."

"You say you were in Germany when Carol Berkowitz was murdered. Can you prove that? You were questioned by town police."

"Yes, and the state police. It was their case. They were satisfied with my answer."

"Did they ask you to prove you were away?"

"No. If you think her death had something to do with the events of Kristallnacht, you would be mistaken. The state police were involved, and they didn't give a damn about her death. You are more ignorant this time than when I last saw you. I confessed to sneaking out of this dungeon and taking the McKay woman to a play and then dinner, and we had a romantic time in a field, and I killed her. You heard me, didn't you? You could have arrested me for that and removed me from this horror. But you were not interested. So here I stay. Now you bring up ancient history that shouldn't matter to anyone. But in the interests of telling the truth, I will help you. Do you understand? But I want something in return."

"You haven't left this place, Hagar. What you know about the McKay murder, you read in the newspapers. You aren't even a good liar. I know Haase likes to rip women apart with his bare hands in a very particular way and watch them bleed to death. It's obvious he killed Berkowitz. But why?"

Hagar crossed his arms over his chest, and his mouth broke into a wide smile. In the confined space of the cell, Hagar raised and lowered his feet in a celebratory dance. His mouth dropped open and his tongue fell out.

Paul slapped Hagar across the face. He grabbed him by the throat. "I hope you die in this miserable shithole."

The door opened, and the guard pulled Paul into the hallway. As the door slammed shut, Hagar pushed his face up against the bars.

"They told me you were crazy, Beirne! The Japs really messed you up. You're a drunk, like all the others."

In the darkened hallway, the guard escorted Paul past the other cells, where the inhabitants stared out their tiny windows. Some screamed at him; others stared. When he reached the outside, he tried to calm himself. The sun was warm for fall, the sky clear, and he found a half circle of chairs under a tree in front of the building. He pictured himself pulling his gun out of his holster, pushing the barrel against Hagar's forehead, and pulling the trigger.

Ten minutes passed before he sat up and looked at the tall building. He walked back through the entrance to the guard's station.

"Do you keep visitor books? Can I see them?"

A few minutes later, he was escorted down a steep, pitch-black flight of stairs that opened into a wide basement. The guard flipped a switch on the wall, and a series of overhead lights lit up in sequence. On the far wall were stacks of bound books on metal shelves. There was no order to it. Books were piled on top of each other. The air smelled of dust and moldy dampness.

"You're welcome to look through those," the guard said. "They aren't well organized, and as far as I know, we aren't careful about getting people to sign in. It's hit-and-miss. I can't stay with you. You'll be down here alone."

"Does anyone else come down here?"

"You mean the patients?" The man laughed at Paul's concern. He turned back towards the stairs. "Turn off the lights when you're done.

You'll find me by the front entrance. Make sure you say something, so I know you aren't still down here. This place gets locked up tight at sundown. It would be hell to be trapped here all night."

Standing in front of the floor-to-ceiling shelves, Paul estimated there were at least two hundred and fifty bound visitor books. He pulled one off the top of a pile and laid it out on a table under an overhead light. Handwriting on a cover page read: JANUARY 1945–JANUARY 1946. He put it back and grabbed the next one. Two hours later, he found the visitor books for 1954. There were books for January and February. An hour later, he found the books for July, August, and September 1954. The pages were laid out on horizontal lines, with the name of the visitor or visitors on the left, the time and date of their visit, and the person whom they were seeing on the far right.

He was halfway through September when the name "Lang" caught his eye. Next to that name was "Baer." No first names. The day of their visit was September 28. In the "Who are you seeing?" box was the name Auggie Hagar.

TWENTY

The first thing he did upon entering the kitchen was pop open a Rheingold. He pushed back any feeling he was making a mistake. Sliding open the door to his deck, he walked to the Adirondack chairs by the creek and sat there until the night sky was bright with stars. The temperature had fallen into the mid-forties, and the chill seeped through his sweater and heavy work jacket. The tide was all the way in, covering the wooden planks of his dock in salt water. It had been a full moon two nights before, a hunter's moon, which swelled the creek. He could smell the wet salt grass. It was lovely.

When he first moved into the bungalow after the separation from Phyliss, he often slept in the chair outside. The small bedroom—there was barely enough room for a single bed and a dresser—brought on panic attacks and intense claustrophobia in the middle of the night. He was trapped on the bottom of the sea again, in total darkness, men around him praying loudly and begging God to save them. Other nights it was the horror of a boy alone in a dark room, the window unlocked, the shutters open. On cold nights he slept on the couch, but on warm nights he slept outside where the night air, the salty smell, and the openness brought on a sense of calm.

Inside, he scrambled eggs. He turned on all the lights in the living room, picked up his markers, and began writing names and commentary inside circles on the sheets of white paper he had taped to the wall.

When he had filled in a dozen circles, he drew lines connecting them. The overall effect was a spider's web that now, as he stared at it, made a measure of sense to Paul. There was a story here, a connectedness.

Across the top of one of the sheets of paper, in black letters, he wrote: **WHAT HAPPENED TO MY MOTHER?** Under it he put **BAER** in one circle and **JOYCE BEIRNE** in another, stepped back, looked it over, and drew a straight line between the two circles. Under that he wrote: **BAER AND LANG VISITED HAGAR.**

After falling asleep on the couch, he dreamed of headless torsos in a ditch. He was half asleep, trying to shake off the nightmare, when there was a knock on the door. The doorknob rattled loudly. Paul got up and let Doc in. He turned on all the lights and went to the kitchen to get the coffeepot going.

"You are finally locking up the house now?" Doc said. When Paul didn't respond, he said, "Get up. Clean up. Put on some clean clothes. Put everything in a bag and go to the laundromat. It's a new day. Show some self-respect for a change or nothing else you want in your life will be possible. Today, you start anew. That means make your bed every morning, clean up the breakfast dishes, clean the bathroom at least once a week. No excuses."

Doc was in his customary suit and bow tie, shoes polished to a high shine. A pocket square peeked out of the suit pocket. Doc's appearance was something to marvel. Paul could not relate the person with his past to the well-dressed man in the room.

Paul looked like a man who'd spent the last few nights sleeping on the grass in his backyard. Unshaven, soiled clothes, his appearance gave off an odor even if Doc didn't stand close enough to him to smell it.

"Are you listening?" Doc said. "Wash everything. Clean up this dump. You are starting over. Have a little pride, Paul, a measure of self-worth."

Doc went to Paul's bedroom. When he came back, he said, "You took down the mirror and put it in the closet? That's how you deal with yourself? Running away won't help you. I want you to put it back up and deal with what you see."

Paul pushed up and went to the bathroom. He rehung the mirror. When he returned to the living room, he threw a heap of clothes and bedsheets on the couch. Doc shook his head at the sight. He looked over the sheets of white paper with all the circles and connecting lines and names circled with markers.

"I'm trying to organize what I have," Paul said.

Doc followed the lines that snaked between names.

Paul said, "I keep going over it in my head, Doc. The names, how people know each other. My father knew Hermann Lang, a Nazi spy who stole the most important secret of the war and gave it to the Germans. That is a given. Lang gets out of prison and, prior to his being deported, comes to Lindenhurst, Long Island. That was in violation of his parole agreement. Certainly, he was to stay in a halfway house until a flight had been booked to take him back to Germany. He was still in federal custody. No way he would be allowed to get the train to Lindenhurst. What brought him here that he would risk being sent back to prison? And he was here at least a day before he was killed. He visited Hagar at Pilgrim State. My father went with him."

He poured coffee into a cup and handed it to Doc, who looked it over before accepting it.

"How often do you wash dishes and clean the kitchen?" Doc asked.

Paul ignored him.

"I mean really clean the place," Doc said. "Take everything out of the cabinets and wash everything down with disinfectant. At Passover I loved to watch my mother clean every inch of the kitchen to ensure there was no *chametz.*"

"Huh?"

Doc ignored him. "Your ignorance is breathtaking," he said. "Americans only know their own culture. Everything else is foreign to them."

Paul didn't want to deal with the criticism.

"The McKay woman did not go to the Alcove to get drunk just because it was an easy walk and close to her house. That's not what happened at all, Doc. She had a purpose that night: to meet either Lang or Haase, maybe Baer. Or all three. Maybe she'd had a relationship with Haase before, and they'd go off somewhere and do what two drunks do to each other. And on this night, following some plan I don't know about, he killed her. To my way of thinking, her going there was to meet Lang, whom she knew from the factory, perhaps to settle something. Something important, as he was violating parole."

Doc said, "Most likely it was to ensure a secret stayed hidden. It's not about money or friendship or having a beer together. It had to be a big secret to take such risk. Perhaps these are events and people who cross paths, who have some prior history. It's not chance, Paul."

"No, no, no," Paul said. "Murders happen by chance or in a moment of anger. That's not this. Lang was in the Alcove arguing with Mrs. McKay. It's no doubt him in The New York Public Library trying to find out what had happened to Burger. He came out to see Mrs. McKay, and then something happened. Perhaps what she said to him changed everything."

"What's Haase or your father got against Lang? I looked over Lang's clothes before the body was claimed, to see if perhaps there was something that could tell us where he had been."

"What did you find?"

"There was a train ticket in the right, back pocket."

"One way or return?"

"One way. That would suggest he had arranged a ride back so he wouldn't get delayed waiting on a train. In his shoes were flecks of sand like he'd been walking in a beach area. Plus, a single scallop shell in his left pocket."

He removed it from his pocket and showed Paul. "Perhaps he picked it up as a souvenir of the day. Maybe it brought back earlier trips out east and he wanted the shell to take with him when he was deported. He comes to Lindenhurst on an earlier train and is picked up. He goes to Pilgrim State to meet Hagar. That's probably mission number one. Get their story straight. Number two is to see Mrs. McKay or both husband and wife. Haase sees her in the bar or knew she would be there. Or maybe all three were to meet there. A reunion of spies. In British crime novels, and in classic spy novels, the questions are answered at the end. That's not life, Paul. Life is an unanswered question. Mysteries stay a mystery. Lang was surely in a hurry to return to the halfway house before they knew he was missing. On top of that, you can't be certain Lang was in the Alcove. Just because his body was found in front of it, doesn't mean he'd been inside. Maybe the German she was speaking with that night was your father."

They were staring at the wall of lines and circles when there was a knock on the door. As Paul approached the door, he saw a man on the front step holding an envelope. When he opened the door, the man said, "Mr. Beirne? This is for you."

Paul took it and saw it was from the mayor's office.

"You have to sign that you got it," the man said, holding out a clipboard and a pen. Paul looked him over, thought for a moment to refuse to sign, but took the pen and scratched his initials on the bottom of the page. He sat at the kitchen table and opened the envelope to find a handwritten note on a plain sheet of white paper:

Dear Mr. Beirne:

This is official notification that you have been fired as the police chief of the incorporated Village of Lindenhurst, effective immediately. The village attorney will compute any money owed to you and will forward a check in that amount to your address.

Sincerely,

Olly Madden, Mayor

TWENTY-ONE

In the morning, Paul went to the garage and put the fishing tackle in the back of the truck. He drove into town and picked up a sandwich and a six-pack of Schlitz. Before he walked to the checkout, he returned the six-pack to the shelf. When he walked outside, he saw the same late-model Ford truck parked on the opposite side of the street. Schmidt was behind the wheel.

Paul tossed the sandwich into his truck and began to walk across the street. As he did, Schmidt looked out the driver's side window, smiled, made a gesture with his hand as if he were firing a pistol, and sped off.

Paul stood in the middle of the street and watched the Ford proceed north on Wellwood Avenue. When he got back in his truck, he drove to Pauli's school. He parked at the curb and looked up at the building, then pulled away. He arrived at the marina a few minutes later.

It only took a few minutes to gas up, and before nine A.M. he was in the middle of the bay, running east along the sandy edge of the barrier beach. Under a bright fall sun, the bay bottom was visible in twenty feet of water. The southwest breeze smelled of brine, wet eelgrass, and tidal mud. Screeching gulls worked the water to the east, and he steered towards them.

Being on the bay, the sky clear overhead, the fall air cool and dry, always raised his spirits. But not this morning. He'd been fired. And he was being watched. Someone followed Pauli home from school. His anger rose and fell along with a feeling of helplessness, of being unable to change his circumstance, trapped again.

Edging closer to the barrier beach, he pulled up the Evinrude so it would not drag on the sandy bottom as the boat drifted. He assembled the four sections of his fly rod, attaching a bright streamer at the end of the leader. Playing out the line behind the boat, he drifted east with the falling tide. He was twenty yards off the sandy edge of the barrier beach in three feet of water. Four deer stared at him from atop the dunes. At one point he put his rod down and sat in the boat, trying to lose himself in the beauty of the bay and the dunes to the south, past which lay the ocean. He felt its massive presence, as you feel something big and overwhelming off in the distance beyond your vision.

The trick to catching a striper on a fly rod was sight casting. He had to pay close attention to the shallow water to spot the shadow or tail of a large bass. If he saw one, he had to cast the line in such a way as to drop the streamer in front of the bass's mouth where he could grab it. It all had to look natural—a bug or small fish on the surface of the water. It also had to float and drift naturally; the line could not pull on it. Otherwise, the bass would know it was fake. They aren't easily fooled. Fly-fishing was the art of the con.

An hour of drifting brought him closer to the bridge. He pulled in his line and gently placed the fragile fly rod on the seat in front of him. He lowered the Evinrude into the water, yanking the starting cord twice before it started. He motored back to where he started, killed the outboard, and started sight fishing again.

Thirty minutes into his drift, he spotted a striper in two feet of water, floating still, its tail going back and forth to hold it in place in the falling tide. He raised the rod to the one o'clock position and played out the line, the tip moving from eleven o'clock to one o'clock, back and forth, back and forth, until he felt he could let the line loose and drop the streamer into the water as close to the bass as possible.

The streamer landed on the smooth surface of the water two feet in front of the striper. The fish didn't move. Paul fast-stripped the line to mimic bait before he jerked up the tip of the rod, pulled the line behind him, let it completely unfurl—he counted off three seconds—and let it loose in front of him. The line unspooled, a rolling curl until it fully extended itself and the streamer landed in front of the patient bass. This time the bass lunged at it, grabbed it in his mouth, and took off with a vengeance, wildly pulling line off the reel until Paul tightened the drag. He let out a happy yell and began to put line back on the reel, but never jerking the rod out of concern the bass would spit out the fly.

Ten minutes later he had the bass close enough to the boat that he could drop his net in the water and scoop it aboard. Gently, he picked up the bass from the net, and with his right hand pulled the fly out of the bass's lower lip. He looked over the fish and its dark stripes, estimated it at twenty-eight inches in length, and let it slip off his wet hands back into the clear water.

❖

Darkness had fallen when he arrived home, his bungalow shrouded in the shadows of oak and maple trees. There was no moon to brighten his path. The salt creek was shrouded in darkness. Still, he could smell it, knew it was there. The creek was his own lighthouse, a mirror that reflected his image back at him, a steady beacon.

He carried his tackle to the back of the garage, then came around the side of the house to his back deck. Stepping into the kitchen, he reached to the wall by the refrigerator and flipped on the overhead light. Behind him was the dark living room. He caught the odor of alcohol exhaled in gusts from a drunk's mouth. Spinning backward, he reached for the wall switch. Baer stood in front of him. Paul stepped towards the door to the deck. His pistol was in the cabinet above the sink.

Baer reached behind him and held up his son's pistol.

"You always kept it there. Not too smart. *Du warst als Junge nie besonders Schlau.*"

"You talk like that when you want to insult me."

"It means you never were very clever as a boy," Baer said. "Too predictable. That's not a good thing for a man in your former profession. It is not in your favor that you are ignoring the messages of people who want you to stop what you are doing. You are being reckless. Have you no regard for your son's safety?"

Baer's eyes were bloodred. His hands shook wildly, a bad condition for a man holding a pistol. As he exhaled loudly, a cloud of polluted air escaped his mouth and slapped Paul's face.

"You've been in my house," he said.

"What are you talking about?"

"Du warst in meinem Haus!"

"Speak English, you dumb Kraut," Paul said.

"You broke into my house and stole paperwork and documents. I want it all back. Everything you took."

"You can't make demands of me any longer, old man," Paul said. "Those days are over. You will tell me about my mother and what happened to her. And now there is another question you will answer: Is Richard Baer your brother?"

Baer glared at his son.

"He was the commandant of an extermination camp," Paul said.

"You are ignorant," Baer said. "The Jews make up stories so the world will give them its sympathy. Very clever, those people."

"He sent you the photo album of those happy Nazis out for a nice break from the slaughter. Picking blueberries."

"You stole that. I want it back."

Paul laughed. "How would you explain that your own brother is hiding under another name?"

"My brother is a hero," Baer said.

"You bought a ticket to return to Germany so you could help him stay hidden, isn't that right? You come from such a distinguished Nazi family, Baer. You must be honored."

He threw a punch at his son's face, but he was slow and uncoordinated. His big body pitched forward, allowing Paul to jump out of the way as Baer landed face down on the kitchen floor. The pistol slid away from him. He pulled his father up from the floor by the collar of his coat, shoved him towards the sliding door and out onto the deck. The old man fell face down again, and Paul yanked him up and pushed him around the house. Up the street, a car's lights winked on. The Ford truck moved towards them. Paul saw Schmidt's face behind the wheel. He shoved his father so hard towards the truck that he fell again.

"Get out of here!" Paul shouted.

The old man crawled towards the passenger side door and pulled himself up. Schmidt leaped out the driver's side door, a Luger in his right hand, pointed at Paul's face. Paul took four steps towards Schmidt and slapped the pistol out of his hand. It clanked to the road, and Paul kicked it towards the curb. Reaching out with both hands, he grabbed Schmidt by the throat and pushed him back against the hood of the car.

"Watch out, Beirne—your day is coming," Schmidt said.

Baer climbed into the truck. Paul came around to the passenger side and, reaching in with his right hand, grabbed his father by his coat.

"Where's my mother?" he shouted.

Schmidt gunned the engine, spun around in the street, and was gone.

Inside the house, Paul put the Luger on the kitchen counter, staring down at it for nearly a minute. He picked it up, removed the magazine from the grip and, pulling back the slide, ejected the bullet from the chamber. His eyes welled up with tears. He pulled open the sliding glass door and stepped out into the darkness obscuring the creek.

TWENTY-TWO

Paul drove to the marina and sat on the dock by his boat. It was early; the sun had yet to top the trees. Sleep had been an impossibility. Before five A.M., he simply gave up and climbed out of bed, seeing his reflection in the newly hung mirror over his dresser.

He was tinkering with the Evinrude, cleaning the spark plugs and running fresh water through the engine, when he looked up. Doc was standing on the dock. Paul climbed out of the boat, wiping the oil off his hands with a rag. He pointed towards the clam shack, and the two men walked over. Paul ordered a dozen littlenecks on the half shell with a slice of lemon and two cold beers. Doc waved off an offer for a dozen of his own.

The man in the shack held up a plastic bag containing fish fillets. "I got blackfish that just came in," he said. "You can have them, Paul."

At Paul's house, Doc watched him fry the fish. Neither man spoke. Paul was quiet, as if talking now with his friend had become a burden. He boiled some small potatoes he'd brought from his uncle's barn. When everything was ready, they went outside and sat at the table on the deck. The air was dry and cool. The deep cold was weeks away.

"I am being watched," Doc said, breaking his silence. "It obviously has something to do with what you are doing, Paul." When Paul didn't respond, Doc said, "I didn't come to America to be watched."

When Paul remained silent, Doc said, "I don't understand how you are going to solve these murders. There are connections and relationships between people that I don't think will be possible for you to put together to fully understand the whole picture. On top of that, you are no longer the police chief. You have no investigatory or arrest authority."

"I don't know about that," Paul said.

"You were fired, Paul," Doc said.

"Whatever I learn, I can give to the DA," he said.

"I don't see you or anyone coming after you making an arrest in the McKay killings," Doc said. "Lang is unknowable. I don't know how you are going to get a grip on it."

❖

Paul was frying an egg in the morning when Cantwell appeared at the kitchen door.

"Early this morning, detectives from the DA's office showed up at Village Hall. They just finished up a half hour ago. They took out dozens of files, cardboard boxes, and cabinets on dollies. Madden showed up while they were carting everything out."

At Madden's house, a line of official cars filled the street and driveway. Paul parked and walked a half block to the house. Men were bringing out boxes. The mayor was standing inside the door, his fist in a detective's face, shouting for the men to get out. The detective turned and walked to the sidewalk, where he spoke with a man carrying a clipboard. Paul stood ten feet from them. As three men headed down the driveway,

Madden leaped off the front porch to block them. When he pushed one of the detectives, the lead detective shouted, "Arrest him now!"

A detective spun Madden around, pushed him up against the side of the house, and cuffed him.

"You will regret this!" Madden shouted. "You can't come marching in here like a bunch of goons."

Two detectives walked the handcuffed mayor down the driveway to a waiting car, out of which stepped Lindsay Henry. As they reached it, Madden saw Paul.

"You miserable bastard, Beirne!" Madden shouted. "You are a dead man."

"Take him away," Henry shouted.

Retreating to the quiet of his house, Paul stood before his sheets of paper. He made a circle around MADDEN and connected it to HAASE with a black line. There were now so many sheets of paper on the wall, he could barely see the wall underneath. He called the DA's office and asked for Henry, who was not available. Later in the day, when he called back, Paul pressed him for information, but Henry was reluctant to talk on the phone. His main question came down to this: What is the relationship between the mayor and a murder suspect?

They agreed to meet at the Sunrise Diner in West Babylon. Henry was waiting on him when Paul arrived. They took a booth in the corner, away from other customers.

"You have Madden? What is he charged with?"

"Interfering with my detectives carrying out a search warrant."

"That's all?"

"I pulled the village code, Paul. The way it's worded, you're an employee of the village board and not specifically an employee of the mayor. He fired you, but he got the support of the board. Now with

Madden's arrest, the board can bring you back as village police chief, and Madden can do nothing about it. If that happens, you can continue the murder investigation."

"Why do you bring that up? Those people don't care about me. They aren't on my side."

"Granted, but they don't want three open murders in their village. It's bad for business. The Chamber of Commerce wants this cleared up. You know Jimmy Burrell on the board?"

"A hack like the rest of them. But enough to say hello," Paul said.

"He called to see what we had on the mayor. He brought up your job. I told him you had to be brought back. He has the support of four of the five trustees to rehire you. Finding evidence to arrest Haase would be your main goal now. That's all they want from you. If you aren't up to the task, I will assign detectives from my office. But arrests have to be made."

He looked across the table at Paul.

"Don't go down any blind alleys or try to settle old grievances. This is your last shot at this."

The morning after the village board meeting, Paul parked behind Village Hall. Downstairs, he found Connie refiling paperwork and Cantwell seated at his desk.

"Connie, please get Mr. Evans on the phone for me," Paul said.

"Yes, Chief." A minute later she said, "Billy is on the line."

Paul picked up the phone on his desk.

"Billy, good morning to you. As you no doubt know, I'm back on the job. I'm calling to tell you that you are fired. I will have any belongings of yours boxed and thrown in the dumpster behind Village Hall.

Don't come here. You will not be allowed in the building. If I suspect you have anything at your home, I will get a search warrant and seize it. Do you understand?"

He didn't wait for an answer. He and Cantwell got in the chief's truck and drove the two miles east to state police headquarters. A trooper manned a desk in the lobby.

"We're here to see Superintendent Homestead," Paul said, removing his wallet from his back pocket to show his badge.

"I don't know that he's here," the trooper said.

"Find out," Paul said.

The man picked up the phone and said, "The superintendent has two visitors." He held his hands over the phone. "What are your names?"

"Deputy Cantwell and Chief Beirne from Lindenhurst," Paul said.

Homestead and Schmidt appeared in the lobby and walked to where Paul and Cantwell were waiting for them.

"We are here for the Haase file," Paul said. "If you won't turn it over, I will get the district attorney to get a court order for it. Do you understand?"

Homestead turned to Schmidt and said, "I don't believe we have that, do we?"

"I can't recall," Schmidt said.

"Go look," Paul said. "I want the file. You have it. Evans gave it to Schmidt. I get it back, or we go to court."

An hour of waiting produced the file, or what Paul hoped was the complete file. It had been a while, and he would have no way of knowing what, if anything, had been removed.

Back at his desk in Village Hall, he went through the file page by page. On the cover, he wrote the names of the dead in a vertical column.

Berkowitz

Lang

Constance McKay

Mr. McKay

When he was home, he went through the boxes of paperwork he had taken from his father's house, loaded them in the back of the pickup, and returned to headquarters. The photo album, and the letters signed "Neumann," would stay in the safe-deposit box until he could come up with some idea of what to do with them.

"Roger," Paul said. "Call the village locksmith and ask him to change the lock on the entrance to the department. You and I will have the only keys. Under no circumstances is anyone upstairs to get a copy. Do you understand?"

"Yes, sir, I do."

"Chief," Connie said. "There was a call while you were gone about an old boat barn down near one of the marinas. Far as I know, nothing was ever done about it."

"Billy wasn't interested," Cantwell said. "Madden told him to ignore it."

"What kind of calls?" Paul asked.

"Squatters living in this old barn. People called and said they were cooking and sleeping there."

"Connie, do you remember a family in the village named Miller? They were in the boat-building business."

"Oh, yes, Warren was the son. I went to grade school with him. He was killed in North Africa. His father was Sloan Miller. Warren's grandfather was also Sloan Miller. He was the one who started the boat-building business in the 1920s. They were busy during the war years building landing craft. They had hundreds of workers living in boarding houses all over the village."

"Is there anyone in the family in the village now?"

"Yes, I believe Warren's widow is in the old Miller house down by the bay. The marina is pretty much abandoned, with some old boat houses still standing. She never remarried after she got that letter that Warren had been killed. Betty Miller."

A half hour later Paul drove up in front of a big house that sat at the edge of the bay. He recognized it as one of the oldest houses along the waterfront. With its faded splendor it suggested a long-gone elegance. After parking in the gravel driveway, Paul walked around the front. Paint peeled off the siding, broken gutters hung down on one side, and the shrubbery along the front had long been left to itself.

He knocked several times, then walked around the side and peered through the windows of the garage. Inside was a 1930s truck. He continued on until he was at the back of the house. A weedy lawn ran down to the bay's edge. A dock jutted out from the yard; half of its planks had rotted away and fallen into the water.

As he turned towards the house, he saw a woman wrapped in a heavy winter coat seated in an Adirondack chair on a back patio. He waved to catch her attention, but she did not see him.

"Mrs. Miller?" he called out.

She turned towards him. As he walked closer to her, she said, "Paul Beirne. I know your face from the newspaper."

She pushed off the arms of the chair, stood up and turned towards the back of the house.

"Why don't we go inside," she said. "It's getting chilly."

Paul followed her through a back door, which brought him into the kitchen. She put a teapot on the stove and turned on the gas.

"Would you have a cup of tea with me?"

"Yes, thank you," he said.

"We can sit in the parlor," she said. A uniformed maid entered the kitchen. "Sally, would you mind bringing us two teas and perhaps a plate of your sugar cookies?"

"Yes, ma'am," the maid said.

Mrs. Miller picked up a cane off the counter and Paul followed her through the dining room and into a large living room. One end of the room was lined with shelves that held dozens of wooden ship models. She took a seat in a corner chair and motioned for Paul to sit next to her.

"It's a shame, this house. It was once the most grand in the village. My in-laws had the Miller Boat Yard over on the east side of the creek. You were not here during the war years, I believe?"

"I was in the Navy."

"This was the busiest boatyard around," she said. "We had workers here twenty-four hours a day, seven days a week. Those landing craft that made the assault on the Normandy beaches? They were built right here."

The maid carried in a tray and put it on the coffee table in front of Mrs. Miller.

"Thank you, Sally," Mrs. Miller said.

She looked at Paul. "Perhaps I am trying too hard to hold on to the past," she said. "My husband cared deeply about the boat-building business. He grew up in it. He was perhaps the company's most skilled carpenter. Before he enlisted, he told me he wanted to become a marine architect when he got home. He dreamed of building magnificent sailboats."

She looked out the windows towards the bay. "When I lost him, the business could no longer carry on. All the government contracts dried up at war's end. We shuttered the yard in 1948. I'd put it up for sale, but I don't have the heart."

"I wonder if you could help me with some research I am doing," Paul said. "I saw a newspaper clipping that, back in the mid- and late 1930s, the local chapter of the German Bund met in one of the boat barns. Do you remember that?"

"Oh, yes, Chief, of course. There were perhaps twenty of them. All in uniform. They'd march down Wellwood Avenue as if they owned the place. Horrid people, all of them. My father-in-law had a different view of them and what was going on in Germany, and he happily let them use the big barn for their meetings. He would often go himself. My father-in-law also went to the Nazi rally in Madison Square Garden in 1939. He communicated regularly with Mr. Lindbergh, who was an ardent supporter of Hitler's and a dyed-in-the-wool Jew hater. In fact, Chief Beirne, Mr. Lindbergh sat in that very seat where you are right now."

"He came here?"

"Along with a small group of local followers. My father-in-law gave them a dinner party. I never knew the purpose of his visit to Lindenhurst, of all places someone of his stature would visit. Warren was as disgusted as I was, and we left for the weekend so as not to see them. I don't know the names of anyone he met. When Warren enlisted, his father roundly criticized him for fighting against the Germans when they were the future he wanted for America. When I received the letter that Warren had been killed, I told my father-in-law. He said nothing. I will never forget that, Mr. Beirne. And he didn't come to the church service I held for Warren. A year later, right out on our dock, my father-in-law put a gun in his mouth. When I went through all his papers, I saw that he was a financial contributor to the local Bund, and also to Lindbergh's organization, America First. The barn the Bund met in, he donated to them."

Paul sipped his tea and sat quietly as Mrs. Miller stared out the window.

"I love looking at the water," she said. "I believe I will die in this chair one day, still looking out at the bay."

She pushed herself up. Paul reached out to help her.

"Perhaps you should go over to the property, Chief Beirne. I called your department to report squatters were living there. Your replacement didn't check it out. He couldn't be bothered."

Paul drove south on Wellwood until he reached a dirt road. He passed the remains of the marina and boat-building business until he reached a small barn that leaned over on its side, part of the roof covered with a tarp. The barn door was off its hinges. On the dirt floor were oil-stained mattresses. A portable propane stove of the kind people take on camping trips sat against the back wall, which was smeared from grease and smoke.

He heard noise and spun around to see two cats fleeing under a broken section of wall. A ladder lay on the dirt floor. He picked it up and leaned it against the back wall. As he did, he could see rafters above him and some sections of floorboard. He went out to his truck and returned with a flashlight.

Leaning the ladder against one of the rafters, he climbed up so that he could see above the ceiling. Sections of floorboards were missing. Bent nails suggested the boards had been pried up with a crowbar. He retreated down the ladder and leaned it against the back wall. The stove was warm to the touch. Next to where he placed the ladder was a pile of coiled rope. Behind the rope was the underside of a part of a table consisting of a thick wooden brace the table rested on that had bolt holes in it where it attached to the tabletop. What caught his eye were faded German words written on the underside of the brace.

A shadow fell across Paul. He spun around to face a man standing in the open door.

"Who are you?" the man said.

"Chief Beirne of the Village of Lindenhurst. How long have you been here?"

"Since the beginning of summer."

"Where were you before that?"

"In the City, mostly."

Paul stepped towards him, and the man stepped backward.

"What is your name?"

"Edward."

"Okay, Edward. This doesn't look like a very nice place to stay, and it will be winter soon. What will you do then? I can find you some help."

Outside, Paul got a better look at him. Something about the way he stood in front of him, with his feet together and his arms straight down along his sides, caught his attention.

"Did you serve during the war?"

The man nodded. "In the Navy."

They had something in common. "You have nowhere to go?"

Edward stared at Paul, raising his right hand toward the barn to indicate he wanted to go inside.

"What is this place, Edward? The owner said a German group met here before the war."

"This was a clubhouse for local Nazis," Edward said. "There was a swastika flag here, under all the trash. I burned it."

"Edward, I am going to go and do some work," Paul said. "I will be coming back to check on you. Are you okay with that?"

"Yes," he said.

"And I can find you a place to live through the county. Do you understand that?"

"I don't want that."

"You can't stay here, Edward."

"There is something here I don't understand."

"What do you mean?"

He didn't answer.

Paul explained he would be back. He got in his truck and drove up Wellwood into the business hamlet. From a booth in front of the library, he called Cantwell and asked him to go upstairs into Village Hall and search property records to see who was paying taxes on the barn. He called Doc and asked him to meet him at the barn. When he drove back, Edward was gone. It was another hour before Doc drove up the dirt road and parked. Paul was inside standing by the table brace.

"Look at the underside," Paul said. "The top of a table would have sat on that, attached by bolts. Tell me what the writing on the bottom says."

Doc bent down to get a closer look at the underside of the brace. There were three square bolt holes in a horizontal line. He strained to read the words.

"In Hamburg I used to be dressed in velvet and silk. I am not allowed to say my name."

Paul handed him a flashlight. Doc shined the light on the words. "In English, it says, I was one of the kidnappers of the Lindbergh baby and not Bruno Richard Hauptmann. The rest of the ransom money lies buried in Summit, NJ."

"What's beneath that?" Paul asked.

"The letters NSDAP," Doc said, pushing himself up. "National Socialist German Workers Party. The Nazi party, Paul."

They loaded the table brace in the back of Paul's truck. Cantwell drove down the dirt road.

"I found the property records," he said. "Someone is still paying taxes on the property. Two hundred dollars a year."

"Who?" Paul asked.

"The clerk in the tax office said that was confidential. She went and talked to her supervisor and came back and said I was not entitled to that piece of information. She was told to keep the records in the safe, away from anyone who asked for them."

"Do one other thing, Roger: call up to Albany and see if you can get the incorporation papers for the Lindenhurst chapter of the Bund. I'd like to see whose names are on it."

❖

An afternoon in the library reading microfiche copies of twenty-year-old New York City newspapers exhausted Paul. Late in the day, he found articles about the governor of New Jersey, Harold G. Hoffman, who was in office at the time of the Hauptmann trial and who publicly expressed doubts about Hauptmann's guilt.

Returning to his office, he made several calls to the state capital in New Jersey. He kept getting people who referred him to other departments, until he was on the phone with a researcher in the archives department at the Rutgers University library.

"The former governor died," the researcher said.

"When did he die?" Paul asked.

"In June. Five months ago."

"Of natural causes?"

"I wouldn't know."

"How old was he?"

"Fifty-eight," the researcher said. "There's rumors that he took his own life. You are a police chief on Long Island? Why are you asking about Hoffman?"

"He played a role while he was governor in delaying the execution of Richard Hauptmann," Paul said.

"Everyone in this state knows Hauptmann kidnapped and murdered that child. He got what he deserved. That was none of Hoffman's business, butting in like that."

"Based on what you know, what was the single most damning evidence against Hauptmann that led to his conviction and execution?"

"Besides he had some of the ransom money? Or that people say they saw him near the Lindbergh house? Or how about Lindbergh saying it was Hauptmann's voice he heard when the ransom money was paid in the cemetery?"

Paul did not appreciate the woman's mocking tone.

"I get your point, but what else?" he said.

"The wood used to make the ladder that was leaned against the Lindbergh house right under the nursery window came from the floorboards in Hauptmann's attic in the Bronx. That enough for you?"

"They proved that?"

"Yes, why? With a wood expert. You sound skeptical."

"Hauptmann decides to kidnap the baby of the most famous man in America and makes a ladder from wood in his own house? So poorly made that it could not be used to support a man climbing up and bringing a toddler down with him. He could have gone to any lumber yard and picked up lumber and made a real one for such a serious task. Why cut it out of his own home, with his own tools?"

"You've read the newspaper accounts?"

"Yes, of course," Paul said. "I can't fathom how a jury convicted him. The ransom money was widely circulated. Many people had it and exchanged it at banks or stores. Ransom money even turned up after Hauptmann was executed. This guy Hauptmann was supposedly a good carpenter, right? But he makes a ladder in sections that's so bad it breaks when the kidnapper comes down the ladder holding the child? You say eyewitnesses saw him near the Lindbergh house? They were told by the prosecution to say that. Lindbergh saying he heard Hauptmann's voice in a dark cemetery is a joke. There's nothing logical about this case. They railroaded the first guy they could hang it on to please the Lindberghs. And on top of all of that—was this really a kidnapping?"

The woman exhaled loudly. She stammered before she found her voice.

"That is disgusting! For someone in your position, that strikes me as very strange. Disloyal, even. Are you some sort of Communist? I can assure you, no one in New Jersey feels the way you do. Everyone involved with the prosecution had an excellent reputation. You're wasting your time with Hoffman. He was a worthless governor. If he killed himself, good riddance. Is there anything else you want?"

"Yes. Could you find the Hoffman obituary for me and tell me what funeral home was used?"

TWENTY-THREE

It was eight in the evening when Paul reached Hoffman's widow. When she expressed a great deal of skepticism as to why he was calling her, he told her of the discovery of the table brace in a barn used by the German Bund and the reference to Hauptmann written on the bottom of it.

"My husband would have been fascinated by that," she said. "It sounds to my ear like a confession of someone who was involved."

"Mr. Hoffman did not believe Hauptmann was guilty?"

After a pause, she said, "What I can say for sure is this: he didn't believe Hauptmann, if he was involved at all, acted alone. He believed the kidnapping could not in any way have happened the way the prosecution laid it out, by one person. And that's assuming there was a kidnapping. He came to believe it could not have happened without the cooperation of someone inside. The inside person is what made it all possible. In the end, after the execution, after my husband had done his own investigation, he told me the entire prosecution case was a fabrication so they could convict and kill this man. The goal from the beginning was to appease Lindbergh, who was such a big figure in America and beloved by the adoring press."

"He believed others were involved?"

"That's the easiest thing to believe, Mr. Beirne. No one outside the immediate family would have known the Lindberghs were there that Tuesday night, staying at the house in the middle of nowhere. They'd never stayed there on a Tuesday before. And without someone telling the kidnappers ahead of time, they would not have known which window was the child's nursery. The ladder was right up against that window, Mr. Beirne. How's that possible without someone inside telling the kidnappers which room was the nursery? And why, of all the windows in a very big mansion, was the latch broken on the shutters on just that one? No one inside could reach out and pull the shutters closed and lock them to safeguard the child inside.

"If he were here today, my husband would say someone inside the house removed the child and gave him to someone on the outside. Whoever this was, they took the child right out the front door. The ladder was just a ruse. A prop. It wasn't used. It was there for appearance's sake. A setup to make it look like a kidnapper entered the house. No one could have climbed up something that shoddy, crawled through the nursery window, grabbed the child, then backed out the window and onto that ladder, all the while holding a toddler. That never happened. You have read, Mr. Beirne, that my husband visited Hauptmann in his jail cell? He offered him a way out of the execution if he would confess and say what he did or who else was involved. Hauptmann said he was innocent, had no role in it, and had no idea who pulled it off. The money he had in his possession the day of his arrest came from his friend, this Isidore Fisch character. Had Hauptmann confessed, there would have been no electric chair. The State of New Jersey murdered

Richard Hauptmann to appease Lindbergh and the howling mob in the press."

"He was framed?"

"Every step of the way."

"The boards in Hauptmann's attic—they were used to make the ladder?"

"Not at all, Mr. Beirne. Another made-up story. Done at the last minute to tighten the case for an execution. When the effort to convict Hauptmann and execute him looked weak, a cop named Bormann went into the attic, pulled up the boards, and a so-called expert said the wood in the ladder came from those boards. One of the many things that intrigued my husband is this very simple fact: on the very day the body of the child was discovered in the woods, not far from the Lindbergh house in an area that had been thoroughly searched, this Mr. Fisch applied to return to Germany. He was a Jew, Mr. Beirne. Doubtless you're up to speed on what the Nazis did to the Jews. So here you have a German-born Jew *returning* to Germany in December 1933, eleven months after Hitler came to power, at a time when thousands of German Jews were fleeing the country. Surely, he would have known just reading the newspapers in New York, and in letters from his family in Germany, what was going on there. Jews were desperate to get out, Mr. Beirne. Yet this German Jew goes back! The testimony described him as poor and down on his luck, yet he purchased a first-class ticket on a boat to Hamburg. My husband was certain he bought the ticket with ransom money."

"Along with visiting Hauptmann in jail, your husband conducted his own investigation?"

"You must understand, my husband had a strong dislike for the officials around him. Schwarzkopf, the chief investigator, was so loyal to Lindbergh he'd have done anything for him. Mr. Wilentz, the prosecutor, had been a friend of my husband's. He once had a lot of respect for him. But he either didn't care he was railroading an innocent man, or somehow, he convinced himself Hauptmann was guilty, so the concocted evidence at least served to send the child's killer to the death house. He believed them both subservient to Lindbergh. The public and the press demanded the killer be executed. But, yes, he did, along with a detective from Burlington County. My husband kept a large number of files of his own, plus material he retrieved from the state police."

"And where is that today, Mrs. Hoffmann?"

"It's safe. Hidden away. And it's going to stay there. I am not telling anyone about it. Maybe he shouldn't have had those records, I don't know. But I just lost him, Mr. Beirne. I hope you understand that. And he certainly didn't help his reputation in recent years. No, I'm not going to help you with that. One day those papers will be returned to the state, but not now. But you must see that even then, it won't make any difference. No one in this state will admit that the trial and conviction were a travesty. Not now, not fifty years from now."

First thing in the morning, Cantwell and Paul drove to the boatyard. The mattress was gone, as was the portable stove.

"There's a sizeable homeless camp of war veterans in the woods south of the psychiatric hospital," Cantwell said. "I've seen tents in there."

Leaning the ladder against one of the rafters, Paul climbed up and shined the light around. When he reached the level of the attic floor, he stepped out onto the floorboards.

"Come up the ladder, Roger," Paul said.

On all fours, Paul crawled to the side of the attic, the boards bending and creaking under his weight, to where several of the floorboards had been pried up and removed, with nails sticking out of the two-by-fours they had been nailed to. Cantwell stood at the top of the ladder, shining his flashlight to where Paul was looking.

"Looks to me like several boards were pried up with a crowbar," Paul said. "Why would someone come here and remove this wood? More importantly, what was the wood used for?"

He remembered the photographs in the newspapers of the ladder leaning against the Lindbergh mansion. He also envisioned the home-made ladder in his father's house that he used to get into the attic. It was well constructed to hold a heavy man, with two-by-fours along the sides, heavy slats for the crosspieces, and dowel rods connecting the sections. That ladder could support a man carrying a child.

"Are you still waiting on someone in Albany to tell you who incorporated the Bund in Lindenhurst?"

"Should have that any day," Cantwell said.

"You didn't drop the ball on that, did you?" Paul asked as they walked back to the car.

At his desk, Paul made calls to New Jersey, wanting to avoid the unpleasant archivist at the Rutgers University library. The newspaper accounts he'd read in the Lindenhurst library, and the copies of the papers he got from the funeral home, showed photographs of the ransom notes from the supposed kidnappers. On each note was the so-called signature of the kidnapper or kidnappers—clumsily misspelled as "singnature" by whoever wrote it—which consisted of two circles, odd lines, with three horizontal square holes, one of which was in the center where the circles overlapped.

He reached a state trooper in Trenton who agreed to make copies of the notes from the police archives.

"Nobody's asked about those notes in twenty years," the trooper said. "Why do you care? I don't get it. I gotta write down something about this request."

"Just write than I am curious," Paul said.

The Trooper volunteered to send a messenger to Lindenhurst with them the next morning.

In the morning, anxious to talk to Cantwell, Paul rang the deputy's house. He could tell he had pulled him out of bed.

"I got the paperwork for the Lindenhurst Bund, Chief," Cantwell said. "It was incorporated in the village in December 1931 by five people: August Hagar, Rudolf Haase, Helmuth Baer, Peter Burger, and Hermann Lang. I also got the property tax records after Mr. Henry called the village for me."

"Who is paying taxes on the barn now?"

"That's curious, Chief. Up through two years ago, it was the Bund chapter itself, with those same names. Then only Helmuth Baer paid them. Last year, no taxes were paid. The village will probably take it over."

Driving to headquarters, Paul rolled the names over in his head. He walked through the back door of Village Hall to his office in the basement. He was pleased to see the door was locked.

"You just missed a courier from Trenton, Chief," Connie said. "He left a package on your desk."

He opened the manila envelope and pulled out sheets of paper, all mimeographs of the originals. A note on the top stated: *These are assembled in the order in which they were received.* He noticed the writing on each of them, with misspelled words that looked embarrassingly amateurish. It also looked to him that whoever wrote these notes wanted the reader to believe the kidnapper or kidnappers were foreigners. On each of the notes was the signature of the kidnapper: three horizonal holes, with one in the middle area where the circles overlapped, and wavy lines.

When Doc arrived, Paul gave him the copies. Looking them over, he smiled.

"Absurd," Doc said. "These were accepted in court? It's a kid's version of what a ransom note would look and sound like. It's someone trying to make himself sound illiterate in English, unable to speak the language because he's Italian or German or whatever. A dreaded foreigner. These are the notes the kidnapper sent? And this symbol—what is it?"

"The kidnapper's 'signature'—which he doesn't know how to spell. It's on each of them. The trial testimony from a handwriting expert was that Hauptmann wrote them all."

"They don't even look the same," Doc said. "Someone testified to that under oath—that he wrote all of them?"

"Yes," Paul said.

"I'd guess the key to this is understanding where this symbol comes from," Doc said.

Paul pointed to the corner of the room, where the table brace was leaning against the wall next to a row of filing cabinets. Doc took the notes, assembled them so they were in a neat stack, and stared at them and the table.

He read the writing on the bottom of the brace, this time in German.

"Ich war einer der Entführer des Lindbergh-Babys und nicht Bruno Richard Hauptmann. Der Rest des Lösegeldes liegt in Summit, NJ."

He put the notes on Paul's desk and sat down, staring at the brace.

"This exonerates Hauptmann, Paul," Doc said. "I can't imagine this being part of a prank. It's in literal German—not the half-assed writing on the ransom notes submitted to the court by someone playing at it. This is a confession. Whoever had this table in 1932 was involved in what happened at the Lindbergh mansion."

Cantwell came down the stairs. "You didn't know about the fire early this morning, Chief? I was just at the fire department talking with the guys. That boat barn we went to near the old marina? Fully engulfed when the boys got there."

"When did you ask Lindsay Henry to call the village on your behalf to get the tax records?" Paul asked.

"Two days ago," Cantwell said.

TWENTY-FOUR

I t was after sundown when he picked up the phone on his desk and called the farm in Cutchogue.

"I wanted to ask you about my mother leaving rosary beads at the farmhouse," he told Anna. "Did she leave anything else? If she was planning on leaving my father, she would have brought her belongings out to the farm. I have a memory of her putting boxes of her things in the trunk of the car, but I don't know when that was."

The next morning, the ringing of the phone awakened Paul. The clock on the wall read 5:10 A.M.

His aunt said, "Martin says she brought one or two boxes of her things a week before her last visit. They are in the workshop, on the shelves above the bench."

Her statement caught Paul by surprise.

"I don't understand," he said.

"Martin never looked in the boxes, Paul," she said.

"Why didn't he look and see what she left there?" His voice rose.

"I can only explain it by saying his sister going missing has always crushed him. He should have told you. I'm sorry. I can only think he pushed it out of his mind because he's always feared the worst. He never believed your father's story that she left him and you."

It was evening before Paul arrived at the farm. His anger at his uncle had been tamped down on the drive east. The kitchen light was on as well as one light in the parlor. He went to his bedroom and quietly put his things away.

In the morning, while it was still dark, he got out of bed, dressed, and walked out the back door towards the workshop near the workers' quarters. The morning air was cold, free of any lingering humidity. A broad sweep of farmland ran to the dark woods overlooking the Sound. The light was on in the first workers' shack, and he could see a silhouette behind the curtain that draped the single window.

The workshop was a shed with a three-quarter-inch plywood workbench across the east-facing wall. Above the bench were pegboards from which hung dozens of tools—screwdrivers, chisels, all manner of wrenches. He pulled on a washer tied to a string and a light bulb on the ceiling glowed. The room was cold, the air thick with dust. A large vise anchored one end of the workbench and an anvil sat on a sawed-off tree stump on the floor. To the right of the door were boxes of potato bags and bags of pesticides and fertilizers, covered with dust. A shelf ran along the top of the wall above the workbench, jammed with toolboxes, pieces of pipe, boxes of screws and nails, and a stack of rubber tractor belts.

Paul pulled himself up onto the workbench. He followed it along until he reached the end, where he found two cardboard boxes. He pulled both down and jumped off the workbench. The cardboard was soft from the years of being left in the workshop. Both had covers on them. It was clear from the dust they had not been opened. Looking at his watch he pulled on the light cord. He returned to the farmhouse, worried Martin was already up and looking for him.

At dinner after a day of work in the barn, Martin said, "The truck will be here later tonight to pick up the bags."

"You go on to bed. I can wait for it," Paul said.

Martin finished his dinner, pushed the plate forward on the table, and went to his desk. Paul could tell his aunt was upset but it wasn't his place to understand the dynamics in the household. He carried his plate to the sink and washed up, stacking the dishes in the rack.

Standing by Martin's desk, he could see his uncle was focused on his ledger books, filling in numbers and estimated prices.

"Do you remember when my mother brought boxes out here for you to keep?" Paul asked. When he didn't look up, Paul said, "Did you look to see what it was?"

Martin put his pencil down and stood up. Anna came in from the kitchen.

"Just before she was gone," Martin said. "Why are you asking me if I looked in it? She was gone, that's all that mattered to me."

Walking away from his uncle, Paul pulled on a sweatshirt and a wool cap and went outside into the darkness. There was no point in confronting his mother's brother all these years later. Inside the workshop, he pulled on the cord for the light. For a moment he stood staring at the boxes on the bench. When Anna came in, he pulled the top off the first one to find a folder filled with recipes clipped from the Lindenhurst *Star* and Babylon *Beacon*. At the bottom of the box were two 1930s copies of *TIME* magazine. He picked up the first one. It was dated June 1938 and featured photographs of two men in a laboratory.

"That's Charles Lindbergh," Anna said, pointing to one of the men.

Paul opened the cover and read: "Charles Lindbergh and his mentor, eugenics researcher Alexis Carrel, at the Rockefeller Institute in New York City."

While he leafed through the pages, a postcard dropped out onto the bench. It showed a photograph of a building, underneath which read *Eugenics Record Office—Cold Spring Harbor, Long Island.* The second box contained recipe books, some women's magazines, and a folder of inky imprints of baby Paul's footprints. He lifted the folder, books, and magazines out and placed them on the workbench. A manila folder filled the bottom half of the box. He pulled it out, slid the box out of the way, and laid the folder on the bench.

In pencil his mother had written: *From my husband's belongings in the safe deposit box at the Suffolk County National Bank.* Next to that she had penciled a date: *February 19, 1939.*

She wrote *my husband* and not his name. Paul tipped it over and the papers fell out onto the bench. He stared at them, momentarily hesitating to go through them.

"I don't understand, Anna," Paul said. "Martin had these for years? He never told me he had my mother's things."

Anna leaned against the workbench. "When Joyce disappeared, just vanished from his life and your life, he was completely stunned and heartbroken. He tried so many times to come up with an explanation—she wanted to flee your father, start a new life away from him, something that might make sense. But he knew it was not his sister to leave her son. Then you enlisted in the Navy and were gone, and for several years we had no idea if you would return. The Navy informed us you were a prisoner of war. He couldn't bring himself to go through her belongings, as it would feel like an admission she would not return. My only guess is he hoped she would come back."

Paul felt a keen disappointment in his uncle but vowed not to say anything to Anna.

After a moment, Anna said, "Why don't you bring that into the house and spread it out on the kitchen table. It's cold out here. The kitchen is warm."

She heated up milk in a saucepan and added a spoonful of powdered chocolate from a tin of Baker's Instant Cocoa. She poured it in a cup and placed it on the table. In the parlor, Martin was asleep in his chair. Paul looked at everything spread out on the table.

The first sheet of paper showed a pencil drawing of the side of a two-story mansion. A circle was drawn around the upper-left window on the second floor. Under it was an arrow pointing to the words "Featherbed Lane." The second sheet of paper showed a diagram of both floors in the house: on the first floor, the front entry was circled, and next to it were the kitchen, study, and stairs to the second floor. On the second floor the drawing showed the layout of the bedrooms and, in the corner that matched up to the window on the first sheet of paper, the word *kinderzimmer* was written in black ink.

"Any idea what that is?" Anna asked.

Paul shook his head. "Kinder means child, I know that."

He picked up an envelope. In it was an invitation addressed to his parents to attend a going-away party on December 5, 1933, in the Bronx, at 1279 East 222nd Street. Inside on a card was written: *Treffen wir uns, um Isidor Fischs Rückkehr nach Deutschland zu feiern.*

"Did your parents know someone who lived at that address in the Bronx?"

Paul shook his head.

Anna picked up the card. "Do you know this name—Isidore Fisch?"

"He was a friend of the man New Jersey executed for the Lindbergh kidnapping. He had the ransom money, and he gave it to Hauptmann. When the toddler was found dead, Fisch went back to Germany."

Anna picked up the *TIME* magazine cover and the card for the Eugenics Record Office in Cold Spring Harbor.

"I remember my mother once saying my father had a job of some sort in Cold Spring Harbor," Paul said.

"Well, your mother saved the invitation, plus this issue of the magazine, for a reason," Anna said. "I think eugenics is the study of how some people are genetically superior and others are inferior. The people who believe in it say there are races, and that the inferior people, like those born with certain disabilities, should be treated differently."

She picked up the second cover of *TIME*, which showed Dr. Alexis Carrel and the words, *Man, the Unknown*. A worn, yellowed, German-language brochure fell out of the magazine as she opened the pages. On top were the words *Gesetz zur Pravention genetisch kranker Nachkommen*, and a date, 25 July 1933. A second sheet of paper, in German, was titled *Meldepflichten missgebildeter Neugeborener*.

Paul pulled open a business envelope and found a stack of $100 bills wrapped in a rubber band. The band broke as he pulled it off. Next to the portrait of Benjamin Franklin was a seal, the words *Gold Certificate* above and below it. Shuffling the bills, he guessed they represented thousands of dollars twenty years ago.

"Gold certificate bills. We had to turn them in at some point in the early 1930s," Anna said. "They are worthless now."

"Why did my mother save them?"

"Your father saved them, and she brought them with her out here for safekeeping. They meant something to her."

TWENTY-FIVE

It was after eight P.M. when Paul drove down Doc's street. He honked the horn as he pulled into the grassy area in front of the house. He knew by leaning on Doc's smarts he was putting his friend's life in harm's way. He found Doc seated at his piano, focused on the keys, both hands moving up and down with a measure of grace that caught Paul's eye. His fingers floated above the keys. Paul felt awed to be in Doc's presence.

He put the manila folder, with his mother's papers and magazines, on the kitchen table. He was going through them when Doc finished playing and joined him in the kitchen.

Doc picked up the *TIME* with Lindbergh and Carrel on the cover.

"I remember a photograph that appeared in the Vienna papers in 1936 during the Summer Olympics. It showed Lindbergh sitting in a box with Hitler at the stadium. He praised the Germans for the development of the aviation industry. This American hero with Hitler watching the games. And this well after the anti-Jewish measures were underway, including boycotts and mass emigration, stripping the professions of any Jews, taking away their citizenship. Their businesses were stolen and handed over to Nazi party members. My father lost all his concert bookings and teaching assignments. A young Nazi named Neckermann took our home and even the Bechstein piano. My father was suddenly a noncitizen. This was two years before Kristallnacht when they torched the synagogues. Lindbergh and Hitler thought the Jews were behind everything and had to be rooted out. The 'Jewish problem,' as it was always called."

Paul handed Doc the invitation to Fisch's going away party in the Bronx. Doc shook his head.

"There is no chance he or his family survived in Germany," Doc said. "Absolutely no chance. Taken to Riga on trains, marched into the woods, and shot. Dumped into mass graves. Fisch was running from something or he was too stupid to know what he was getting into by going back to Germany."

Doc picked up the drawings of the outside of a house and the sketches of the rooms inside. He pointed to the circle drawn around the window on the corner of the second floor. He looked over the *TIME* that had Carrel on the cover touting his new book, *Man, the Unknown*.

When he finished reading, he said, "Lindbergh was close to this man? This Carrel was a Frenchman. I've read about his medical work. He was a Nazi through and through. A believer in the master race and that the inferior races should be weeded out. Lindbergh is this man's associate? How can Americans see this man as a hero or some sort of larger-than-life figure?"

Doc picked up the German-language brochure.

"What is it?" Paul asked.

"A Reich law gazette, advertising the passing of a new law in July 1933. That's seven months after Hitler comes to power, and look what these savages are doing. It reads, 'The Law for the Prevention of

Genetically Diseased Offspring.' It is a sterilization law, Paul. Forced sterilization on those who didn't fit the new ideal. My brother and I were both surgeons in Vienna. All the Austrian newspapers wrote about this. The doctors, we all talked about it. The Nazis passed all kinds of racial laws in the winter and spring of 1933. Fisch went back to this because he had to."

He picked up the paper titled *Meldepflichten missgebildeter Neugeborener.*

"This is a decree written by a man named Wilhelm Stuckart," Doc said. "It reads 'Reporting Obligations of Deformed Children.' It came out in Germany after the war that Stuckart had a Down syndrome child, a son. He had him gassed."

"His own son?" Paul asked.

"He wasn't 'perfect.' Imagine having your own son put to death because he doesn't fit your ideal. That was probably the least of the horrors those people unleashed."

"At the trial, it was Hauptmann's defense that the ransom money he had on him and in his house was given to him by Fisch at that going-away party," Paul said. "Something like fourteen thousand dollars in gold certificate bills was found in Hauptmann's house. Another thirty thousand or so has never been found. My father bought a ticket to Germany in February 1933. I was probably told he was working on a job somewhere. He was gone for several months. I do remember my mother and me staying on my uncle's farm for a long stretch of time. For a month or so, I went to the Cutchogue school."

"Did your parents have any money?"

"No. Always fighting over money."

"How would your father pay for a first-class boat ticket?"

"I don't know," Paul said.

He pointed to the stack of $100 bills on the table.

"Those are my father's gold certificates that were supposed to be turned in. That's how the authorities zeroed in on Hauptmann. He had them, and it got him executed."

TWENTY-SIX

They call it 'rice pudding,'" Lindsay Henry said.

He was seated with Paul at the Sunrise Diner. "Get someone a job, Madden gets a percentage. Same with a raise."

"I want to arrest Haase for the murder of Mrs. McKay," Paul said. "I'm not interested in Madden's extortion schemes."

"You don't have enough," Henry said. "You have to work with what you have not what you'd like to have. In New York State, the law is such that it's not exactly illegal to kickback to a political leader for a job. I can hold on to the case and move ahead for a trial. That will take up the next three to five months. After that, a judge will likely dismiss all kickback charges. That's all the time you have, Paul, before Madden fires you again."

Paul spent the rest of the morning on the phone. The archivist at the New Jersey State Police office mailed Paul the list of serial numbers on the bills that an associate of Lindbergh's passed to a man in a cemetery in the Bronx. To Paul's mind, this was one of the stranger aspects of the kidnapping case, with Lindbergh insisting no police be present.

He called the Eugenics Record Office in Cold Spring Harbor. After a lengthy explanation from a secretary that the office was no longer called that, Beirne asked if she could look for employment records from 1930 to 1933.

"I believe my father might have had a job there," Paul said.

"Is that what you're looking for?" she asked. "I ask that because this office used to advocate for immigration to be limited and the so-called defectives to be registered and sterilized so they wouldn't reproduce. Would your father have worked in that sort of environment?"

He gave her his number, and later in the day, she called back. Helmuth Baer did contract work at the lab in 1931. "I can't explain what 'contract work' means, however. The contract was with three other men. Helmuth Baer, a Rudolf Haase, and a Hermann Lang. A Mr. McKay is listed as a subcontractor, but it doesn't say what the work was."

"Do you remember if Dr. Carrel and Charles Lindbergh were there at about that time?"

"Oh, yes, that is clear from the records. They worked closely together. Lindbergh looked up to Carrel. He saw him as a hero."

At home, Paul began another review of the boxes of material piled up on the kitchen table, on the coffee table in the living room, and on the floor in small mountains. He reread all the newspaper accounts of the Hauptmann trial, adding new dates to his chronology and timeline on the sheets of white paper tacked to the living room wall.

In red letters, he added a new date to the existing line he had for Fisch returning to Germany: the day the toddler's body was found was the same day he applied for the paperwork to leave America. He taped another sheet of white paper on the wall. In black marker, he wrote under the year 1931: *Baer, Lang, and Haase do some sort of work at Eugenics Lab/ likely met both Carrel and Lindbergh there. McKay was also there.*

Paul was making another pot of coffee when he heard the mail slot open and clank shut. He sorted the mail on the kitchen counter and was happy to see an envelope from the New Jersey State Police. He peeled open the envelope to find five sheets of paper filled with serial numbers in three columns on each sheet. He retrieved the bills his mother had saved. He was on the fourth sheet of paper when he found sequential serial numbers that matched the bills she had hidden on the Cutchogue farm.

He wrote on the wall, in large black letters: **Baer has Lindbergh ransom money from 1932. $32,000 in 1932 dollars. Approximately $35,000 was never accounted for**.

The phone rang.

"The Haase woman called looking for you," Cantwell said. "She said she got beat up badly."

Paul picked up Cantwell at Village Hall, and twenty minutes later they pulled down the driveway of a farmhouse in South Huntington. Houses had been built all along the north side of the property, and the frames of more houses were going up south of the farmhouse. He removed his pistol from the holster and put it in the glovebox. Cantwell did the same. A woman in a flannel shirt, work pants, and knee-high rubber boots answered the door.

"Nach wem suchst du?" she said as she pushed open the storm door.

Paul said, "Neither of us speak German."

With difficulty she said, "My English not so good."

"We're looking for Mrs. Haase," Paul said.

"Wer bist du?"

"I'm Paul Beirne, chief of the Lindenhurst Police Department. This is Deputy Cantwell."

They followed her through a dining room, into a kitchen and out the back door, and along a brick path to a greenhouse fifty feet behind the farmhouse. Charlotte Haase was leaning against a worktable covered with flowerpots and bags of soil, her arms folded across a turtleneck sweater, her long hair tied tightly behind her head. Both eyes were black almost to her chin, her right ear was twice its normal size, and her lower lip had been stitched together. A bandage ran from her right cheek, under the lower lip, to the left cheek almost to her ear.

"When did this happen?" Paul asked.

"Last night. Very drunk. He goes to bars to find women he can screw. I waited up for him this time. He just started hitting me. It woke his mother. She came downstairs and started hitting him to get him to stop."

"Does he know where you are?"

"He doesn't know my friend," she said.

"If he can find you, he might kill you this time."

"He's been going to my cousin's house, thinking I am there."

The woman, standing by the door, said, *"Sie können ihn nicht verhaften und vor Gericht stellen, wenn Sie sich weigern, zusammenzuarbeiten."*

Paul shook his head in frustration.

"She is saying I don't have to cooperate with you," Charlotte said. "You should be able to arrest him without me."

"She doesn't know what she's talking about. You would let him get away with this?" Paul said.

"I have no choice. You don't understand. I'm trapped. Without him, I have no way to support myself. I have no money. I have no place to live. I have to go back to him. I have two boys to look after."

"If I arrest him, a judge can hold him on high bail he couldn't make. You could stay here or find somewhere else to go."

"I don't have a dollar to my name," she said. "Besides that, there is his mother. You have no idea what that woman is like, what she is capable of. She's as crazy as he is. This family, they're all sick."

She stopped talking, putting her right hand over her mouth to prevent further truth from leaking out.

Cantwell turned away.

"If you arrest him, he will kill me the first chance he gets."

"So why am I here? What's the point of telling me he beat you up?" When she didn't answer, he said, "You know what he did to Constance McKay?" He stepped closer to Charlotte. "He shoved his hand right up her vagina and ripped her wide open. Do you understand that?"

The other woman shouted at Paul.

"What is your relationship with Olly Madden?" Paul asked.

"*Sag ihnen beiden, sie sollen gehen*, Charlotte," the other woman said.

"Tell her to shut up!"

"She wants you to leave. This is her house. If she calls the police to remove you both, he might find out and know where I am. You have to leave," Charlotte said.

TWENTY-SEVEN

Paul drove to the Haase house, parked and waited. An hour later, a taxi proceeded down the street and pulled into the driveway. Charlotte stepped out. Haase and his mother came out of the house. The two boys stood in the doorway. The mother pointed her fist at her daughter-in-law and shouted at her, her arms pinwheeling over her head.

When Haase saw him, he ran down the driveway. "You get out of here! Get out of here!"

Haase's mother shouted at Paul in German. He backed up towards his car and watched as Charlotte walked past her mother-in-law and into the house.

❖

When Doc arrived at Paul's house, he went into the living room and examined all the new information that had been added to the wall.

After several minutes, he said, "Have you read Sherlock Holmes?"

"No, I haven't."

"Do you read books, Paul?"

Paul ignored the question.

"I read the German translations when I was a kid." He saw on the kitchen counter a copy of *All Quiet on the Western Front*. "Are you reading this? I will take back my comment if the answer is yes."

Paul shook his head. "That's my son's book. He asked me to read it. He had it for a school project. If his grandfather comes to the house, he has to hide it from him. He told Pauli it was trash written by a traitor."

"Did you read it?"

"I haven't got around to it yet," Paul said.

"Erich Maria Remarque. A great novelist. He fled the country. The Nazis couldn't get him, so they executed his sister. They cut her head off. We all read it. I read it so many times I can recite entire pages from memory. Here we go: 'The fight ceases. We lose touch with the enemy. We cannot stay here long but must retire under cover of our artillery to our own position.'"

He paused for a minute. "I could go on. It sold out in every Vienna bookstore when it came out. It was a sensation. That book by Remarque and hundreds of others were piled up in the street in Berlin outside the Opera House and set on fire," Doc said. "A sickening scene. A mountain of banned books on fire."

"When was that?"

"May 1933. We saw the photographs in the Vienna newspapers. A mob of Brownshirts throwing books into a bonfire. Any Jewish author had his books burned, along with Heinrich Mann and Thomas Mann. The point you should remember about Holmes is this: 'When you have eliminated the impossible, whatever remains, however improbable, must be the truth.'"

Doc spread both arms out to encompass the sheets on the wall.

"There are more than just a few things going on here, Paul. But there's one thing that stands out, however improbable: Lindbergh didn't want his own son. He was a believer in eugenics. The son wasn't perfect in the racial ideal Lindbergh and his friend Carrel believed in. Think of what Stuckart did to his own son. Lindbergh arranged with someone to hand off the child and to stage it like a kidnapping, complete with ransom demands. If you take Hauptmann out of the picture—if you say, as an exercise, he didn't have anything to do with the taking of the child or the child's death, and if the ladder wasn't used to take the child out of the building—then all you have left is Lindbergh on the inside. There is no other explanation. A criminal gang didn't show up that night and grab the boy. No housekeeper, no staff person, the boy's mother, was going to steal the child and sneak him out of the house. That didn't happen. He did it. No other explanation works."

"Think of the material my mother saved," Paul said. "If something happened to her, it would be there for someone to find. She feared my father would get rid of her. So she saved that for me, Doc. It's all about the Nazi view of getting rid of people they don't want. The whole trial story is absurd. Lindbergh was so big, such a hero, no one could see him involved in his son's disappearance, even when the case against this Hauptmann fellow was illogical and concocted. Lang, my father, and Haase worked with Lindbergh and Carrel in Cold Spring Harbor. McKay was also there in some capacity. They all met there. Carrel is a true believer in getting rid of the people he sees as unworthy of life. Surely, he and Lindbergh talked about that philosophy. Maybe Lindbergh talked to Carrel about his own child."

Pointing at names on the wall, Paul said, "I think the stealing of the bombsight and the spies are a separate story. The names overlap, before the war over a common cause."

In the morning, he picked up Doc and they drove to the Bronx and found the house at 1279 East 222nd Street, where Hauptmann lived at the time of his arrest. The house sat on a corner lot, a three-story apartment building next to it. A woman came out of the house and stood on the front step.

"*Dürfen wir mit Ihnen sprechen, Frau Hauptmann?*" Doc asked.

"*Bitte geh weg,*" she said.

"Mrs. Hauptmann, it's important we speak to you," Paul said. As he was about to ask Doc to translate for him, she stepped onto the sidewalk.

"What do you want?" she said.

Her appearance surprised Paul. She was well-spoken, with a self-confidence he picked up immediately. He was relieved she spoke good English. He stepped closer to her and saw a young man standing behind the door.

"Mom, don't talk to them," he said. "Come back inside."

"Your husband—" Paul said.

"—was murdered by the State of New Jersey," she said. "Everyone on the prosecution team knew Richard had nothing to do with it. They sat back and let him be executed. Who are you? What do you want?"

"Mom—come back inside! Don't talk to them!"

"There is some new information on the case," Paul said. "Could you please hear us out. I believe we can help—"

"What new information? The truth has always been in plain sight. People of all kinds knock on my door every week with their crazy ideas. One man has come repeatedly to tell me he is Lindbergh's son. He wasn't killed. 'I'm him,' he tells me."

She stepped directly in front of Paul. "You don't understand. I told them the truth. Richard worked during the day and picked me up at my job in a bakery that evening. He never drove to New Jersey to steal that child. What could he have possibly done with a child? Bring him to our house? You could bring them the people behind this, the very people who took and killed that child, and New Jersey wouldn't care one bit. If you know anything about this case, you know that Richard worked the very day of the supposed kidnapping. The authorities even rigged the employment records to show Richard didn't go to work that day. That's the length they went to frame him. He wasn't an hour away in New Jersey climbing a ladder, crawling through an open window when the Lindberghs and their staff were downstairs, and taking a child. You don't understand, do you? Please leave. I don't want to hear anything."

Doc stepped backward toward the car. Paul reached out to touch her arm. "Mrs. Hauptmann, please."

She turned and went back into the house.

For five minutes, while Doc sat in the car, Paul stood on the sidewalk outside the house, hoping Mrs. Hauptmann would see he had not left. At one point, she looked out the front windows at Paul, then drew the blinds.

Two hours later, Paul pulled into a gas station in Hopewell, New Jersey. When the attendant came out to fill the car, Paul told him what they were looking for.

"The old Lindbergh house? People come by every day, wanting to know how to find it."

He went inside the station and came out with a hand-drawn map. Pointing to a line on the map, he said, "That's Featherbed Lane. There's no sign on it, or there was, and someone took it for a souvenir. But just follow this map, and you'll get to the house."

"Who owns it now?"

"Lindbergh never spent a night in that house after someone took his kid out of it," the attendant said. "A couple of years ago, the State of New Jersey bought it as a home for juvenile delinquents."

Paul followed the map, getting confused at one point on a dirt road and turning around to find his way back to where he was. Holding the map up in front of him, he turned onto a paved road and then made a sharp left onto a dirt road, which brought him through a grove of trees until they approached the mansion. He parked in the front with a group of other cars, and both men got out. Paul retrieved a manila envelope, out of which he pulled the two sheets of paper with the hand-drawn diagrams of the two-story mansion. They walked around the side of the house, where Paul stopped and pointed to the second floor.

"The second-floor window, all the way on the left," he said. "It is circled on the paper. That's the window to the nursery where the toddler was sleeping."

"Only someone inside the house could have made this map, Paul," Doc said. "No one else could possibly know the exact layout of the rooms, let alone when the child was put to bed."

"Not a single fingerprint was found in the room," Paul said. "It was all wiped down, every piece of furniture. No dirt from the outside. Then what would the kidnapper do? Climb back out the window and down the ladder, holding on to the kid, walk a half mile up the road to his car, and just drive off? Murder the child with a blow to his head and dump him by the side of the road on his way back to the Bronx? With all the roads blocked by the police? And what after that? Hope he can make some money with the ransom notes even though the child is dead? That's the whole story?"

"I can see someone handing him the toddler out of the window, but not one man climbing up and through the window and taking the child, then backing out again," Doc said. "No kidnapper, no matter how brazen, would take a child from an occupied house, let alone this particular house and this particular child. Beyond that, a kidnapper wants to make money off the act and then return the child. This child was killed and dumped by the side of the road."

A uniformed security guard came around from the side of the house.

"Hey! You can't be here! Move away from the house!"

Paul held up both hands. "We'll leave," he said. "No problem. We were just curious."

"You and a million other people," he said.

TWENTY-EIGHT

The next morning, Paul found a note from Cantwell on his desk: *At the high school. Principal says someone broke some windows in the cafeteria.*

Paul wrote on it: *Will be at the library looking at old newspapers.* He put it on Cantwell's desk.

At the library, Paul asked for microfiche for the *New York Times* for all of 1939. He started on January 1, 1939 and began rolling the microfiche reel quickly, stopping only at front pages. Within a few minutes the February 21, 1939 edition of the paper appeared on the screen. The story ran down the left-hand side of the paper, with the headline: 22,000 NAZIS HOLD RALLY IN GARDEN.

Paul called Doc at the funeral home. He and his assistant had just picked up a body at a nursing home in West Babylon and were preparing the corpse for a viewing in the afternoon. Doc said he was going into the City the next day with his brother to see a Bach concert at Carnegie Hall.

"I'd like you to do some research while you are in there," Paul said. Any guilt Paul felt about pulling Doc into this story had faded. "Go to the public library on Fifth Avenue and read the microfiche from different newspapers about the trial of the four men who landed in the submarine in Amagansett. I need to know more about them. But particularly Burger. Also get the name of the prosecuting attorney. I hope he is alive, and I can reach him."

❖

"His name is Frances Biddle," Doc said.

He was calling from a phone booth outside the library, traffic noise heavy in the background.

"He was the attorney general at the time and the chief prosecutor against the spies. He was also one of the judges at the Nuremberg trials after the war. There were four Germans who landed in Amagansett: Ernst Peter Burger, George Dasch, Herbert Haupt, and Heinrich Heinck. All four of them had lived in the United States. Some became citizens before returning to Germany. Dasch was a waiter at the Heidelberg Restaurant in Yorkville, and he cooked at Camp Siegfried out east on Long Island. They were recruited by the Abwehr to return as spies on the *U–202*. That's all in the newspaper accounts."

Doc stopped for a moment.

"Paul, are you aware Lindbergh gave a speech in Iowa on September 11, 1941? That's two years after the start of the war, and it was known what the Germans were doing with the Jews in eastern Europe. In his speech, Lindbergh said, 'The three most important groups who have been pressing this country towards war are the British, the Jews, and the Roosevelt administration.'"

The next morning, Paul reached the former attorney general at his home on Cooper's Neck Lane in Southampton. After a few minutes of chitchat, Paul asked about the four men who landed in the *U-202*.

"I'm retired now," Biddle said. "The Nuremberg tribunals were exhausting. When I returned to New York, I decided I wanted to spend my fall afternoons by the fireplace looking out at the ocean. It's a lot more pleasant than sitting in a courtroom hearing testimony about mass murder and extermination squads. And I have so many regrets. Sometimes, sitting here by the ocean, I feel overwhelmed by them."

"Regrets about the war crimes trials?"

"We tried some of the leaders and hanged some of them. But they were the bureaucrats. They sat at desks and had thousands of others carrying out the actual killings. Those men returned to society in Germany when the war was over, and some of them now occupy important positions in the West German government. From what I read now about the German unwillingness to confront the truth of the past, I doubt much more will ever happen. The real killers simply faded back into civilian life."

Paul went through an explanation of the events in Lindenhurst, saying he wanted to learn more about the Bund and its members.

"Four others landed in Florida," Biddle said. "We had a military tribunal for them, convicted all eight, and executed six of them in the electric chair. Dasch and Burger returned to the American Zone in West Berlin to live out their lives. They were both deported in 1948. Burger was killed when he returned. There were accounts he was run down in the street by a drunk driver the week after he got home. It was ruled an accident."

"In my father's papers were records of a Wilhelm Stuckart," Paul said. "Do you know that name?"

"A believer in euthanasia for those deemed unfit," Biddle said. "Do you know about the Wannsee Conference? He attended that. It was there, around a big table in a Berlin mansion, that they mapped out the 'Final Solution.' Tell me, why would your father have papers about him? And why are you interested in the four men who landed in Amagansett?"

"I think it ties into everything else I'm looking into," Paul said.

"Stuckart was killed just last year. Another car accident. There was a lot of speculation that it was not an accident at all. But no one has taken responsibility."

"Did either of the spies say anything before they were deported?" Paul asked. "What were they doing here? Why did they come?"

"It was all about espionage, but frankly I thought that was just a cover story. It seemed very weak to me. It was suggested by Burger when he was interrogated after his arrest that he, among the others, had a personal reason to return to New York. Unfinished business. But he never said what that was. It was also fascinating to me that Burger was at the Beer Hall Putsch with Hitler in November 1923. He was in that very early group of Hitler followers. They were idolized by the Nazi Party and given medals and honors. On the day of his arrest in New York, Burger had that medal in his pocket. He emigrated to America in 1927 and became a citizen, only to return to Germany."

"In reading everything, I don't really understand how they were caught so soon after arriving here," Paul said.

"Someone within a day of their landing on a Long Island beach called the FBI anonymously and said where they were staying in a Manhattan hotel. This person named the hotel and the room numbers. Whoever that was wanted them arrested and out of the way. That person surely knew they'd be convicted and executed. Perhaps it would be helpful to you if we talked later this morning or early afternoon. I'll review my files before you call back."

It was just after two P.M. when Paul reached Biddle, who was seated in his study by a fireplace, as he could hear wood burning.

"Do you like the ocean, Mr. Beirne? A delicious fog has rolled in. It's very quiet, and if I stand outside, I can hear the waves on the beach. Several times we've heard whales passing by. I could spend whatever time I have left in this house looking out at the ocean."

Paul heard papers shuffling.

"It's impossible, Mr. Beirne, to understand the eight Germans who landed on our beaches from U-boats, as well as the large Nazi spy ring that was put on trial in Manhattan early in the war, without understanding the Bund here in America. You know about the Duquesne spy ring?"

"I've read the newspapers."

"Those people had been here for years and still were loyal to the Nazi ideals," Biddle said. "Their goal was both sabotage and to find ways to steal things that could be smuggled back to Germany to help in the war effort. It was also to raise money, for the Bund here in America, but also for the budding Nazi party in Germany, so that it could do better in national elections. The 1932 elections in October were particularly critical. Remember, we didn't get into the war until late in 1941, so these Germans in places like New York City could do their espionage and smuggle what they found on German ocean liners headed back to Hamburg. The theft of the blueprints for the Norden bombsight was a huge benefit to the Germans. It was curious to me when we questioned Burger and agreed not to send him to the electric chair that he knew Lang from when they were both working in New York City and on Long Island. There was a string of bank robberies in and around New York City. It was figured the Bund was behind them.

"It's always been my view that the four men on the submarine that landed in Amagansett had arranged ahead of time for safe houses and people who would look after them. They didn't come cold; it was all prearranged. People who had been active in the Bund in the 1930s, who went back and forth to Germany for various reasons, and who were alerted ahead of time that these men would be coming. That way they could be looked after the moment they got here and not left to their own devices."

"They all knew each other?"

"Yes, to one degree or another. Burger spoke fluent English almost without an accent. He knew people in New York City and in the big Bund chapters on Long Island. To this day, we don't know who turned them in. My guess would be one of their contacts, as no one else would know they were here."

"What was the date they landed in Amagansett?"

"June 12, 1942."

"This person who turned them in," Paul said, "whoever it was, wanted them caught and arrested?"

"And executed—out of the way," Biddle said.

TWENTY-NINE

ootsteps pounded on the staircase to the basement. When Paul looked up, Cantwell was standing over the desk. The phone rang. Paul picked up and listened to a man describing shouting at the Haase house.

"Chief, I live two doors from these people. You've got to put a stop to this," the man said.

Charlotte was standing in the driveway when they arrived at the Haase house, her arms folded, head bowed, as Haase's mother screamed in her face. When Paul jumped out of the car, Haase's mother ran down the driveway waving her fist at him.

"Du kommst hier raus, du lügender Hurensohn," she shouted at Paul as she got within a few feet of him.

He reached out, put his hand on her face, and pushed her backward. He walked towards Charlotte, who had both hands over her face.

"He hit you again, did he? Tell me what happened."

"Ich erzähle dir nichts," she said, dropping her hands to reveal a swollen and bloody nose.

"Speak English!" Paul shouted.

"I am not talking to you," she said.

"You will talk to me," Paul said, grabbing her arm and pulling her down the driveway and away from the house. At that moment, Haase burst out of the front door of the house, waving his fists.

"Get off my property, Beirne! Get off my property!"

Cantwell grabbed Paul's right arm and pulled him away from Haase.

"You don't have the right to beat the hell out of your wife," Paul said.

"We are leaving here, Chief," Cantwell said, grabbing both of Paul's arms and pulling him to their car. As they reached the curb, an elderly man appeared in the middle of the street.

"Dear God, Chief, these people are white trash. You've got to get them to stop all of this. I'm sick of it. And you tell me what the mayor was doing here just an hour ago. He and that German woman were shouting at each other in the driveway, and that old Kraut came out to break it up."

Paul walked back up the driveway.

"Why was Madden here, Mrs. Haase?"

"Get off my property," Haase said.

A few minutes later they pulled up in front of Madden's house on a cul-de-sac east of Wellwood Avenue.

"You know this is a bad idea, Chief," Cantwell said.

"If you don't want to be here, leave," Paul said. "I'll walk back to the station."

"What is wrong with you? You have no reason to confront Madden. If you do, once again you'll be out of a job. Just pull away before he comes out and sees us."

The side door of the house opened, and Madden stepped out. When Paul went to open the car door, Cantwell jerked him back.

"Come on, man," he said. "For once use your head."

Paul drove down his father's street. His car was parked on the oyster-shell driveway by the garage. He drove to the end of the cul-de-sac, killed the engine, and sat there for thirty minutes, unable to make up his mind as to whether he would knock on the front door. He proceeded down the street, parking opposite his father's house. He got out of the car. The front door opened, and his father stuck his head out. Then he stepped out, the door closing behind him. His shotgun was draped over his wrist.

"You have no business being here. *Sie können nicht ohne die richtigen Papiere auf mein Grundstück gehen.*"

"We need to talk," Paul said.

Baer took four strides forward, pushing Paul backward. The barrel of the shotgun was pointed at Paul.

"Put that away," Paul said. "Let's talk about what I took and what you have in the house. And why you are packing up to leave. Where are you going? Why now?"

"We are not talking about anything," Baer said. *"Verschwinde jetzt, bevor ich meinen Anwalt anrufe und dich wieder als Polizeichef entfernen lasse."*

"I don't want to keep saying it," Paul said. "You've been in this country long enough to speak properly, even though you are a traitor and a murderer. I don't want to hear your Kraut tongue!"

Baer's mouth twisted as he tried to push the words out. "I will get my attorney to put a stop to this."

"Why do you need an attorney?"

"To protect myself from people like you."

"If living here was so awful for you, why didn't you return to Germany and live there? You went back in February 1933—what was that trip about? You took my mother to Isidore Fisch's apartment in December 1933 for a going-away party. How did you know him? Hauptmann was there. You must have seen it when Fisch handed him a box to keep while he was away. What did you think when Hauptmann was executed for a kidnapping and a murder he had nothing to do with?"

Up the street a man shouted, "I've called the police! They are on their way!"

"How did you know Fisch, to be invited to his going-away party?" Baer said nothing.

"Put the gun down, Baer," Paul said.

"Geh und fick dich."

As Cantwell drove up, Baer retreated into the house. Paul stood on the walkway, staring at the front door. Cantwell approached him and tried to pull him away and back to his car. Paul angrily jerked his arm away from Cantwell.

"Paul—listen to me. I'm trying to help you—"

"Leave me alone," Paul said. He walked to the door and pounded his fist on it.

"You are going to talk to me! Do you hear me? You are going to tell me who you are!"

Cantwell tried to pull Paul away once more. "Come on, we are leaving here," he said.

Slamming his fist on the door again, Paul stepped backward.

"Let's go, Paul," Cantwell said. "There's nothing here."

An hour later, a courier arrived at police headquarters with a letter from Brady Whitener. Paul had to sign for it. It ordered him to be in his law office at three P.M. that day, with or without an attorney.

"Do you want me to go with you?" Cantwell asked.

They arrived at Whitener's law office on Montauk Highway in Babylon and were ushered into a paneled conference room with a long oak table and fancy portraits of partners in the firm lining the walls. A receptionist told the two men where to sit, and another twenty minutes went by before the door opened and in walked Whitener and Baer. Whitener held a briefcase stuffed with paperwork under his right arm.

"You can leave, Deputy," Whitener said, staring at Paul but ignoring Cantwell.

"Roger, wait for me outside," Paul said.

"Okay, Beirne," Whitener said. "Here are my instructions: Do not go near my client's house ever again. Do not approach him in the village or in a bar or restaurant. Do you understand?"

"Your client?" Paul said. "You really represent a high-class clientele, Whitener."

"So here is how this will go down: While I am here, you will ask the questions you want. And nowhere else. You have one shot at this—do you understand? I will advise Mr. Baer whether to answer any question. This is your only opportunity. But go ahead—tell us what you got."

Staring at his father, Paul said, "What was your relationship with Hermann Lang?"

"Who?" Baer asked.

"Hermann Lang," Paul said. "You formed a Bund chapter with him in Lindenhurst. Where were you the night he was murdered?"

Whitener reached over and touched is client's arm. "Do you know that name? If you don't, say you don't."

"I don't know that name," Baer said.

"That man was run over by a train," Whitener said. "How's that my client's affair?"

"Mr. and Mrs. McKay? Ever meet them?"

"No."

"Ernst Peter Burger?"

Baer leaned back in his chair, a smile on his face.

"How do you know him?" Paul asked.

"He doesn't know the name, Beirne," Whitener said. "Next."

"August Hagar?"

"No idea," Baer said.

"Richard Baer? He's your brother. You have a photo album of Baer and his friends having a picnic near an extermination center."

"Who cares about that? Besides, that has nothing to do with anything, and my client will not answer it," Whitener said. "You stole that from his house, so whatever you think it is today is irrelevant."

"You have a wireless radio in your attic. What was that used for?"

"Wait. Hold on. Who is this Burger fellow?" Whitener asked Baer.

"Never heard of him."

"You, August Hagar, Lang, Burger, Haase—all of you formed the Bund chapter in 1931. Lang is dead. Burger is dead. What's left of that gang is you, Hagar, and Haase."

"So what?" Baer responded.

"You had a clubhouse in an old boat barn."

"As he said, so what?" Whitener said.

"I found the underside of a table there," Paul said.

Whitener laughed.

"It has writing on it. A confession. It says Hauptmann had nothing to do with the Lindbergh child's death and the missing money is buried in Summit, New Jersey. It's not buried there. You had the missing money, Baer. You kept it. My mother hid it. She wanted me to find it."

Baer's expression went dark. "Your mother—what did she do?"

Whitener pounded the table. "You're wasting our time!"

"She betrayed me—"

"How did you know Isidore Fisch?" Paul asked.

"Some Jew," Baer said.

"So you knew him?" Paul said.

"Not really."

"He sent you an invitation to his going-away party when he fled to Germany," Paul said. "You must have been on good terms with him. Why? My mother saved it, along with a lot of other things of yours. I have it all. She figured it all out, Baer—and left it for me."

"She figured what out?" Whitener said. "Stop wasting our time!"

"He went back to Germany, that's all I know," Baer said. "But he can't help you. He's dead. His whole family, none of them could have survived. Jews, all of them."

"Hauptmann was at that party—"

"Shut up!" Whitener shouted at his client.

"How did you meet him?" Paul asked.

"Don't answer that!" Whitener shouted. "Move on."

"You went to Germany in February 1933, days after Hitler came to power. Why did you go?"

"I have relatives there," Baer said.

"Nothing wrong with making the trip," Whitener said.

"How did you pay for it?"

"With money."

"You paid for your first-class boat fare the same way Fisch paid for his, isn't that right?"

"With what?" Whitener asked.

"Lindbergh ransom money," Paul said.

"Enough of this nonsense. You can leave now, Beirne," Whitener said, standing up. He waved his arm at Baer. "No more talking. Shut up. The case you are referring to resulted in the conviction and execution of the murderer. Everyone knows that. That case is closed and done. You bring up this old crime because you hate your father and you have made absolutely no progress in solving murders in our village. This only shows how incompetent you are."

Paul stood up and leaned over the table into Baer's face. "There were tens of thousands of dollars in missing ransom money that were never accounted for. You had them. I have them now."

Whitener shouted, "Shut up!"

"Do you remember the night of February 20, 1939?" Paul asked.

"No," Baer said. "I have no idea about a date that long ago. *Sie behandeln mich, als wäre ich ein Verbrecher. Wie würde ich mich daran erinnern, was ich vor so vielen Jahren in einer Nacht getan habe?*"

"What about March 1, 1932?"

Whitener shouted, "Shut up!"

Paul came around the side of the table behind Whitener, who stood between the two men.

"Get out! Get out!" He pushed Paul towards the door and pulled it open.

"You had two postcards from my mother in your desk that I found, Baer. They are postmarked after February 20, 1939. Where was she?"

Whitener grabbed Paul's arm and led him to the door of the law office.

THIRTY

When they arrived back at headquarters, Connie was hovering over the phone.

"That was Lindsay Henry again," she said. "He's very eager to talk to you."

He went to his desk and dialed the district attorney's office.

"A judge just tossed all the charges against Madden," Henry said. "By law, it means he goes back to being the mayor. The first thing he will do is fire you again and the board will go along with it."

He was home an hour later when Cantwell called.

"We have an hour to clear out our stuff," he said.

"Roger, grab all the investigative files, all the photographs, the autopsy reports. Box it all up and start stacking everything by the back door. I'll be there with the truck. Grab the table brace that's leaning up against the wall behind the filing cabinets. But don't bring it out until I get there."

In his house, Paul gathered up all his boxes and loaded them in the back of the truck. He pulled down the sheets of paper from the living

253

room wall, folded them, and put them in another box and carried everything to his truck.

When he pulled up behind village hall, Cantwell was bringing out the boxes. Paul parked next to the door, jumped out, and loaded the boxes in the bed of the truck. A minute later, Cantwell came out with the table brace. Paul thrust the truck into first gear and turned out of the lot onto Montauk Highway. A few minutes later, he pulled into Phyliss's driveway. Pauli was throwing a baseball against the garage door when Paul got out of the car. His ex-wife appeared on the back deck.

"Can I leave some material here for one night?" he said. "I have no other place to take it right now."

"Don't bring your troubles into this house, Paul," she said. "What have you gotten yourself into?"

She stood over the side of the truck, reaching down to open one box to see photographs taken the morning Constance McKay was found dead. She grimaced, turned away. Paul and his son carried the boxes and the table brace to the back of the garage, pulling down the door when they were done. Paul put his arms around his son. Phyliss stepped closer to both of them.

"What is going to happen?" Phyliss said. "Don't put us in danger."

"I will be back to get everything," Paul said.

❖

Early the following morning, Paul was awakened by the phone ringing. It was the doctor at the psychiatric hospital. He dressed quickly and thirty minutes later picked up Doc. The two men drove to Pilgrim State.

"Mr. Hagar is in our hospital in one of the other buildings," Dr. O'Connell said. "He was admitted two days ago. Thallium sulfate was found in his bloodstream. How it got there, we have no idea."

"How would he have ingested that?" Paul said.

"It's water soluble," Doc said. "Completely tasteless."

"Did he try to kill himself?" Paul asked.

"There is no thallium sulfate anywhere on these grounds. Rat poisons like cyanide, yes, but they are locked away in the groundskeepers' building. He had no cyanide in his system, just the thallium."

"You people can't do anything right," Paul said to the doctor.

Doc paced from side to side in the office, looking out the glass wall to the roomful of patients affixed to their seats. Most were sleeping, their heads slumped over. Others stared back at him. A man in a white gown stood up from his seat and approached the glass window of the office until he was just a few feet from Doc on the other side. The man pointed to his forehead.

"You do lobotomies here?" Doc asked.

"We find it quite effective to change bad behavior," she said.

"Why don't you just put people up against a wall and execute them?"

"I don't know who you are or who you think you are," she said, "but this is your last visit to this hospital."

Her office door opened, and an attendant placed the visitor's log on her desk. She opened it and scanned the pages until she found what she was looking for.

"The morning he got sick, he had a visitor, but the man refused to sign his name, and no one enforced it. He sat with Hagar in an approved area under supervision."

She stared at Doc until he turned away from her.

"I want to speak to the guard who signed this visitor in and see if he can describe him," Paul said.

"You may not," she said. "I've had enough of you and your associate here. You can both leave."

Paul slammed his fist onto the page. "Someone poisoned Hagar. It was either the visitor who saw him that day or someone who works here."

"It is more likely," she said, "that someone gave him the poison because he wanted to end his life. He knew he was scheduled for a lobotomy. I would suspect someone on the staff."

"That's murder," Paul shouted, so close to her face that she stepped away from him.

"He tried to kill himself. You can both leave now," she said.

Doc said, "Paul, let's go."

"No. I want security to take us to the hospital. I want to see this man."

Two uniformed security men appeared at the door of the doctor's office.

"We are not leaving," Paul said. "You are not dismissing us. Do you understand? I want to talk to Hagar."

"You have no authority here," she said. "We are a state institution. You can't threaten me and get away with it." When Paul didn't respond, she said, "He can't talk. He's in a coma."

"I don't believe you."

She looked at the guards. "Take these two men to the hospital. Let them see Mr. August Hagar for themselves. After that, escort them off the grounds. If they come back, call the state police and have them arrested for trespassing."

Doc and Paul walked to the elevator and rode to the lobby level. Doc put his hand on Paul's shoulder; he pushed it away. They were escorted out a back door and onto a landscaped patio where a sign read: FOR

Employees Only. They walked down a stone path to a two-story brick building and entered through a side door.

Inside, a guard stood behind a desk. The guard standing next to Beirne said, "These men are looking to see Mr. August Hagar."

The guard at the desk said, "Come with me."

He exited the door, the others following him. When they came around the side of the building, he pointed across an open field towards where a van was parked. A crew was digging a hole in the ground.

"That's him there," the guard said. "In the box."

THIRTY-ONE

An hour after leaving the facility, Paul turned down his street. Four cars and a pickup truck were parked in his driveway. The front door of the house was open. He banged his fist on the steering wheel as he jumped out of the truck. He ran inside. Madden was standing in the living room. Evans stepped out of the kitchen.

"You removed material pertinent to a criminal investigation from headquarters," Madden said.

Schmidt emerged from Paul's bedroom. "Nothing there, Mr. Mayor," Schmidt said.

"Where have you taken it?" Madden said.

"Get out of my house," Paul said. Schmidt pulled his pistol from a hip holster.

"We have a search warrant to be here," Madden said. He pulled a folded strip of paper out of his pocket and slapped it across Paul's face. It fell to the floor.

"Where is the material you removed from headquarters?"

"If it's not here, it might be at Liebmann's house," Schmidt said.

"We will go there next," Madden said. "Go through the garage again, trooper."

All the cabinet doors in the kitchen were open and the drawers pulled out. Plates, bowls, glasses, and utensils were dumped on the floor. In his bedroom, the mattress had been pulled off the bed and leaned up against the wall. The drawers of the dresser were pulled open, the contents dumped on the floor.

Screaming into the windshield, Paul drove to the funeral home and then to Doc's house. He was standing outside by the curb as Schmidt and Evans stood in the door. He looked at Paul, raising both hands in a sign of helplessness. He stood next to Doc and watched as Schmidt and Evans came in and out of the house.

"I've seen this before," Doc said.

Paul drove to Phyliss's house. In the kitchen, Paul told his son that the material they put in the back of the garage was going to Cutchogue where it would be stored in the tool shed. He repeated it to make sure the boy understood where everything would be. The boy threw his backpack over his shoulder. His mother picked up his cereal bowl from the kitchen table and put it in the sink.

Paul stepped towards the back door. Phyliss leaned against the kitchen counter, her arms folded, staring at him.

"You think telling a young boy all of that is a good idea?" she said.

His eyes were on the kitchen cabinets, which were the nicest parts of a house built in the early 1920s. Upon his return from Asia, unable to get a firm grip on his life, Paul had bought cherry boards from the lumberyard. He set up a carpenter's shop in the garage, and over the first ten months of his return, built and installed the cabinets. He remembered Phyliss telling him they were so beautiful she could never sell the house. They looked almost the way they did on the day he installed them.

"I am in a hurry," he said. "They went to my house this morning and they are now at Doc Liebmann's looking for everything I have collected. They would need a search warrant to come here."

He loaded the boxes and the table brace into the back of his truck. She stood by the door. He backed out of the driveway, turned south to catch the highway east. He was at the end of the street when he saw in his rearview mirror a half dozen cars pull in front of Phyliss's house.

❖

It took the better part of a day to clean up the house from the mess Madden's people had made. He stayed off the phone. For nearly two hours, he sat at the kitchen table making notes on legal pads. When he was done, he drove to Doc's and then to his father's house.

He and Doc walked around to the deck and into the kitchen, where his father was waiting on them.

"What do you want?" he said. He pointed a finger at Doc. "What is he doing here? I don't want him in my house."

"We need to talk," Paul said. "Your particular preferences are of no interest to me."

Baer lunged for the phone on the counter by the refrigerator. Paul got there first and pushed his father away. He pulled the phone off the counter, yanking the cord out of the wall, and tossed it on the floor.

"Worüber willst du reden?" Baer said.

"'What do you want to talk about?'" Doc said.

Pushing his father into a seat at the kitchen table, Paul said, "You will speak in English. Do you understand?"

"Sprich nicht in diesem Ton mit mir. Du wirst mich respektieren."

"What now?" Paul said.

"'Don't talk to me in that tone. You will respect me.'"

Paul laughed. He pulled papers that had been in his father's house out of his coat pocket and laid them on the table.

"You were a participant in the Beer Hall Putsch in 1923," Paul said. "I saw that medal in the drawer by your bed, next to your Luger. So were Hermann Lang and Ernst Peter Burger. Such an elite little group of hardcore believers. You have that history between you."

Baer stared at Paul so intently both Doc and Paul had to look away.

"So what?" Baer said. "What does that mean today?"

"It means you all have something in common—in Germany and here," Paul said.

"Loyalty is a concept you don't understand."

Paul cut him off. "You had a chance encounter with a man named Alexis Carrel."

"I met him in Cold Spring Harbor. He was a scientist doing eugenics research."

"Lindbergh was there. You met him, too. Who proposed removing Lindbergh's son from the house? The child was somehow deficient? Didn't fit the ideal?"

"Sie erfinden dies, während Sie fortfahren."

"'You are making this up as you go along,'" Doc translated.

"The testimony at the Hauptmann trial was that the boy had some sort of health issues. There was no kidnapping, was there? Hauptmann is picked up by the police and they find some of the ransom money in his house. You saved letters from him. You knew Isidore Fisch."

"We went over this," Baer said.

"Why did my mother keep the Lindbergh ransom money and the boat ticket?"

He said nothing.

"You knew Richard Hauptmann had nothing to do with the taking of that child or his death. How did you feel when you read in the papers he had been executed? Did that bother you at all?"

"Du erzählst Lüge um Lüge, weil du so viel Groll gegen mich hast."

"'You are telling lie after lie because you hold so much resentment against me,'" Doc said. "'All you care about is getting even with me.'"

"Lang got out of prison and was to be deported. Yet he came to Lindenhurst, where he was murdered. Why was he here? It wasn't about the money you kept, because it is worthless today."

"He was run over by a train. That's what the paper said."

"He was hit in the back of the head with a steel rod and placed on the tracks to make it look like he was just another drunk run over by the train," Paul said.

"Nonsense."

"He came to see you and the McKays."

Baer looked away.

"Tell me, Baer," Paul said. "Tell me how it all went down that night in New Jersey in 1932."

The old man's face fell to his chest. He stood up and, wobbly on his feet, reached for the back of the chair. Doc, holding his arm, guided him back into the seat. The act of kindness angered Paul. He jerked Doc's arm off the chair. Doc stepped back.

"Someone in the house brought the child out and gave him to you. Or was it Hagar who took the child? No one used that ladder."

He shook his head.

"You made the ladder from wood you pulled out of the Bund headquarters in Lindenhurst."

Baer looked up. "I didn't hurt the child. The child was alive when we left."

"Oh my God," Doc said softly.

"Where did you take him?" Paul asked.

"Hagar took the child somewhere near the house. They never went on any of the roads."

"Oh my God," Doc repeated.

"You killed Lang and Mr. McKay. Haase killed Mrs. McKay. Burger was deported, and he died in Germany. And Hagar was poisoned in the asylum. Everyone connected with the Lindbergh case is dead—but you and Haase. And you are leaving the country."

Baer tried to stand up but fell back into the chair. This time Doc did not offer any assistance.

"You assumed Haase would ultimately get arrested and the state would strap him in the electric chair for killing Constance McKay and that would be that. Did you know Haase was going to meet her and kill her that night?"

"I didn't hurt the child," Baer said. "That was never the plan. The child was going to be adopted—"

Doc covered his face with both hands. "I can't believe what I am hearing," he said. "These people are monsters."

"How clever that the death turns into a ransom demand to raise money for the Bund and the party in Germany," Paul said. "Everyone knew all along the baby was dead, and you asked for money to bring him back. A cruel hoax. Who wrote the ransom notes? Whose writing is on the table brace? It's yours, isn't it?"

"You came here to confront me about an old murder case?"

"No," Paul said. "I'm no longer the police chief. Besides, no one is interested in the truth of the Lindbergh case. It ended when Hauptmann was electrocuted. You could confess to it and New Jersey wouldn't care."

"So you are not investigating the McKay murders? This is not about them. Then what do you want? What are you here for?"

"I want to know what happened to my mother."

THIRTY-TWO

M an konnte nie darüber hinwegkommen," Baer said.

"'You never could get over it,'" Doc said.

"Du hast mich beschuldigt, dass sie nicht hier ist."

"'You blamed me for her not being here.'"

"You took her to a Brownshirt rally in Madison Square Garden, and I never saw her again. She didn't run off with someone. I came home from school. You were in the living room. I asked you where Mom was, and you said you didn't know. I asked you again and again, and the answer was always the same. You got sick of the questions and told me to shut up and forget her. The day I enlisted and was leaving for California, you took me to the train station. On the platform, I asked you again. Do you remember what you said?"

The man, mute, stared off into the distance.

"You told me some story about her falling in love with a man and leaving you and me behind," Paul said. "You lied about that, and you've lied about it ever since. Every time you open your mouth, you lie. You took your young American son to Nazi marches in Lindenhurst, and for Nazi weekends at the Bund camp out east. You introduced a boy to that."

Baer walked down the hallway towards his bedroom.

"Where are you going?" Paul said.

"Ich muss dir nicht antworten."

"'I don't have to answer to you,'" Doc translated.

"Where is my mother?" Paul shouted.

Doc grabbed Paul's arm. "What is he doing?"

Paul stepped towards the hallway just as his father emerged from his bedroom and moved back towards the kitchen, the Luger in his right hand.

"You ask me about your mother," he said. "I will tell you the truth, and you will accept it and get out of my house. Do you understand? Your mother is dead. You've been to the insane asylum. Maybe you should start there."

"What are you talking about?"

Doc said, "Paul, please. Back out the kitchen door."

"Deine Mutter ist tot."

"He insists your mother is dead," Doc said.

"Then tell me where she's buried. When did she die? Where is the death certificate? You are trying to collect on a life insurance policy. You must know when and where she died. She sent you a postcard after the rally in the Garden. Where was she then?"

Paul and Doc backed up to the door, slid it open and emerged on the deck. Baer's neighbor was raking leaves. He stopped what he was doing.

"I didn't harm your mother," Baer said. "She is dead. They took her life."

Stepping onto the deck, Baer pointed the Luger at his son. Doc closed his eyes.

"Where is my mother?"

Staring at his son, Baer turned the pistol around, pushed it into his mouth, and tripped the trigger. The explosion shattered the top of his head, covering the sliding glass door behind him with blood and chunks of brain matter.

Doc screamed, "No!"

Paul's knees collapsed under him. Doc reached to help Paul, and the two men stumbled off the deck to the grass. The glass patio door shattered, shards falling on Baer's body and covering the deck. The neighbor ran over and pulled up short when he saw the body. An expanding pool of blood covered the deck under Baer's destroyed skull. Paul stumbled towards the salt creek, falling and getting up, making it only halfway before he fell again. He wretched onto the grass. Behind him, Doc leaned against a tree, covering his face with both hands.

The first to drive onto the property was Evans, followed by Schmidt. Fire trucks and an ambulance appeared. Paul stayed twenty yards away as state police went in and out of the house. Evans retrieved a blanket from the trunk of his police car and covered the body. Doc walked to where Paul was seated in the grass near the edge of the creek. His face was pale, his breathing labored. Doc walked over to the ambulance parked on the side of the house and spoke with an attendant. He returned with a blanket and a medical kit. The attendant draped the blanket over Paul's shoulders. Doc felt Paul's pulse. He helped him stand. The attendant took one side and Doc the other, and they walked him to the back of the ambulance.

As they reached the ambulance, Schmidt stepped towards Paul. "Hey, Paul, I'm sorry about this—"

Paul grabbed Schmidt by the throat with his left hand and rammed his right fist into his face. The force sent Schmidt to the ground. He jumped on Schmidt's chest and with both fists slammed his face and the side of his head. Doc tried to pull Paul up but couldn't. Evans shoved Doc so hard he fell against the back of the ambulance. Then he pulled Paul up. Schmidt jumped up and swung a wild fist at Paul's head. When he missed, he pulled out his pistol and pointed it at Paul.

"You should be dead, Beirne," Schmidt shouted. "I should have done it when I had the opportunity."

THIRTY-THREE

Paul fled east.

For part of each day, after he helped Martin with the equipment, he walked in the woods along the Sound. On good weather days, he drove to the Wickham farm and walked through the apple orchard to the edge of the creek and dropped a clam rake into the tidal mud. There was an orderliness, a rhythm to the farm, in the lines of apple and peach trees in the fields and in the vibrant salt creek. Standing in clear saltwater, subject to the pull of the tide, felt like a spiritual experience, something that took Paul outside of himself. On this farm he felt a strong sense of place, a belonging. Sunday morning, he went with Anna and Martin to Mass at the Irish chapel in Cutchogue. His uncle was unable to walk even a few feet without having to stop and wheeze in enough air to power his next step.

Back at the farm, Paul retrieved all the research material he kept there, loaded everything into the truck, and drove west.

❖

Each afternoon when Pauli got home from school, Paul drove to the house to see his son. Some days he picked up the boy at school, as the restrictions Phyliss had in place had been removed. She had not said anything to Paul about it; he didn't know why. It was Pauli who told him his mother had sat him down at the kitchen table and said arrangements with his father would change.

They went into the village and got ice cream and Paul dropped him off at his mother's. For several days in a row, Phyliss asked him to stay for dinner and help Pauli with his homework. He didn't ask about McGregor, and she didn't bring him up.

Most Sunday mornings, Paul took his son to Mass at Our Lady of Perpetual Help on Wellwood Avenue. On one of those Sundays, Paul, Phyliss, and Pauli drove to the creek behind his father's former house. From the back of his truck, Paul retrieved the urn containing his father's ashes and they walked to the salt creek. The tide was falling. They walked out onto his father's dock. Paul, standing over the water, overturned the urn, and the ashes sprinkled into the falling tide.

It was the end of something, Paul felt that keenly. He hoped he could cast off the loathing of his father, the hatred he had long felt, and get past it because he knew it would only weigh him down.

❖

The following weekend, Paul loaded a cooler of drinks and food into the truck, along with sleeping bags, blankets, changes of clothes, and the duffel bag Phyliss had prepared. He separated the top and bottom pieces of the two surf rods and put them into their leather containers. Two Luxor reels wrapped in linen cloth were packed in his heavy canvas lure bag, where he kept his knives and other gear.

He grabbed his surf waders off a hook in the back of the garage and a smaller pair for Pauli.

At the clam bar at the marina, Paul bought three dozen littlenecks they would open later. As he made an inventory of everything he was bringing, his son ran down the dock towards him and climbed on board, a broad smile on his face. Paul's emotions went soft seeing his son. At the top of the dock, Phyliss waved at Paul.

The sky was luminous, a deep blue that settled the mind. A high mountain of smoke-gray cumulus clouds crossed the western sky. Rain was not expected for several days. Cold was another matter, with temperatures expected to dip into the forties by midnight. Sleeping on the beach would be challenging, but he was confident he could find enough driftwood for a fire. He cast off the bow and stern ropes and climbed into the boat.

"You want to start her up, Pauli?" he said.

He squeezed the bulb on the gas tank to prime the carburetor, made sure the engine was in neutral, and pulled hard on the cord. The engine turned over. Paul pushed off from the dock with one of the oars and Pauli steered the boat out of the marina into the welcoming open water of the Great South Bay.

Paul pointed to a spot off to the right, and Pauli turned the Evinrude and steered the boat into shallow water by the barrier beach. As he did, the boy pulled up the outboard so that the shaft and propeller were out of the water. Paul stepped out into a few inches of saltwater and pulled the boat up onto the sand. Pauli walked along the bottom of the boat and climbed onto the bow and jumped out. He let out a happy yell as his feet sank into the sand.

They unloaded the boat and when they were finished pulled it farther up onto the beach, above the high-tide line. Paul pulled the anchor out, made sure it was tied off to the cleat on the bow, walked it out ten yards, and buried its sharp edges in the sand. They carried their cargo up a narrow deer path to the top of the dune. In front of them was the ocean. As far as they could see east and west there was no one. They dropped down onto the beach and proceeded another fifty yards or so before putting everything down. Paul pulled the surf rods out of their cases, put the pieces together, and attached the heavy reels. He drove two surf spikes into the sand and planted both rods in them, so they stuck up into the air like flagpoles.

Out of the tackle bag he retrieved two wooden fishing plugs called Junior Atoms. He'd always had good luck with them. He pulled fishing line off the reels, slid them up through the guides to the tips, and then strung out a good ten feet of line before attaching a swivel and then the lures. Carefully, as he had recently filed the hooks on the lures, so they were very sharp, he hung them from the bottom guides on each rod, and with a crank of the reel, tightened the line.

A few minutes later Pauli returned with an armful of sticks and chunks of driftwood and sections of washed-up boards. Paul retrieved the army surplus shovel he had brought, the blade of which folded out, and dug a shallow pit. When he was done, Pauli dropped the smallest sticks into the hole, stacking the larger pieces on the side. They pulled on their rubber waders, retrieved the rods from the spikes, and walked clumsily to the surf.

At the water's edge they separated by about fifty yards. Wading out into the surf, Paul felt the salt spray in his face and smiled at the briny taste on his lips. The sound of the waves crashing on the sand was lovely. Paul let the lure loose from the bottom guide, flipped the bail on the reel, and slid the line over his index finger. In a smooth motion he pulled the rod back over his right shoulder until the tip was nearly parallel with the water, then pushed it forward, releasing the line and sending the lure, a floating surface plug, nearly one hundred yards in front of him, past the line of swells. He turned to his left to see his son doing the same. He waved to him.

Paul spotted gulls diving into the water two hundred yards to the west. He shouted to his son and pointed towards the birds. Paul walked down the beach towards where the birds were working. Pauli cast the plug as far out as he could, then retrieved it, jerking the rod tip up so that the plug danced on the surface of the water. Paul could see the tails of large, striped bass slapping the surface as they chased bait fish.

"Pauli—look!" He pointed to the churning surface of the water moving east along the back edge of the waves.

The boy reeled in the lure, then cast again, the plug landing twenty or so yards to the east of the wild water. As it hit the surface the plug jerked below the water as a bass tried to swallow it and took off, the rod bending over sharply and pulling the boy off balance.

Paul shouted. As Pauli reeled in the line, he backed up onto the sand and five minutes later pulled a striped bass out of the water. It was fat and heavy. They walked towards the tackle box, where Paul retrieved a pair of pliers with which he pulled out the lure.

"Thirty, thirty-five pounds," Paul shouted, slapping his son on the back. The boy beamed.

Paul laid a flat board the boy had scavenged for the fire on the sand and gutted and scaled the bass. Pauli took a pack of kitchen matches from the tackle box and lit a clump of beach grass at the bottom of the hole. When it began to burn, he laid on small sticks and then larger ones. After it had burned down, Paul piled rocks around the edge of the fire and placed an iron skillet over the coals. He dropped butter into the skillet and, as it simmered, one bass filet. He removed the bag of littleneck clams and opened them, one by one, handing them over to his son to eat.

"Do you think driftwood smoke smells differently from a regular wood fire?" Pauli asked.

"It's because the driftwood was in saltwater for so long before it dried out under the sun on the beach. It gives the fish such a great flavor."

They ate on paper plates and the boy pronounced the bass the best he ever ate, and the potato salad his favorite of all the things his mother made. After dinner they cleaned up and walked to the edge of the surf as the sky to the west lost its brilliant blues and yellows and darkness fell across the beach. They were the only two people in a theater watching something magical unfolding on a stage in front of them.

Pauli crawled into his sleeping bag. Paul placed more sticks on the fire to keep it going. Their silence was broken when Pauli sat up.

"Will you ever tell me what happened to you in the prison camp?" he said.

The question caught Paul by surprise. He looked at his son, unsure how to respond.

"Mom said you never told her," Pauli said. "She wanted you to bring it up but you never did. Will you tell me one day?"

He looked at his son but didn't answer.

❖

In the morning, before sunup, the waves crashing on the beach wakened Paul. He unzipped his sleeping bag, sat up, and was greeted by a damp fog. To the east, the horizon glowed a pale yellow and orange through the fog. He pushed himself out of the bag and stood up. He could see his breath. From his backpack he pulled out a sweatshirt. He retrieved his boots and laced them up. When he was done, he piled two pieces of driftwood onto the still-hot coals from last night's fire. The wood began to smoke, crackle noisily, and burst into flames. When Pauli awoke, he would be warmer, and when the fire died down, he could throw the iron skillet on the coals and fry bacon and eggs.

Looking east and west on the beach, there was no one. The sky to the east brightened as the fog lifted, and he welcomed it and the warmth of the moment. There was a light southwest breeze. The tide was coming in.

THIRTY-FOUR

I t was later in the week when Paul jerked up in bed. He did not know what had stirred him, and as he was thinking about it, a memory returned, unwelcome. This one was about his dead father. Paul spent hours each day and night thinking about his father's life and death as part of an unsuccessful struggle to let go of it. This memory concerned an unanswered question he had carried around with him since childhood.

Did his old man try to kill them both by drunkenly overturning his rowboat, with its Evinrude outboard motor that never worked properly, while they were fishing in the Great South Bay on a late fall day?

It was a matter of family history that the boat turned over, his father clung to the side of it, and he did not help his son, all the while wailing away in German. They were fishing between Lindenhurst and the sandy line of the barrier beach. Few boats on the water in those pre-war days. They were straight out from the village marina fishing with squid when his father failed to start the outboard so they could change positions.

"God damn Evinrude!" he shouted, yanking on the cord so hard the boat rocked back and forth. *"Das verdammte Ding ist nutzlos!"*

Even as a teenager, Paul knew to keep his distance from his father when he blabbered away in Kraut and drank too much. But there was no escaping in a nine-foot rowboat.

"Ich hatte dich vor Jahren wegwerfen sollen!"

Sitting up in bed, he could hear his father's voice. The worst part of the memory was watching his father stand up in the boat. He was well over 240 pounds. The cooler in the boat held twelve bottles of Rheingold. When they pulled away from the marina that morning, Paul watched as his father drained the first eleven, a cigarette clutched between yellowed fingers. The boat rocked, flipped over, and threw both of them into the water.

"Ich will hier nicht sterben! Ich will hier nicht sterben!" he had shouted as the boat drifted in the outgoing tide towards the inlet and the open ocean.

Paul got out of bed and went to the bathroom and pissed. In the kitchen he made coffee. There were a few slices of bread left for toast. As he waited for the coffee, he heard his father's words that day, which he later translated with the help of an English-German dictionary his mother gave him: "I don't want to die here!"

Oh, YOU don't want to die here!

After breakfast, Paul retrieved the two postcards his mother had sent his father the day after the Madison Square Garden rally. The postmarks were worn. But he could see part of a word within the postmark, which appeared to have been deliberately smudged. He read it as "grim," the first letters faded. After "grim" was "N.Y."

He put the postcards back in the box and drove to the asylum. Inside at the security desk, the guard recognized him. He signed in and the guard escorted him to the basement, flipping on the series of overhead lights across the ceiling of the cavernous room.

"There are two kinds of records here, if you can find them," the guard explained. "First, there are visitor records: people who come to either visit someone or check someone in. Second are records of procedures done on patients."

He pointed to the far end of the basement. "For that, you need to start somewhere over in that mess," the guard said. "Good luck."

Going through the stacks of bound visitor books frustrated Paul. No one cared to keep records in an organized way. The books were tossed in heaps; some had slid off shelves and landed on the floor, where they stayed. It was hours later, after finding no books before 1941, that he decided to come back the next day.

He returned to the asylum the next morning, signed in at the entrance, and was escorted to the basement. For the next four hours he went through dozens of visitor books. Then he found it.

At 2:50 P.M., February 20, 1939, Helmuth Baer arrived at the intake center, as it was referred to in the ledger, with his wife, whose name he wrote down as Joyce Baer. An employee had written: *Schizophrenic, talks suicide, must see medical staff. Husband says he can't control her due to her explosive anger spells.*

That's not my mother, Paul thought. *He's making it up.*

Ripping out the page, he walked to the far side of the vast basement, where books marked SURGICAL/MEDICAL were stacked on shelves and thrown about. Another two hours of looking, and Paul found the surgical records for the first four months of 1939. Next to his mother's name, someone had written: *Husband insists on procedure and signed the required paperwork. Prefrontal lobotomy performed 10 A.M., February 21. Patient assigned to a room. Complications required her return to surgery.*

"She mailed the two postcards that morning, then was operated on," Paul said out loud.

He read it again, as if saying it over and over would ease the horror of the words. He walked across the wide room, back and forth. He remembered with clarity coming home from school that day and asking where his mother was. He stared at the document as if the facts would change if he kept reading the words. The doctor's signature filled a box in the next column: Jonathan Herr, MD. Paul ripped out the page. He bounded up the stairs and went to the security desk in the front of the building.

"Can you tell me if a doctor named Jonathan Herr still works here?" he asked the guard.

The man shook his head. "I have no idea," he said.

"I need to find him," Paul said.

"Only thing I can suggest is check with the employment office," the guard said. "It's here on the first floor, in the back of the building."

A minute later, Paul pushed open a door. He told the woman at the desk what he was looking for.

"Dr. Herr? He was our primary surgeon for many years. He retired at least ten years ago."

"Do you know where I might find him?" Paul said.

"Well, I was here when he retired," she said. "He was in his seventies then. I suppose he could still be around."

"I need to know where he is," Paul said.

"I told you, he retired many years ago."

"I don't care. I want to find him."

"Why?"

"Just tell me where I can find him."

She left her desk and came back a few minutes later, handing Paul a slip of paper with an address on it.

"I don't know if the address is any good or if he's still alive," she said.

He found the house an hour later on a street in Smithtown. He parked, walked up, and knocked on the door. Several minutes passed before Paul heard shuffling inside. Peering through the glass on the door, he saw an aged man navigating his way to the front door with a walker. When he reached the door, he fumbled with the lock.

"Dr. Herr?" Paul asked.

"Yes?"

The sight of the man, who was thin and had great difficulty holding himself erect on the walker, drained the anger out of Paul. For a moment he thought he should not have come.

"I would like to talk to you about my mother," he said.

"Your mother?"

"Yes. Her name was Joyce Baer."

The man shook his head. A long moment passed. He pulled the walker back a bit and reached towards the door. "Would you like to come in?"

THIRTY-FIVE

It was a clear fall morning, a Sunday, when Paul drove into the village. Temperatures had fallen but were not yet the kind of cold that kept people indoors. That was a while away. Leaves had been falling off trees for several weeks; some were already bare.

He stopped at the railroad crossing where Lang was found. With no car behind him, he sat at the wheel, the engine running, looking down the tracks towards the Alcove Bar. A car came up behind him and honked.

At his former house, he picked up Pauli and Phyliss. No one spoke in the car on the drive to the cemetery. Dr. Herr was waiting for him. He was with a woman Paul guessed was a health aide. The doctor, too frail to stand, hovered over his walker.

A few minutes later, Martin and Anna pulled in. Martin's face was flushed, his head downturned. He picked his way forward with a cane. Towering overhead was the asylum. Spread out before them was the open ground of the state cemetery. Paul shook his uncle's hand and kissed his aunt, who was carrying a spray of roses. Anna wrapped her arms around Pauli and Phyliss.

Using his cane, Martin approached Herr. "I don't understand this, Doctor," he said. "What is this place?"

"It's where the lost are buried," Herr said, reaching out to shake Martin's hand. He let it hang there before he pulled it back.

"What did you do to my sister?"

"I tried to help her have a better life," he said.

"There was nothing wrong with her," Martin said.

"In those days, a husband bringing in his wife and requesting a procedure was enough."

"You told my nephew she died on the operating table," Martin said.

"She had a stroke," Herr said. "I couldn't save her. You must remember—"

Martin waved his right hand at the doctor and turned away.

"Do you remember where she was buried?" Paul said.

"I was there that morning," Herr said. "I was deeply bothered by her death."

Herr raised his right arm and pointed towards the middle of the field. Paul helped Martin navigate the uneven ground. They stopped where Herr had pointed. A rusting metal marker was stuck in the weedy ground. On it was stamped 5459.

"That's it," Martin said. "Dear God." He covered his face.

Anna placed the roses on the ground by the metal marker. She and Martin crossed themselves.

"God bless you, Joyce," Martin said. He tried to say, "I'm so sorry—" but the words were lost.

Another ten minutes passed before they walked back to the cars. Herr was waiting for them.

"Was Baer with her when you cut into her brain?" Martin asked.

"No," Herr said.

"Was she allowed to make calls after he dropped her off?" Martin asked.

"Baer insisted she not be allowed to use the phone," Herr said.

"And that was enough?" Anna said.

Martin stepped closer to the doctor, who had both hands on his walker.

"You murdered her," he said.

"Her husband brought her in."

"That's all it took. Bring her in. Drop her off. I don't want her anymore. You deal with her. And based on nothing but his lies, you cut into her brain. You tortured her."

Paul stepped between Martin and Herr. He reached out and gently put his hand on his uncle's arm.

"Please, Martin," Paul said.

"Your 'procedure' killed her," Martin shouted. "And they threw her body in a mass grave. A nameless number. People treat their dogs better than you treated my sister."

"I did what I could," Herr said. "The husband brought her in and I was charged with dealing with her issues. The operation might have helped her. Looking back—"

"She had no 'issues' except a monster for a husband. I don't want to hear it!" Martin shouted. "You are a fraud."

"He is to blame, not me!" the doctor shouted. He covered his face with both hands and sobbed.

The health aide steered Herr into the car, helping him get seated. She came around and opened the driver's side door. She started the engine.

Paul dropped off his son and Phyliss and drove to the funeral home. Doc was downstairs, putting paperwork in cardboard boxes.

"The village board revoked my contract to do autopsies," he said. "And there have been more threats, Paul. Several yesterday, one this morning. A man's voice. He said, 'We'll burn your business down.' My brother is moving to Israel. He's quitting America. He wants me to go with him."

THIRTY-SIX

At his father's house, Paul reorganized his material, shifting papers from one box to another. This would now be his archive and his new home. It was slightly larger, with more room for his research. He would give up the bungalow he moved into after the separation and leave the sorrow behind.

He called a locksmith in the village and asked him to change the locks on the front door and the new rear sliding door. He bought shelves from the hardware store in the village and set them up on the wall behind the couch.

In the evening, he wrote letters to authorities in New Jersey on yellow legal pads and took them to the library to type. The first batch went to New Jersey Governor Alfred Driscoll, and then his successor, Robert Meyner. He summed up what he had, asking that an investigation into Hauptmann's conviction be opened. Neither responded. The second and third batches went to local district attorneys and, when none showed any interest, he wrote to members of the state legislature. More silence.

At the bottom of one of the boxes was material Doc had given him. He opened an envelope and found a role of Kodak TRI-X black-and-white film. In another box he found the McKay woman's purse. Opening it, he pulled out the gold locket with the tiny photograph of a blond-haired boy.

❖

Before eight A.M. the next morning, the phone rang. It was Connie. Charlotte Haase was looking for him.

When he pulled up in front of the Haase house, he sat in the car for a few minutes. As he got out of the car, Mrs. Haase walked towards him. They walked up the driveway, and through a metal gate she pushed open and shut after Paul had entered the backyard.

"Where is your husband?" he asked.

"The other night, about seven o'clock, there was a knock on my door. When I opened it, I saw a young woman. She asked for my husband. I said I didn't know where he was. He was gone. She wouldn't listen. She said, 'I am going to the police about him.' I asked what she meant. She said he met her in a bar in Levittown and she left with him in his car, and he tried to rape her. She said she pushed him away and got the car door open, and he said to her, 'I will do to you what I did to that woman in Lindenhurst.'"

She walked towards the back of the yard, where a rusting metal fence ran along the property line. Behind it was a house with a trash-filled backyard. She led Paul to a hole in the ground. A shovel was stuck in a pile of dirt next to it. On a wooden table were flowerpots, bags of potting soil, and a glass jar, the top layered in rust.

"The night that woman was killed, Rudi came home very late. I was in bed. I heard water running in the bathroom. I got up and I opened the bathroom door. He was standing over the sink, washing blood off his arms and clothes. I screamed. He pushed me out of the door. When he came out, he threw me his bloody clothes and told me to go to the basement and wash everything. I did as I was told. After Rudi had gone off to bed, I went back to the basement and found his belt on the floor. It was soaked in blood. I took the belt, rolled it up, put it in the jar, and buried it in the backyard."

He walked to the table and picked up the jar. The belt was inside.

"Have you opened it or tried to remove it?"

"No," she said. "Will you put him away?"

"I will find him. And more importantly, you will have to testify in court, in front of him, about the night you saw him washing off blood in the bathroom. Do you understand that?"

She nodded.

"You have to do that, or he won't be prosecuted. You are the major evidence against him."

In the kitchen, Paul picked up the phone on the wall and called Cantwell. He told him where he was.

"You can't be there," Cantwell said.

"She invited me here," Paul said.

"Is that legal?" When Paul didn't answer, he shouted, "Is that legal?"

Paul hung up.

Charlotte made coffee on the stove. As the coffee percolated, she made toast and brought it to the kitchen table, along with butter and strawberry jam.

When she poured the coffee, she said, "If he knows I have talked to you, he will come here. Rudi will kill me. He knows what I saw."

"We will find him and bring him in," Paul said. "He won't get bail, so you don't have to worry about that. The district attorney's office will take over the case."

She stumbled trying to find the right words in English.

"To be truthful, I am surprised you are still alive," she said.

He stared at her.

"After you were at the lawyer's office, your father came here to meet with Whitener and Rudi. Your father told them what you said. Rudi said you should be killed."

"My father heard that?"

"Yes. He said nothing. Neither did Whitener. Instead he called the mayor on the phone and they talked for a few minutes. Before, when you were here, you asked about the mayor. The mayor and I, we had a friendship. A *beziehung*. A relationship. He came to the house early on the morning the woman's body was found to tell Rudi to change the tires on his car."

"How did he know your husband killed the woman?"

"That morning, after Rudi came home, he went to bed and slept. When the house was quiet, I called the mayor to tell him what had happened. He knew about the murder before you did. Later that morning, Madden came to the house. He told Rudi to say nothing about the murder on the telephone. He thought if Rudi was arrested, his *beziehung* with me would come out. He cared for his politics because he was making so much money doing it."

THIRTY-SEVEN

A check with the Department of Motor Vehicles brought Paul and Cantwell to a house on a working-class block of homes on quarter-acre lots in Uniondale. For two days, they sat a half block from the house before they realized the upstairs was home to a family of four, and the basement was occupied by a man living alone.

Paul walked up the driveway to the back and found a trash can filled with empty liquor bottles and torn-up bills. On one from the Long Island Lighting Company there was a name: Rudolf Haase.

On the morning of the third day, they arrived at the street a little before six in the morning. Fifteen minutes later, Haase got in a pickup. They followed the truck to a street in Hicksville where a row of houses was under construction. A large sign nearby read: BILL LEVITT IS BUILDING YOUR DREAM HOME. They pulled up alongside the pickup as the man was stepping out.

"Rudolf Haase?" Paul said. "Do you have a minute for us?"

The man stuttered something in German. "You were told to stay away from me," he said.

Cantwell walked around the right-hand side of the truck and peered into the cab.

"What's this about? I am here to work. My boss is expecting me."

"Not today," Paul said. "You're coming with us to answer a few questions."

"My boss will fire me if I don't show up. This is all I got."

"I couldn't care less about your job situation," Paul said.

Cantwell stood behind Haase, Paul in front of him. Paul grabbed his arm and turned him around towards the car.

"Put your hands on top of the car, Haase," he said.

After frisking him, Cantwell pulled his arms behind his back and cuffed the wrists. They led him to their car and placed him in the back seat. Thirty minutes later, they pulled behind Village Hall and brought Haase downstairs. Connie jumped up from her desk.

"Oh, my," she said. "I wasn't expecting this today." She put on her coat and picked up her purse. "I hope you know what you're doing." She fled up the stairs.

Cantwell directed Haase to a chair opposite Paul's desk.

"I don't understand," Haase said. "What am I doing here? I want to call my lawyer to put a stop to this. You have been told—"

"Playing stupid is not going to help you," Paul said. "Nor is your dirtbag lawyer. What is going to help you is to tell us the truth and then let us figure out what to do with it. Do you understand?"

He nodded.

"You were in a bar and met a woman and you got her in your car, and when she tried to get away, you told her you would do to her what you did to that woman in Lindenhurst?"

Haase's mouth dropped open, revealing black-and-brown teeth.

"I don't understand," he said.

"No more 'I don't understand what I'm doing here.' Just tell us the truth. If we have our facts wrong, after we hear your story, maybe we can take you back to your job. But first we need to hear the truth. You were in a bar. You met a woman. You got her in your car. You tried to rape her. You mentioned a woman from Lindenhurst."

No response.

"And that would be the McKay woman, right?"

"Du erfindest das alles."

"Don't give us your Kraut bullshit." Paul slammed both hands on the desk.

Cantwell stepped away from Haase. Paul could see his deputy was in over his head. Trying to free himself from the handcuffs, Haase pushed back in his seat. He was such a big, awkward, and ungainly man that Paul thought the wooden chair would collapse under him.

"I'd like to go to the bathroom," Haase said.

"Piss in your pants. We need to get some things cleared up first."

Haase leaned forward, staring at Paul, breathing in and out heavily through a gaping mouth.

Paul said, "The mayor kept your wife informed?"

"I don't know what you mean."

"Your wife was screwing the mayor. He told her and she told you what to do and what not to do," Paul said.

"Charlotte wouldn't fuck me. I doubt she'd fuck any other man." He smiled.

"Whatever she got out of him kept you from being arrested," Paul said. "He didn't want you arrested because he thought it would come out that he was screwing your wife."

Leaping to his feet, Haase struggled to balance himself. With his arms pinned behind his back, he fell into the chair, which collapsed under him. Cantwell pulled him up and set him back on another chair.

"You piece of shit," Haase said.

"'Get rid of the tires. Don't talk on the phone.' Let's get your story straight: The woman in the bar, Constance McKay, you tried to rape her. Then, for thrills you shoved your hand inside her and ripped out her insides."

"She was dancing on the tables and pulling her dress up. Anyone could see that. When I got up to leave, she walked me out the door and got into my car. She was in there the night before, too. She was with another German who was there. Maybe he's the one who killed her."

"You mean Lang. Your old friend from Bund days," Paul said. "She was no stranger. You knew her, Haase. From something twenty-two years ago. And Lang knew her, too. She said something to him that caused great alarm. Isn't that right? She issued a threat to Lang, to expose something."

"I didn't kill Lang," he said.

Haase tried to stand again. Cantwell put his hands on Haase's shoulders and pushed him back into the chair.

"You assaulted her with your fist," Paul said.

"I took her home," he said.

"This latest incident. When you picked up a woman in a bar, and you told her where you lived. A stupid move on your part, Haase. You will be held in the DA's lockup without bail pending a trial six, eight months from now. You will not be released. We will gather evidence on the murder of Constance McKay. That must have been some night, Haase. Sitting in a bar, listening to the World Series. This was the night Willie Mays caught that ball at the warning track, right?"

"This never happened. *Sie erfindet diese ganze Geschichte, um mich in Schwierigkeiten zu bringen.*"

"Speak English," Cantwell said.

"This bitch, she just wants to get me in trouble."

"Before we drive you to the lockup, tell us about how you shoved your hand into Mrs. McKay's vagina, and she bled to death in a field north of Lindenhurst Village. You did to her what you did to Carol Berkowitz."

The mention of the name momentarily stunned Haase. His lips fluttered but no words came out.

"That was you, Haase," Paul said. "And you killed the McKay woman, too."

"She asked for a ride home."

"You drove her to a field by the railroad tracks, pulled off the road, and you murdered her. You went home after killing her. Your clothes were covered with blood. What did you do with them, Haase?"

"I don't know what you are talking about. I gotta piss," he said.

"We know what you did with them," Paul said. "We have your bloody belt."

Haase's mouth dropped open and he let out a scream.

Paul leaned down, his face a foot from Haase's. "You will die in prison, Haase," he said, slapping him hard across the face.

THIRTY-EIGHT

After Lindsay Henry's detectives had taken Haase away, Paul drove to the Haase house. He left Cantwell in the office to get a grip on himself. When he arrived, he found Charlotte Haase standing in the driveway waiting for him.

"Am I safe?" she said as Paul walked up the driveway.

He told her Haase was in custody and would appear before a judge in Riverhead at ten A.M. and would be held on very high bail.

"What about your sons?" Paul asked. "What are you going to tell them?"

"What does a mother tell her boys about their father butchering a woman?" Her hands rushed to her face. "What words, in German or English, are there for that? There is a death penalty in this state?"

He nodded. *It wasn't just one woman*, he thought.

"I will sit in the front row and watch him choke on his last breath."

At six A.M. on a Friday morning, the day after Charlotte Haase had completed her testimony before the grand jury, Paul, Cantwell, and two detectives from the district attorney's office pulled up to the home of Olly Madden. The house was dark. The two detectives walked up the driveway to watch the back door. A light in a second-floor bedroom flicked on.

Paul banged on the door. He heard footsteps on the stairs, and the door swung open. Madden stood there in a bathrobe.

"What's this?" he said.

Paul stepped inside, his left hand on the mayor's shoulder to push him out of his way. Cantwell went to the back door to let in the two detectives. The three men went to Madden's office in the den and began collecting papers and file folders. Soon they were carrying a filing cabinet out the front door to a waiting truck idling in the driveway.

Standing on the stairs in her bathrobe, Madden's wife cried out, "Why are they here, Olly? What did you do? Tell me, what did you do?"

Paul walked into the kitchen and threw the search warrant on the kitchen table.

"Check the basement, upstairs, if there's an attic, then the garage," Paul said to Cantwell.

"You can't do this! You have no authority. I fired you." Madden lunged at Paul, who pushed him back.

"You can check with the district attorney on what authority I have," Paul said.

"Olly, what do they want?" his wife cried from the stairs.

Madden dialed a number and shouted into the phone. When he got off, he pointed a fist at Paul and said, "You won't get away with this."

Paul stepped towards him. "It will be wonderful to see you behind bars," he said. "And you might want to tell your wife before she reads it in the newspapers that you were screwing Haase's wife."

He said it loud enough to make sure Madden's wife heard him.

Cantwell handed Paul a thick ledger book and a large envelope. He turned the envelope over on the kitchen table and out spilled thousands of dollars in cash.

"There's fifty, sixty thousand there, Chief," Cantwell said.

Madden reached out to grab it. Paul pushed him away and opened the ledger. Hundreds of pages held names and businesses in the left-hand column and dollar amounts on the right. He recognized many of the names as village employees. He could also see dozens of businesses, local and countywide, that were doing business with the mayor and the amounts they were paying him. One line read: *Jimmy McGregor. $100 a week.*

"Take Madden upstairs, Roger. Take the two detectives with you. Watch Madden get dressed. Watch him take a shit. Watch every drawer he opens. But search everywhere. Take whatever time you need. He's probably got more cash hidden somewhere."

He turned to Madden, whose wife fell to her knees on the linoleum floor and sobbed.

"Mayor, you are under arrest for a variety of charges related to providing confidential law enforcement information to a murder suspect through your sexual relationship with his wife."

Paul led a handcuffed Madden out the front door. Schmidt pulled up and jumped out of his car.

Madden screamed, "Help me!"

Reaching under his coat, Paul pulled out his pistol and pointed it a few feet from Schmidt's face. He led Madden by Schmidt, who stepped out of the way, the gun still at his face. Behind Paul, Madden's wife, screaming, collapsed by the front door.

❖

When Doc arrived at Baer's house, he found it challenging to navigate around all of Paul's boxes. It was later in the day when he pulled the ransom letters out of a box. As he did, he saw the table brace leaning against the wall by the front door. He kneeled to read the handwriting on the underside. He held the ransom notes together, taping them on the kitchen table so they were lined up perfectly. He held them to the bolt holes on the underside of the brace. The holes on the notes lined up perfectly with the holes on the brace.

"Look," he said.

Paul kneeled next to Doc.

"The ransom notes were written by someone who used the bolt holes and the lines on the wood around the holes as the signature," Doc said. "Paul—the ransom notes were written on this piece of board. The holes line up, the lines all line up. The notes were written on this by someone saying Hauptmann had nothing to do with the taking and killing of the child."

The following morning, Paul brought Doc's roll of film to headquarters.

"I imagine it's pretty much the same as the pictures I took that morning," Cantwell said. "I can't imagine there's anything different on it, Paul. But we can develop it to be sure."

Paul followed Cantwell into his makeshift darkroom. In the tight space, Cantwell had set up a fold-up table on which sat three trays. Pointing to the trays, Cantwell explained that the first one contained developer, the second a stop bath, and the third a fixer. The liquid in the third tray was about an inch deep.

"I learn more every time I do this," Cantwell said. "The next step has to be in total darkness."

All the lights in the office were turned off. Cantwell and Paul stepped into the darkroom. Cantwell pulled the thick curtain closed behind them. Picking up the roll of film, Cantwell unspooled it and, holding both ends of it, ran it through the developer in an up and down motion for ten minutes. After that Cantwell moved the film to the stop bath. He repeated the same motions he used in the first tray, making sure to coat the entire strip of film with the liquid. Finally, he moved to the fixer tray and repeated the procedure for another ten minutes. Then he reached up and pulled on the string and the light bulb glowed red.

Paul watched as Cantwell placed the film in a tub of clean water, thoroughly rinsing it for nearly thirty minutes. No one spoke. Pulling the film out of the tub, Cantwell ran it between two fingers to squeeze out any water, and then reached up and hung the film over the line that went from one wall to the other.

Two hours later, Paul returned to find Cantwell ready to make prints. Using a magnifying glass, Paul looked closely at each frame on the film. He stopped at one.

"Look, Roger," he said, handing Cantwell the magnifying glass. "It's looking east—over the body towards the woods. Do you see something in the trees?"

Cantwell stared at the negative through the glass. "A figure of some kind."

He pulled the curtain shut again and flicked on what he called a safelight on the ceiling. He placed the one frame they had looked at in the holder of an enlarger and cast the image onto a small easel. Both men stared at the image, which to both looked like a sea of green leaves, trees, and near the middle the shape of a person.

"I can print that," Cantwell said. He put photo paper on the easel. "This part is a little tricky because I have to gauge the exposure time so the image turns out okay on the photo paper."

After a few minutes Cantwell dropped the exposed paper in the developer tray. He rocked the tray to make sure the chemicals in the developer touched every part of the exposed paper. The paper was swimming in the liquid. Thirty seconds later, the image on the paper was clearly visible to both men. It appeared as they were staring at the paper. As the minutes ticked off, the image grew darker and darker.

Cantwell then moved the exposed picture to the second tray. A few minutes later he dropped it in the stop tray. After he rinsed it off for a few minutes, Cantwell hung it from the line with two clothespins.

Leaning towards the image, Paul said, "That's my father."

"Why is he there?" Cantwell said.

"It must have all been prearranged," Paul said. "Otherwise, he wouldn't know to be in the same spot where Haase killed her. He must have wanted to know it was carried out. Think of it this way, Roger: Lang hears something from Constance McKay. He tells Baer and Haase their twenty-two-year-old secret is about to be blown. Lang and the McKays have to be killed to keep it covered up. One thing leads to another. Baer or Haase poisons Hagar."

"Your old man is dead, Paul. You can't ask him what he was doing there. This makes Haase the last person with any knowledge of everything you want to know about."

❖

Paul pulled himself out of bed and went to the kitchen to make coffee. While he waited, he laid out the blown-up photograph Cantwell had made. He stared at the grainy image in the woods fifty yards east of where the body was found. In another box he retrieved the purse and removed the locket. The photograph was too tiny to really get a good look at it, and was heavily worn, as if the McKay woman frequently took it out of the locket, looked at it, and put it back.

An hour later he stood in the darkroom with Cantwell. He watched him remove the photograph from the locket with a pair of tweezers and place it on the worktable. He took a close-up photograph of it. He then repeated the process until, later in the morning, Cantwell hung the print on the line. Both men were looking at a photograph of a blond-haired boy. Three, maybe four years of age.

He called Doc, and he and Cantwell drove to Baer's bungalow. Doc was waiting inside. Paul pinned the enlarged photograph to the wall, stepped back, and stared at it. Out of a box he found the newspaper coverage of the Lindbergh case. On the cover of a 1932 edition of the New York *Daily News* was a photograph of the kidnapped Lindbergh child.

"It's the same child," Doc said.

"I don't get it, Paul," Cantwell said.

Doc spoke first. "The McKays were going to take possession of the boy."

"That makes no sense," Cantwell said. "If they were involved, why would they keep a picture of the boy? Anyone looking at it—wouldn't they know it was the Lindbergh kid from all the newspaper coverage? They couldn't keep a kid everyone could see is the Lindbergh son."

"You are not looking at this right," Doc said. "They weren't going to get the child. That was the feel-good cover story. The McKays believed that was the plan. But the people who took the child weren't going to remove him from the house and give him away to a willing couple. That may have been the plan to make everyone involved feel they weren't committing murder, but that was never how it would end. Constance kept the photo to herself as a memory. She at least *believed* she was going to keep him. She threatened Lang when he arranged to meet her that night. It also means she was the one who gave Lang the blueprints for the Norden bombsight."

THIRTY-NINE

The morning that a jury was to be picked in the Haase case began with Brady Whitener telling the judge an agreement had been reached to spare his client the electric chair. Paul, seated in the front row, jumped up.

"What?" he shouted. The judge banged his gavel. "I was told to be here this morning for jury selection. Now you've cut a deal, and I didn't know about it?"

The assistant district attorney approached Paul, who waved him away. The judge banged the gavel again.

"Take the defendant away while we take a break," he said. A minute later Paul, Whitener, and the prosecutor stood before the bench.

"I want to know why I wasn't told," Paul said.

"You know now," Whitener said. "My client will take a plea in exchange for life in prison without the possibility of parole. If that isn't enough for you, then you are a very bitter man."

"I want to talk to him," Paul said to the judge.

"What for?" Whitener asked.

"I'm not talking to you," Paul said.

Whitener scowled. "Why do you want to talk to my client?"

"I have questions for him," Paul said.

"One of your many conspiracy theories, Mr. Beirne?" To the judge, Whitener said, "Your honor, this is highly unusual."

The judge turned to the bailiff. "Bring the defendant back in for the sentencing." To Paul, he said, "After the sentence, stand up and approach the bench. Make a motion and I will rule on it."

The sentencing took less than fifteen minutes, with Haase reading from a typed sheet of paper how he met Constance McKay at the Alcove Bar, how they left together, and when she mocked him for being too drunk to have sex, he ripped her open with his right hand and left as she bled to death.

When it was over, four sheriff's deputies escorted Haase to the courthouse garage, placed him in a van, and drove him to the county jail. There he was brought to a locked room with a table set in the middle. When he walked in, handcuffed, he smiled at Whitener and glared at Paul.

"What do you want?" Haase asked.

"You aren't going to fry," Paul said. "You must be happy."

"I will be free one day," Haase said. He looked at Whitener. "My attorney tells me there are plenty of grounds for the conviction to be thrown out."

"You pleaded guilty, Haase," Paul said. "You said you did it. There's nothing to be thrown out. Your lawyer is lying to you. You will go far upstate to some hellhole, where you will rot in a small cell for the rest of your life. You will die in your cell and get planted in an unmarked grave. You will become a number kept on a list in some state office that will ultimately be lost."

"Enough," Whitener said. "Is this what you wanted?"

"Why did you kill Mrs. McKay? It wasn't over sex, was it? And what about Carol Berkowitz? Both murders have something in common, don't they? And not just how you did it."

"That was not part of the plea," Whitener said. "Shut up, Rudi."

"And tell me, how did Helmuth Baer know to be there? I have a photograph that shows him in the woods near where you killed Mrs. McKay."

"I don't know what you are talking about," he said.

"Hauptmann was a friend of yours."

"The friendship was between my mother and his widow."

He stared at Paul as if he were about to say something dramatic.

"March 1, 1932. You were there that night in New Jersey," Paul said. "Baer was there. Hagar bashed the child's head in. How did you arrange with someone in the house for the child to be handed over to you?"

"Shut up," Whitener said.

"You all met at the lab in Cold Spring Harbor. McKay too."

Whitener pulled on Haase's arm to get him to stand. He refused, shoving his attorney hard against the door.

"You figure it out," Haase said.

"We know how the ransom notes were written," Paul said. "Did you or Baer write them?"

"Shut up," Whitener said.

"The McKays thought they were going to take the child. But that was never the plan, was it?"

"No one cares one bit about that case," Whitener said.

He pulled Haase up from his seat and pushed him towards the locked door. Paul stepped towards Haase and grabbed his shirt. The deputy entered the room and pulled Haase out of the door.

FORTY

Two days before the start of Hannukah, Paul picked up Doc and his brother in Queens and drove them to Idlewild Airport. They had a four P.M. Pan Am flight to London. From there they had reservations aboard an EL AL flight to Tel Aviv. In the car, Doc tried to make small talk about leaving America when for so many years it was the only place where he and his brother wanted to live.

At the curb, standing by the car, Paul reached out to hug Doc. A light snow fell, dusting their shoulders.

"I feel like I am running away," Doc said. His brother entered the terminal.

"Goodbye, Paul," he said. He stepped away, then turned back towards Paul. "In Jerusalem, my brother and I will say Kaddish for our mother. She was murdered May 17, 1944. Unless you have some objection, I will say one for your mother, too."

❖

Paul spent Christmas morning sitting in an Adirondack chair on the dock behind his father's former home. He could hear Christmas music coming from the village. The cold had deepened; the creek was nearly frozen over. He made a note to check it in the morning to see if it was thick enough to take Pauli ice-skating. Buried inside a thick coat, a wool hat pulled over his head, he felt warm.

Two letters had arrived the day before. The first were forms to sign reinstating him as the police chief of the Village of Lindenhurst. Several times he picked up a pen to sign them. Each time he pulled back. The forms went into his desk drawer. The second letter was from Anna.

Martin is in the hospital, Paul.

It was early on the morning of the twenty-sixth when the phone rang. His first thought was that it was his aunt telling him Martin had died. But it was the warden at the Alden Correctional Facility.

"The prisoner you are interested in?" he asked. "He died last night."

"From what?"

"A bad fall," the warden said.

"Is it suspicious?"

"Everything in here is suspicious. Prisoners kill prisoners. It's common."

"Would you let me know when you bury him?"

"You'd come up here for that? What the hell for? He's dead."

"I want to be there."

"You'd better hurry, then. It's tomorrow afternoon in the prison cemetery outside of town."

In Buffalo, he rented a car at the Hertz desk. He arrived at the cemetery a few minutes before the prison truck pulled in with the casket in the back, followed by a hearse from a local funeral home. Out of it stepped Haase's two sons.

The light snow that began the day had turned into a heavier snowfall. Paul worried about being able to fly back to Long Island. He did not want to linger here. He watched the burial from a distance. On the opposite side of the cemetery a backhoe growled. The sons stood by the grave, hands folded in front of them.

The man on the backhoe shouted, "Come on! Let's get going! I got three more of these to do today, and I don't want to stand out here in the cold!"

When they were done, he watched the hearse proceed down the road, the brake lights bouncing up and down in the potholes and glowing through the falling snow like clusters of lightning bugs on a summer night. The backhoe pushed dirt into the hole, the rocks and clods of hard earth striking the coffin with a hollow thud.

He waited for the backhoe to move away and walked to the grave. A metal rod with a plaque at the top with D-3139 stamped on it stuck out of the cold earth.

Standing over the fresh dirt, Paul reached down and unzipped his fly. Then he pissed on the grave.

POSTSCRIPT

June 15, 1955—Greenport, NY

By the time Paul arrived at the commercial fishing dock at the entrance to the harbor, the sky was a rich blue, free of any clouds. Paul, his son, Phyliss, and Anna Beirne, along with a boat crew, left the dock right at nine A.M. aboard Martin's dragger, the *Predator*. Today was the boat's last run. In the days ahead it was to be sold for scrap. The morning's plan was to head to The Ruins. Standing on the bridge, Paul stood next to the two urns in a box. The pilot navigated east into Gardiners Bay. The pilot had a chart spread out on the console with numbers circled: 41 08'29"N/72 08'46" W. Paul recited the numbers out loud from memory.

He pointed to where he wanted the boat to stop. When they arrived, the pilot cut the motor. Anna stood by the side of the boat. She held Martin's urn; Paul held his mother's. He pulled a piece of paper from his pocket, looked out over the water, and said, "Blessed are the poor in spirit, for theirs is the kingdom of heaven. Blessed are the meek, for they shall possess the land. Blessed are they who mourn, for they shall be comforted."

As the ash drifted across the water, death over life, Pauli wept. His parents put their arms around him and watched the ashes drift away.

AUTHOR'S NOTE

There are scores of books about the Lindbergh case. Many take the position that Richard Hauptmann was framed by the State of New Jersey to please Lindbergh, a national icon. The American press convicted Hauptmann the moment he was arrested. With the press hounding him, his attorney too inept to do even a minimum defense, and the prosecution determined to do whatever they could to convict and execute him, Hauptmann did not have a chance.

Research by Lise Pearlman speaks to the relationship between Lindbergh and eugenicist and Nazi follower Dr. Alexis Carrel. She has broken new ground in her research. The writing of retired Rutgers University professor Lloyd Gardner asks many critical questions about the events that led up to the removal of the Lindbergh child from the house and what followed.

Carrel worked for the Rockefeller Institute in New York and moved to France to serve the Vichy government during the occupation. He died in France in 1944. He believed in sterilization of people he deemed unfit, and he wrote that some people should be "provided with suitable gases [that] would allow for their disposal in a humane and economical way."

Carrel was like the Nazi Wilhelm Stuckart, who supported efforts to eliminate members of society the Nazis wanted removed, particularly "deformed" children. He attended the Wannsee Conference in January 1942, where plans to exterminate eleven million Jews in countries overrun by the Germans were laid out in precise numbers.

He was such an ardent believer in eugenics that he had his one-year-old son, Gunther, who was born with Down syndrome, gassed. Stuckart barely paid a price in post-war West Germany for his crimes; he was killed in a suspicious car accident in 1953.

In October 1938—one month before Kristallnacht and more than five years after harsh anti-Jewish measures were taken against the German Jews by the government—Lindbergh proudly received the Service Cross of the German Eagle from Hermann Goering at a dinner in Berlin.

In 1940, in a letter to his treasury secretary, Henry Morgenthau Jr., President Roosevelt wrote: "If I should die tomorrow, I want you to know this, I am absolutely convinced Lindbergh is a Nazi."

In a further indication of what sort of man he was, and wanting to spread what he believed was his Aryan DNA before his own death, Lindbergh secretly fathered children by women in Germany. He also had six children with his wife, Anne Morrow Lindbergh.

In June 2003, the *New York Times* published a story headlined THIS CASE NEVER CLOSES about the discovery of the table brace. Credit for this remarkable discovery goes to Mark Falzini, a state police archivist in New Jersey. He retrieved a crate stored in a warehouse. Inside it was a board upon which were words clearing Hauptmann of any role in the kidnapping.

Mr. Falzini made an additional and even more remarkable discovery: the holes in the board lined up perfectly with the holes on all the Lindbergh ransom notes. In other words, the ransom notes were written on this table, with words on it that state, "I was one of the kidnappers of the Lindbergh baby and not Bruno Richard Hauptmann."

The Höcker Album is one of the most remarkable photographic histories of the men who carried out mass murders at the Auschwitz-Birkenau complex in Poland. The album contains 116 photographs, including those of Richard Baer and Josef Mengele, the Angel of Death, while they were happily gathered at an SS resort doing sing-alongs and gathering blueberries. Before this album was discovered there had been no photographs of Mengele at the complex. He died in 1979 in Brazil while in hiding.

An anonymous individual donated the album to the United States Holocaust Memorial Museum in 2007.

Richard Baer, hiding under the name Karl Egon Neumann, was captured in Germany in December 1960. He died in pre-trial detention in June 1963.

One of the many riddles of the Lindbergh case is the story of Isidore Fisch, a German Jew living in the Bronx who was a business partner of sorts with Hauptmann. His giving Hauptmann a box of ransom money sealed Hauptmann's fate. How Fisch came into possession of the money is not known, although thousands of dollars of the ransom money were seen in multiple places in New York City after the kidnapping and murder of the Lindbergh child.

Fisch returned to Germany in December 1933, eleven months after Hitler came to power and well after antisemitic measures were enacted by the government. Fisch died of tuberculosis in 1934.

Records at Yad Vashem in Israel show that none of Fisch's family members survived. All were murdered at extermination centers in Poland.

Lily Stein was deported to Europe. She never told her story, and her fate in Europe is unknown.

ACKNOWLEDGMENTS

I want to express my gratitude to Leslie Wells, an exceptional editor who helped me make the transition from journalism and nonfiction to fiction. I also want to thank Michael Carlisle, at Inkwell Management Literary Agency in New York, who showed the manuscript to Pegasus Books and whose guidance I have counted on since he represented my last nonfiction book, *The Long Night*.

Jessica Case, the deputy publisher at Pegasus Books, has been a strong supporter of *The Ruins* since she acquired it. I also want to thank Pegasus Book's publicist, Julia Romero, for getting word out about the novel to the reading public. A first novel could not have found a better home.

Many years ago, I read Frederick Forsyth's first two thrillers—*The Day of the Jackal* and *The Odessa File*. Forsyth had been a journalist who turned events he had reported on into novels. His mix of actual events and fiction was powerful and, for me, showed a way forward.

"Fiction reveals truth that reality obscures."
—Ralph Waldo Emerson